Lucy Hawking has written for the *Daily Mail*, *The Times*, the *Telegraph* and the *Evening Standard*. She lives in Cambridge.

Also by Lucy Hawking

The Accidental Marathon

JADED

Lucy Hawking

headline
review

First published in 2003 by HEADLINE REVIEW
An imprint of HEADLINE BOOK PUBLISHING

This edition published in paperback in 2006 by HEADLINE REVIEW
An imprint of HEADLINE BOOK PUBLISHING

2

ISBN 0 7553 0696 1

Typeset in Meridien by Palimpsest Book Production Limited,
Polmont, Stirlingshire
Printed and bound in Great Britain by
Clays Ltd, St Ives plc

Headline's policy is to use papers that are natural, renewable and
recyclable products and made from wood grown in sustainable
forests. The logging and manufacturing processes are expected
to conform to the environmental regulations of the country of origin.

HEADLINE BOOK PUBLISHING
A division of Hodder Headline
338 Euston Road
LONDON NW1 3BH

www.reviewbooks.co.uk
www.hodderheadline.com

For W.

With very grateful thanks to everyone who helped;
in particular, Tif Loehnis, Marion Donaldson,
my family and my friends

Prologue

It was the final insult. Not only had the mineral water contained too much calcium, the stretch limo been too short, the hotel suite an unacceptable colour, the entourage too small, the country too poor and dusty and the mosques too loud. Now the world's most beautiful woman, a creature of such astonishing proportions and startling physical beauty that it was impossible not to stare at her, had finally arrived at the shoot, a mere four hours late, to find they'd sent the wrong photographer.

Balanced on two vertiginous spike heels, her endless legs led to perfectly sculpted hips and waist, unfeasibly buoyant breasts, long, slender arms, wide collar-bones and a swan-like neck surmounted by a face that was currently twisted into a mask of spitting fury. Her famously wide mouth was contorted into a snarl which threatened to push her upper lip into her nostrils if she extended it any further.

'They promised me Mario!' the model shouted, stamping her foot so hard on the antique mosaic in the hotel lobby that it cracked. 'Not that . . . thing!'

The object of her venom, a tiny dark-haired girl decked out in ancient denim, was sitting on a tapestry sofa, calmly smoking a cigarette. Stylists were fluttering around the supermodel like a flock of exotic butterflies around a hibiscus flower.

'But, sweetie, we're going for a very different look,' said the unfortunate magazine editor who'd landed this particularly difficult

shoot. 'We want to get away from pure fashion, take you in a new direction, much grittier, more contrast. The agency loved it – they want to show your depth and spirituality.'

The photographer lit herself another Marlboro Light. Colonel Gaddafi, she reflected, had been a breeze compared to this woman. It wasn't her usual sort of assignment. She'd only taken it for the money.

'I'm calling Mario,' said the model, stabbing at a minute phone which one of the minions had immediately produced for her.

'Tell him I said hi,' said the photographer, smiling sweetly.

The world's most beautiful woman stopped mid-dial and stared at her.

'You?' she said, wrinkling her nose unattractively. 'You know Mario?'

'Min Haskell's the name,' said the photographer calmly. She'd never met him in her life but it seemed worth a try.

'Min's pictures are world-class,' gushed the editor. 'She's tipped as a rising star.' Having hired Min in a moment of panic, the fashionista was fervently hoping her own career was not about to grind to a halt. It was true she had implied to the model agency that the great Mario Testino would be doing the shoot, and she had certainly tried to secure him. Failing that, she'd run through her contacts list, only to come to the rapid conclusion that this trip was jinxed. In desperation she'd called Min, a young photographer who a few weeks before had randomly wandered into the office with her portfolio. To the journalist's amazement, Min was already in Morocco where the shoot was to take place and so was hired on the spot. Explanations, the fashion editor had figured, could wait for later, a decision she was regretting now that moment had actually arrived.

'But she's so scruffy!' exclaimed the confused model.

Min, who'd spent her whole life dealing with difficult people, was unfazed. 'I'm here to make you look good,' she said gently. 'It doesn't matter about me.'

The collection of make-up artists, hairdressers, therapists and stylists stood stock still, not daring to breathe. The supermodel opened her huge violet eyes very wide, a sure sign she was thinking.

'You'd better,' she proclaimed petulantly. A sigh of relief that the shoot was still on swooshed around the marble lobby.

The supermodel had never worked with anyone as quietly self-contained as Min and found it unnerving. She'd tried throwing an experimental tantrum when told they were to travel to the desert by Land Rover rather than the usual stretch limo with complimentary chilled Krug in the passenger drinks cabinet. Min just stood there watching with a resigned expression on her face. Given no placatory comments to feed her tantrum, the model soon ran out of steam.

'When you're ready,' was all Min said. In the silence that followed, somebody sniggered.

Back at the hotel that evening, Min stood on the terrace watching the stars bloom in the night sky over Marrakech. The shoot had been a huge success. Her pictures shattered the hackneyed image of this particular model, casting her in a softer, more vulnerable light. The editor was delighted and even the model grudgingly admitted they were good. In some of the photos she was no more than a speck in the distance anyway, when Min found someone or something more interesting to focus on in the foreground, meaning the world's most beautiful woman found herself playing second fiddle to a camel, a beaming small boy or a swarthy old man in an off-white turban.

'What's next for you?' said the fashion editor, joining Min after extensive telephonic negotiations on the subject of childcare for her three little ones, complex arrangements which appeared to have broken down totally the moment she left the country. She'd had to bribe the day nanny to stay on as the overnight nanny, whom she was starting to think might have a drink problem, had yet again failed to show up.

'Another beer, I think,' said Min who was very tired. Maintaining her professional detachment could be quite draining, so very different was it from her personality in real life.

'Where are you based?' asked the journalist, who was curious about this talented unknown with her mass of black ringlets, slight frame and torn rucksack.

'I have a sofa in Notting Hill,' said Min. 'And that's about it.'

Chapter One

The streets were unusually quiet. Only those who still hadn't heard the news were at large. 'This is my gift to you,' said the rotund African taxi driver as his cab pulled away from the Gâre du Nord. 'I bring these beautiful oils and spices back from my home in Senegal so that my car will smell delicious and you will take the aroma of love with you throughout your time in Paris.'

The couple on the back seat exchanged glances. The aroma of love was quite strong. 'Do you think we can smoke?' the man whispered to his girlfriend.

'*Excusez moi, monsieur*, she said in hesitant French. '*Est-ce qu'on peut fumer?*'

'*Mais non!*' said the taxi driver, banging his hand on the steering wheel. 'I am telling you! I have brought the essence of the warm, scented air of Africa to perfume your journey through the city of Paris so that your stay here will be full of good omens for the future of your lives!'

The man in the back fingered the ring box in his pocket. The prospect of presenting it that evening to his beloved was making him jittery with nerves. Having no reason to suspect he was suffering from an excess of romantic fear, she assumed it was lack of nicotine that made him so twitchy.

'And you want to smoke cigarettes! It is for you that I make the air sweet so you will breathe it and be filled with peace and

5

joy.' The driver swung his car around a corner.

They emerged on one of the main boulevards of Paris, broad and gracious, with the Arc de Triomphe at one end, the Eiffel Tower visible on the other side of the river. It was the vista of a thousand romantic postcards and the sight the man had hoped would help swing the answer to his proposal from 'probably not' to '*oui*'.

However, the good omens of Africa were not much in evidence that June day for the inopportune lovers and their scented driver. They seemed to have driven straight into hell. Marching down the boulevard towards them came columns of shaven-headed, jackbooted fascists, moving in formation as tightly and cohesively as a Roman legion. They punched the air with their fists, shouting: '*La France – libérée!*' Approaching from the opposite direction came a more raggle-taggle but no less impassioned and menacing force, holding huge placards, flags and burning brands. '*France pour tous!*' they roared, advancing inexorably towards the rapidly shrinking no-man's-land where the unfortunate taxi had stalled, its driver frozen with terror.

Throughout the spring France had simmered with discontent which had, on this particular day, erupted into open rioting on the streets of Paris. The far right had made it to the last round of the French presidential elections. If their leader, a silvery old fox called Le Maître whose avuncular air concealed a will of steel, won at the ballot box, France would fall under the sway of the fascists. Policies advocated by Le Maître included a ban on immigration, special tax breaks for 'real' French people, women to be restricted to a maximum of twenty-five hours' work a week and, most bizarrely, the return of the French monarchy. Although France had been a Republic since the Revolution of 1789 had summarily despatched the then occupants of the throne, there was no shortage of trash royalty drifting around the nightclubs of

Paris, Monte Carlo and New York, claiming that were there ever a French crown, it would belong on their head. So Le Maître's announcement that he intended to return France to a monarchy had sent frissons of delight throughout the so-called nobility of France and the pretenders to the throne, a clever move which united the upper classes with Le Maître's otherwise working-class supporters.

Having been an underground movement for so many years, with secret meetings and clandestine membership lists, Le Maître's supporters had decided to express their ebullient joy at finding themselves only a few steps from holding power in the Republic of France by staging a meticulously planned but unannounced march across Paris. As soon as their left-leaning opponents heard the fascists had suddenly appeared on the streets, they rallied as fast as possible, abandoning their faith in democratic peaceful protest to fight this menace to the bitter end. With no time to plan, the intellectuals, artists, immigrants, teachers, doctors and ancient members of the Free French, the Second World War resistance group – anyone, in fact, who found the idea of France returning to the control of a repressive and brutal regime abhorrent – left their house to join the opposition. Armed with anything that came to hand, brooms, chair legs, breadboards or carving knives, they squared up with grim determination to the vile threat that faced them.

A mounted policeman banged on the roof of the fragrant cab with a truncheon. '*Evacuez la voiture!*' he commanded. The lovers needed no telling, one dashing across the street to the right, one to the left. The driver hesitated, loath to leave his pride and joy to the destructive forces of the riot. '*Evacuez. . .*' the policeman started to shout again, but it was too late. A bolt of flame hit his horse's hindquarters, causing it to rear up and crash down, both hooves through the windscreen straight into the face of the Senegalese *parfumier*, shattering his skull and causing fragments of brain, bone and hair to splatter across his cab in a fountain of bright red blood.

High up on the fifteenth floor of a nearby building, a group of men watched the battle unfold from the plate-glass calm of an air-conditioned conference room.

'How the hell did that taxi get on to the road?' exclaimed a youngish man.

'This is the beginning of the end, *mon ami*,' replied an older one. 'These are dark days.'

'Oh, look, I can see one of the passengers,' said the first man. The girl had managed to slip through the rapidly assembling cordon of policemen but her companion had not been so lucky. He had run slap into a wall of riot shields and been tossed back into the crowd like a leaf.

'Wrong place, wrong time,' said his companion. 'You have to be so careful.'

'Gentlemen,' came a peremptory voice from the centre of the room. 'We must not be like Nero and fiddle while Paris burns. We have our own revolution to attend to.'

The matter to which he referred was an enormous and far-reaching deal of international importance, the finishing touches to which the assembled company had been struggling to finalise for some weeks now.

'This,' he continued, 'is the very stuff of business in the twenty-first century.'

A sparse, granite-faced American spoke up. 'Percy, we're as committed as you to this deal. But as matters stand, we can't close today.'

The tension in the room ratcheted up another notch. The younger man who'd been standing at the window asked to excuse himself for a minute.

'If you must,' snapped Percy, his boss.

In the cloakroom he splashed his face with cold water and studied his reflection with a grimace. He looked drained, which was just how he felt, lacking a shred of motivation to go back in and thrash out the closing details. He'd have a quick smoke to sharpen himself up and, once restored, rise to the challenge.

As he puffed hurriedly in the Gents, he heard the sound of running feet, a door slamming, and the unmistakable sound of a gunshot.

He stubbed out his cigarette in the basin and edged towards the conference room where he put his ear to the door. He heard someone say *'Mais – qu'est-ce qui se passe? Qui êtes-vous?'*

Another voice, and a strangely familiar one at that, replied in accented but faultless English. 'Comrades,' it said, 'as you are no doubt aware, a fraudulent fascist is attempting to impose himself upon the people of France. He must be stopped before he gains legitimate power.'

'Holding innocent people hostage will not help you oppose him,' said someone else.

'I agree,' said the mystery voice. 'As individuals you are entirely insignificant. But speaking collectively you can send a message to the dirty capitalist world. You must tell Le Maître that under no circumstances would your bank do business with his government, and that you utterly condemn him. I have no intention of hurting you. At least, not yet,' the voice added reassuringly. 'Our demands are very simple but until they are met, you are prisoners in this room and I will pick you off one by one if you do not do as I say.'

'Now, just hang on a minute,' blustered Percy's voice.

Another shot rang out. *'Comprenez ça?* Or perhaps, Monsieur, you require a further demonstration? *Non? Alors*, what do you say to my proposal?'

But the lone hijacker must have been more of an idealist than a pragmatist to imagine he could hold a room full of extremely powerful and strong-willed men hostage without encountering any form of opposition. The investment bank's security guards burst into the room, tackled him brutally to the ground and smashed his face on the floor. They strong-armed him out of the conference room, pausing to frisk him for additional weapons next to where the young banker stood watching in the hallway.

'Ah, William Gadget,' the intruder said. 'We meet again.'

'Christophe!' said William, horrified, realising now why that voice had struck a chord with him.

Dripping with blood, the other man sneered, 'I hope you don't think I have forgotten?' With that he tilted back his head and spat in William's face.

At number forty-two Cornwall Crescent, London W11, the home of William Gadget Esq., it had been an Albert day in much the way it was every Monday, Wednesday, Thursday and Friday. Albert was William's cleaner – or rather his antiquated manservant who came five times a week to do the washing up, change the light bulbs, pick up the dry cleaning, refresh the bathroom and tackle other sundry tasks that somehow fell beyond Will's remit. He had inherited Albert, who was seventy-one, from the previous owner of the flat. When Will bought this bijou nook of Notting Hill from a fellow banker who was getting married and thus being forcibly evicted by his new wife in order to experience domestic bliss at first hand in a semi-detached house in the suburbs, he had been specifically asked to retain Albert as part of the fittings and fixtures of the flat. Having no aptitude for cleaning himself, William readily agreed and now found himself in the enviable position of having 'staff'.

He walked into his flat with the familiar sense of pleasure his impeccably tidy surroundings always gave him. His blond wood floors, white walls, fully fitted kitchen with five-ring Smeg hob, and double sink all gleamed. As well they might, given that they were cleaned five times a week and that the only item William made use of in the kitchen was his fridge. As far as he was concerned, attempts to cook would only lead to the production of some inedible fodder and a depreciation in the value of his flat thanks to the damage done to the white goods. So he let well alone and contributed to the boom in the service sector by patronising local restaurants. This left him in the somewhat peculiar position of being able to pontificate knowledgeably on the global economic outlook whereas you could fox him entirely by asking him the price of a loaf of bread. However, this wasn't the sort of query people often put to him so his utter lack of perspective on the day-to-day outgoings of a household passed largely unnoticed.

The bathroom was perhaps William's favourite place. It was entirely lined in black marble, which could have been tacky but in fact made a pleasing contrast to the whiteness of the rest of the flat. It had a shower, which bombarded him from three different angles with a cascade of specially softened crystal drops, and a stand-alone bath with Jacuzzi features. But his love for his bathroom was more abstract than sybaritic enjoyment of the de luxe fittings. Every time he went in there, he was reminded that money can't buy happiness and that cheered him up enormously. Alas, he liked to think to himself as he stood under the power shower, I am indeed doomed to misery! How much happier would I be now if only I didn't have all this!

William, of course, was an extremely wealthy young man, having rented out his generous quota of brain cells to Pollinger's, a large and respected investment bank in the City of London, for the last ten years. The money he accumulated through the flexing of his considerable cerebral power often went on the purchase of the sort of liquid products which serve to destroy grey matter at a frightening rate. This paradox was clearly not one that was sustainable in the long run but as he was only thirty-two, had earnt more in his first year at his first job than his father had in his pre-retirement year at the County Coucil, owned his flat and had no responsibility other than to himself, then a fondness for champagne or vodka martinis was hardly a cause for great concern.

His return to London, a city of quiet grey streets and gently falling rain, had been delayed thanks to the impassioned turmoil in the capital of France, meaning his train only drew into the Waterloo Eurostar terminal that afternoon. He and Percy had sat in silence on the journey. The unlucky Senegalese taxi driver had not been the only casualty of the riot. The nameless lovers had failed to find each other, the billion-dollar deal had not gone through, and Percy's hatred of his employee had set like concrete.

Percy would never have voluntarily chosen William as second-in-command for such an important deal. His idea of a subordinate was just that – someone who would unquestioningly follow the orders given by Percy himself. William was used to the management style of Joren, the boss he'd worked with for the last ten years at Pollinger's, a keenly intelligent man who believed in involving his whole team in the decision-making process. Joren liked to consult, to discuss, to show those working for him his rationale for proceeding down any particular route. Percy was quite the opposite, wishing only to dictate a strategy and have it accepted as gospel. William baulked at this, doubting the older man's judgement and expertise. Matters had come to a head at the Paris meeting when William had flatly contradicted him over the conference room table, not something he would have done to Joren, but then not something he would have needed to either.

Joren, however, had recently vanished from the office. After a strange period of silence it had been announced that he had met with an accident while riding his Ducati too fast in the rain. Visitors were not allowed in the intensive care unit where he lay in a coma, so the Mergers and Acquisitions team were told, but they would, of course, be kept updated on his progress. Much to William's horror, Percy had then taken over the bank's most important deal.

By the time William arrived back at his desk in the open-plan M & A office at Pollinger's it was already late in the day. His nerves were in tatters after the events of the Paris trip but he knew he just had to get through the next few hours as normally as possible, then he could go home and try to make sense of it all. He flopped down into his chair, rested his forehead on the desk and closed his eyes to allow himself one brief moment of darkness and peace. It was soon shattered.

'William,' said a voice, 'I need to meet with you.'

'Not now, Bert,' said Will. 'Can't you go and victimise some female too young to be able to see through you?'

Bertrand, a super-suave American, was the office Lothario, despite the fact that his seduction technique consisted of bombarding his victim with glances, e-mails, phone calls, flowers and champagne until she agreed to have sex with him, after which he dumped her. His line was that he was working with his therapist on commitment issues but at present it would ruin everything if he were to take a step he was as yet psychologically unprepared for. He'd gaze deeply into the girl's eyes and say, 'I really like you, that's why I'm being honest. Because I don't want to hurt you.' William knew this because Bert had done it at least three times with various female colleagues who had then cried on Will's shoulder. Now, when they got an attractive new woman in the division, Will always took the opportunity to introduce the American as 'Bertrand, an immoral, philandering bastard who'll try and break your heart'. The new woman then either thought Will fancied her himself (well, maybe he did), and was trying to put Bertrand down, or else that he was joking, and found out the hard way.

When Will blearily opened his eyes he saw the American fuming with annoyance. Fabrizio, his other colleague, looked up from reading a Formula One magazine hidden inside the *FT* and shot Will a complicit smile. Bertrand turned on his heel and walked off.

'How was gay Paree?' asked Fab.

'High jinks at the Moulin Rouge as usual,' said Will, sitting up and looking around him. It took him a minute or two to realise why the office seemed so different. In his absence, someone had installed TV cameras in M & A.

'What's all this?' he said to Fabrizio.

'Corporate Reality,' said Fab. 'It's a new team-bonding exercise. They film us for a week and then we watch the footage with a psychologist.'

'If I wanted to be on Big Brother, I'd go and flaming well audition!'

'Message to William: Read memos.'

'Oh, God. It's not enough we have to slave away all week, we then have to watch ourselves do it afterwards. Tell me there's a point?'

'We're going to be able to identify personal weaknesses, time-wasting activities and any unresolved tension. Our daily sessions in the "diary room" will help to clarify our issues, and then we carry on as a happier, friendlier organisation,' parroted Fabrizio.

'I'm *not* hugging you,' said Will.

'You're breaking my heart,' said his friend flippantly.

Will kicked his desk leg in annoyance. This was the final straw.

'Got something to hide, have you?' asked a returning Bertrand.

'You know I don't.'

'Time will tell,' said Bert smoothly. 'Everywhere's been wired. Even the rest room.'

'So we'll finally get to see how you keep your hair so neat. The secret of The Bertrand will be out.'

'He's loving it,' said Fabrizio as Bertrand's back disappeared from view.

'Does it not strike you,' said Will, 'that when they do this on television the least popular contestant is voted off daily?'

'It had crossed my mind,' said Fab. 'While the party line dictates that another recession is a technical impossibility, the formation of the planets, the movement of the tides and the inexplicable panic among small furry animals would indicate otherwise.'

'The day shall come when even the investment banker shall be cast on to the street and made to work for a living,' said Will. 'Is this the beginning of the end, o far-sighted one?'

'Such is our business,' sighed Fab. 'While everything appears to the outside world to look good, there's a chance of maintaining the possibility that it actually is. If the façade crumbles, even a little bit, it could tip the movement inexorably downwards. What if Pollinger's have actually woken up to the fact they can't afford their highly staffed operation any more? A review of working practice carried out to create a leaner, more efficient organisation might not send the same panic signals to the rest of the City that mass redundancy would.'

'You're very blasé,' said Will suspiciously. 'What's going on?'

Fab smiled. 'I'm leaving. I've got a new job.'

'As what?' demanded Will, in panic that his last ally was leaving.

'Financial adviser to Ferrari. Fast cars, beautiful girls, world-wide travel and, most importantly, a first-class ticket out of this hell hole. Farewell, my friend.' Fab stood up. 'And fuck you, Pollinger's,' he said, directly into one of the cameras.

Bertrand approached with a smile on his face.

'Will,' he said, looking particularly predatory.

'Bert,' said Will politely.

Suddenly he realised what Bertrand reminded him of: the

shark at the London Aquarium, swimming around its tank looking sleek, menacing and utterly amoral. As Bert walked towards him, he almost saw a dark fin cutting through the surface of the sea. It was too late to run away from the dreadful monster gliding into the shallows. Will felt jaws close over his leg and saw the water round him turn red from the blood which was spurting on to the foam-washed beach. He tried to run but the creature was too strong, too deadly, for him to fight. His mangled corpse thrashed hopelessly while passers by watched in horror unable to help as he . . .

'Will,' repeated Bertrand, 'are you OK? You look kinda pooped.'

'I'm fine,' he replied haughtily. 'It's just this new raw vegetable diet I'm on. It makes me look a bit strange.' This was a total lie. He had no idea when he had last knowingly eaten a vegetable but since he'd discovered you could blame the otherwise obvious effects of a hangover on a detox diet, there had been no stopping him.

'Will,' said Bertrand who had clearly been told that addressing people by their first names as often as possible was a good way to assert yourself, 'Percy wants me to come in with you on the Tellcat deal.' The look of innocence on his face didn't fool William for a minute. He felt fairly sure Bert was trying to provoke a reaction which could then be criticised by the psychologists when the office footage was shown. He struggled to keep cool.

'Tellcat is mine, Bert, and I've worked very hard on it. You can't just cut in at the end because you want to boost your bonus.'

'Sorry, Will.' He shrugged. 'I'm only obeying orders.'

How much damage had been done to the human race, thought William bitterly, while using that excuse? He could, he supposed, go and ask Percy if what Bert said was true. However, given that

Will had got off on the wrong foot with Percy on their very first day working on Tellcat, and only got more wrong-footed as time wore on, he knew he had no goodwill to draw on with his boss. Given his state of mind, evasive action seemed the best hope. He took himself away to a quiet little bar he knew for a few refreshing drinks, and when he returned, it was time for his 'diary' session.

He entered the consultation room which was made out of a few screens jammed together in a corner of the office.

'Hello, William,' intoned a disembodied voice. 'How are things going for you today?'

'Well,' he temporised, 'obviously we face challenges on a daily basis, but that is only a reflection of the fact that we are number one in an industry which takes no prisoners. We remain secure in the knowledge that we have great leadership, with an ethos of professionalism, dedication and intelligent awareness that comes directly from the top.' What crap, he thought to himself.

'Yes,' said Dis Vox. 'But how do you feel yourself?'

'The pressure to perform is one I have become used to over the years so I . . .'

'So you're not tense?'

'Sure, but only because I'm working so hard.'

'How about relationships between the team?'

'Great, really great. Fabrizio is a star and I absolutely feel he's got what it takes,' lied Will.

'How are you getting on with Bertrand?'

'Tricky. My feeling is that he's homesick. He might be better suited to somewhere like, say, Delaware.'

Delaware was the back room of the entire bank. Effectively, Will was saying Bertrand was only fit to count stapler supplies for the rest of his working days. It was a brilliant insult, subtle but deadly, and he was delighted finally to have a chance to use it.

He left the consultation room and popped in to the bank's corporate affairs and promotions office. Gav, whose domain this was, had promised to fulfil a little commission for him. However, the flamboyant and verbose head of communications, whose desperate desire to direct pop videos was reflected in the funky recruitment material his department produced – portraying life in investment banking as only a heartbeat away from life on the road with a boy band – was absent. Instead the production company masterminding Corporate Reality was in residence, but at that moment their sole representative was a techno nerd wearing a Death's Head T-shirt.

'I've come for a tape,' said Will. 'The guys who usually work here said I could pick it up after the weekend.' It hadn't been hard to persuade Gav to waste some of the bank's resources by making Dallas, William's actor friend, a professionally polished version of his show reel to send out to casting agents. In fact he had been positively thrilled and had promised that Dallas' talents would be displayed in such a way that any agent worth their salt would be beating down his door the moment they clapped eyes on his work. William had wondered quite how Gav would effect this miracle from footage of Dallas picking his nose for an advert in the Netherlands, posing as a customer in a building society training video or waddling across the stage in a large feathered suit in a panto last Christmas. But he hadn't wanted to dent either side's enthusiasm for the project, so had kept quiet.

The Death's Head nerd looked horrified at having to interact with another human being but Will spotted a note pinned up which read, 'William Gadget, to collect, tape GD34/7'. The T-shirt duly scrabbled around like a hamster and eventually found the video, which he handed over. In a fit of jubilation that another Tuesday in his life was over, Will waggled the tape at the young chap and said: 'When the world sees this, there'll be a revolution!'

Given the odd look he got in return, Will decided he must be drunker than he thought. Unable to face another round with Bert he gave his desk a wide berth and exited by the back door en route for Notting Hill.

Chapter Two

At 8.04 that Tuesday evening the doorbell of flat three, forty-two Cornwall Crescent rang. It was, predictably, Dallas, an actor whose last break had been playing a dead body in *Casualty*. His Mother Goose had caused quite a stir, however, so he still had intact his dreams of a red carpet, adoring paparazzi and a golden mask on a stick awarded to him by Kate Winslet. He had composed his Oscar-acceptance speech so many times now he'd started to feel it was a work of Shakespearean proportions.

'Hi, Will,' said Dallas, sauntering into the top-floor apartment. 'I was about to go home, you took so long answering the door.' He was wearing an extremely strange pair of trousers. His fashion sense had always erred on the side of eccentric but ever since he'd started going out with a stylist, it had crossed the border to just plain weird. He'd met Luella, the love of his life, on a shoot where she was trying to turn him into Mr Tomato! for a ketchup advert. The pair of them had laughed so uproariously that they'd been thrown off the set and told they'd never work again in consumer advertising. Neither of them had cared, frankly. They'd left together and gone to Soho where their first date was at a £1 peep show followed by an in-depth discussion on their mutual love of narcotics. They'd been together ever since. Perpetually broke, ridiculously in love and usually high, the errant couple were pretty much welcome wherever they went.

Dallas made straight for the fridge and rootled around until he emerged from its capacious, chilled depths with a can of beer. It struck Will that, once upon a time, his mates arrived with a bottle or a few tins. Now they more or less let themselves in, raided the cupboards, left laundry for Albert, used the Jacuzzi and made a few phone calls. Will didn't mind – what was his was theirs. He just couldn't remember when they'd stopped asking.

'Had an audition today,' Dallas said proudly.

'Any good?' Will forced himself to ask.

'Amazing, Will, amazing! It's for a production of *Tale of Two Cities*, done soul-style. You know, gospel backing, bit of James Brown, set in Harlem and Brixton, really funny and alternative.'

Will felt compelled to point out, 'Dal, you're white.'

He looked wounded.

'But I can *act* black.'

'Yes, sure, you'll be great,' Will added hastily. Arty people can be easily hurt and, God knows, have a hard enough time without their friends putting them down too.

'Hey, I called your mobile and this weird guy answered.'

'Oh, yeah, I left it in the office. I expect it was one of the cleaners. What did you want?'

'Just to remind you to get that tape for me.'

'In the briefcase, man. Over there. And don't say I never do anything for you.'

Dallas extracted the video Will had collected from his office and hugged it to his chest. 'My show reel! My greatest hits!' he said happily. 'Oh, Will, I can't thank you enough!' Dallas was hoping that this tape, with its footage of his finer stage moments, might be enough at least to let him get a foot through the door with a Hollywood talent agency. 'I'm sending it off immediately. You are a star!'

The door bell rang again. Will went over to the window and peered out.

'Aren't you going to answer it?' said Dallas.

'Just checking to see who it is.'

'Why don't you use the entry phone?'

'Because then they'll know I'm in,' said his friend, still peering through the blinds.

'Who will?' said Dallas, perplexed.

'Just, anyone,' said Will going over to the entry phone.

When he finally got round to opening the door, his guest had been waiting for a while.

'Bit of a time lag,' said the pleasant-looking if rather short man standing there. It was broadcasting's Jemal Haque, an old friend of Will's.

'Come in, then,' said Will, and turned and headed back to the sitting-room with his new guest following.

'Hi, Jem,' said Dallas who was reclining on a huge *café au lait*-coloured suede cushion, drinking a can of beer.

'Hi, man,' said the latest arrival. 'What happened after I left?'

'Oh, it was quite funny . . .' Dallas started.

'Left where?' interrupted Will.

'Erm,' said Jem, trying to sound nonchalant, 'Dal and I bumped into each other last night, quick drink . . .'

'What time did you get home?' Will interrogated them.

'Oh, goodness, I should think, well, about three,' said Jem sheepishly.

'Dallas?' said Will sternly.

'Ah,' said the actor. 'I didn't really look at my watch – there was a sort of accident, you see, when Luella tried to jump on the bar to dance on it. She leapt right over by mistake and landed in the beer tray so I had to help her out.'

'Poor you,' said Will. 'How very distressing. How is Luella? Still propping up the economy of Colombia?'

'We thought you were in Paris,' said Jem.

'Well, I was,' said Will forcefully. 'And I was having a shit time and I felt very down and not one of you even bothered to call to see if I was all right. I'm fed up with this. Whenever you lot have a problem, you're straight on the phone to get me to sort it out, but when I'm having a hard time, it's just, oh, Will, he's being demanding again.'

Having worked himself up into a frenzy, he tried to light a cigarette but it flew out of his shaking hands and landed on the floor, imbued with so much kinetic energy that it bounced around for a few seconds before coming to a standstill. Jem and Dallas exchanged horrified glances while Will flounced off to the kitchen.

'Oh, dear. Oh, dear,' said Jem.

'He's getting worse,' said Dallas.

'I'd go and talk to him but last time I tried, he told me to sod off,' said Jem.

'We've cabled HQ and reinforcements are arriving,' said Dallas.

'Ah, yes,' said Jem. 'The cavalry is on its way.'

'Rides into town tonight,' said Dal.

'I'm pinning my hopes on it,' said Jem.

'You're not the only one,' said Dal.

The doorbell rang and rang all evening. Each time Will jumped out of his skin and then went through the rigmarole of twitching back his fashionable flat blinds to check who the new guest was before double-checking via the entry phone. He was much more polite to his later guests than he had been to the two old friends who'd arrived earlier but he was drinking manically, with two raised red spots appearing high on his cheek bones. Something was clearly amiss.

By the end of the evening, they'd accumulated an out-of-work web designer called Jason who'd been sacked when his boss had taken a spoonful out of what he'd thought was

Jason's sugar jar for his tea and discovered it was in fact speed, a brace of Swedish IT consultants, a somewhat bruised but still very chirpy Luella, and a random girl Will had once met on a business trip and then never quite been able to shake off. The Chablis washed down the chicken tikka masala they ordered in nicely and all of them were pleasantly drunk in an acceptable weeknight fashion, except for Will who appeared increasingly miserable and nerve-wracked as the night wore on, and the random girl who was beginning to see that she might not have a beautiful future with him after all.

In all of these respects it was a perfectly normal Tuesday night. Will's evenings mostly consisted of passing the time one way or another. But that evening, he was paranoid about getting visitors he didn't want and obsessed with the absence of the one person he really wanted to see. Yet again, she hadn't turned up.

He'd been expecting her since Monday but a delay of a mere twenty-four hours was nothing in the life of Ambrosia Mathilde Sevigny Angelica de Beaufort Haskell, also known as Min, also William Rodney Gadget's oldest friend. The last e-mail from Morocco had been characteristically vague about her potential arrival time, but he kept hoping it would be on the sooner side of later.

He hadn't seen her for months so even without the cryptic message he would have known to expect her small person to land on his doorstep any day now, full of tales of outrageous fortune, having been deported or stuck in an earthquake or stalked by a psycho or whatever new adventure had befallen her in her nomadic life. So regular was this pattern that he'd given her a key so that the next time she arrived at 6 a.m. with a Bosnian boyfriend in tow, she could let herself in without disturbing him. She would stick around for a few weeks, promising Will she'd look for a proper job and settle down, and the next thing he'd know, a once-in-a-lifetime opportunity would lure her to Acapulco and she'd be gone again. She was without doubt the most annoying person he had ever met with the greatest capacity to cause trouble and the most casual way of shaking it off and moving on.

Surprisingly, Will and Min had first met at primary school: not that it was odd that they should both have attended school. The anomaly was that these scions of the houses of Gadget and de Beaufort Haskell should have found themselves in the same educational establishment.

The coffee morning côterie of South Berkshire had been overjoyed by the potential for endless speculation as to why the de Beauforts, those vair, vair posh people, should have decided to send Min, their fifth child, to a state school when Leonora, Henri, Maxim and Selena had been lavishly and privately educated. One rumour was that she wasn't even a proper de Beaufort, which when you saw teeny-weeny little Min (short for Miniature) next to the strapping, firm-jawed, broad-shouldered elder children certainly seemed plausible. The eleven-year age gap between her and her nearest sibling also added credence to the theory that she was the product of an illicit relationship by a member of the extended de Beaufort family which reached right across Europe, taking in various deposed royal families and endless pseudo-counts and marquesas. Some even claimed a Lear jet from Monte Carlo had landed in the grounds of Chieverley, the family home, and deposited baby Min, presumably with some form of explanatory letter pinned to her shawl.

Of course, William didn't know or care anything about this when he was five. Only years later did his mother tell him of the gossip that had spread like an out-of-control bush fire once Min became part of day-to-day suburban life. The other de Beauforts had only ever been glimpsed, passing through the town in sports cars or towing horseboxes to their next eventing triumph. They were like exotic rare animals with their enviable arrogance, beautiful clothes and palpable lack of doubt in themselves or their position in the world. Will's first memory of Min was of a small girl with fluffy dark hair, standing pressed against the institution-green railings of the school forecourt, looking hopelessly down the road for someone to come and collect her. His mother was always bang on time. Before long the admirable Mrs Gadget noticed that Min was the only child always lacking a parent to run to when she came out of school. At home one evening she said with great determination to her husband Phillip, 'I can't bear it any longer.'

'Is that so, dear?' he said, happily unaware that if a woman said that to her husband twenty-five years from then he'd be out of the house clutching his divorce papers, having forfeited half of his income, his abode and his pension, and could look forward only to a future of seeing his kids one Saturday a month when they'd tell him how boring he was.

'No, I've made my mind up,' said Mrs G decisively.

'Very good,' said Phil, pursuing a particularly recalcitrant piece of Cod Mornay.

'I'm going to phone those people,' said his wife, throwing down her serviette.

She marched to the telephone and purposefully dialled. At the other end it rang and rang and rang.

Eventually someone picked up.

''Allo,' said a sleepy voice. It was Sylvie de Beaufort, a woman of fabulously faded elegance whose idea of a busy day was a late-morning cocktail on the chaise-longue while playing opera classics on a wind-up gramophone.

'Hello,' said William's mother in her best voice. 'This is Mrs Phillip Gadget.'

'*Chérie*, Ambrose is out collecting rubbish from ze garden. You will have to call anozzer time.'

Ever since Chieverley had been opened to the public, Ambrose de Beaufort, Min's supposed father, had developed a peculiar mania for cleaning his grounds of the litter the polloi inevitably dropped. He had been known to stalk visitors through the park waiting for a fragment of paper to escape their grasp at which point he would leap out at them and bellow, 'Would you do this in your own bloody garden?' thus terrifying them to bits. His proud boast was that he could 'Spot a bit of litter at a hundred yards!'

The invasion of people who'd traditionally been excluded from Chieverley by its encircling walls had clearly been too much for the old man and he'd hit on garbage disposal as a way to channel his hatred and contempt of anyone who'd actually pay to see someone else's house. His idea of a top night out was to patrol the gardens in the hope of finding a stray Coke can which he would then bear back to the house in triumph, proclaiming, 'How much worse would it have been if we'd let those National Trust buggers get the place?'

'I would like to invite your daughter to come to tea after school,' said Mrs Gadget firmly.

'Ah, *chérie*, she would love to, but she iz in San Moritz. I don't think she can make it,' said Sylvie regretfully.

'I mean your youngest daughter, Ambrosia.'

'Ah, Min. You want to see Min. Yes, of course, absolutely. Tomorrow?'

'I'll pick her up from school and bring her home for tea,' said Mrs Gadget. 'What time would you like to collect her?'

'Bof! Er, I'll have to ask Mrs Norris and then perhaps you call me and then . . .'

'Well, we look forward to having her.'

'You are very kind,' said Sylvie. 'I'm sure Min will be very 'appy with you.'

Whether Sylvie was completely off her head at that moment or whether she had a rare flash of prescience is not known. For Min was very, very happy with the Gadget family. Brought up in the glory and splendour of Chieverley, she took instead to their proudly purchased, conscientiously tidied and completely modern house as though it were a dream come true for her. For once she left school when everyone else did, had fish fingers for her tea, had her unruly hair plaited by Mrs Gadget and settled down on the three-piece suite to watch *Blue Peter*. Neither Ambrose, nor Sylvie, nor Mrs Norris turned up to collect her on the first occasion so she stayed the night and burst into tears when she saw the Winnie the Pooh duvet cover Will's devoted mother had put on her bed, declaring it was the loveliest thing that had ever happened to her.

That day set the pattern for the future. Min came home with Will after school every day to sit in the kitchen while his mum taught her to make cheese straws and let her help mix a sponge cake, or showed her how to knit in the front room. The de Beauforts, only too happy to have found an unpaid source of diversion for a child they obviously couldn't cope with, let Min more or less live with the *famille* Gadget, *mère* and *père* of which grew to love her as the daughter they couldn't have.

Admittedly, this doesn't make the de Beauforts sound like great people but they weren't bad at heart and even their neglect of Min was not born from lack of love. It was more that by the time she came along – wherever she came from – they were too old, too worn out, too broke, too drunk, too absent-minded, too disorganised and probably too selfish, to care for another child. They'd successfully brought up four splendid specimens and doing it all over again was too much for them. Chieverley was crumbling about their ears, their debts were mounting, and they quite simply lacked the resources in every sense to look after Min.

While she longed to be part of the Gadget family, perversely William was fascinated by the glamour of Chieverley, that huge stone house set in soft green parkland with its itinerant inhabitants who'd always just arrived from somewhere exciting and were on their way to somewhere even better. It was so beautiful yet so messy that you could do anything you wanted there without a mother in an apron telling you to pick your socks up off the floor. He loved the chaos as much as Min loved the orderly nature of his house.

Whatever the circumstances of Min's birth, one thing was clear. Someone died and left her a serious amount of money when she was eleven. Instead of following Will – as she passionately wanted – to the local grammar school, she was whisked off to a very expensive boarding school on the outskirts of Paris. While she was there Ambrose died of a heart attack, brought on, some said, by the discovery of some particularly raunchy female underwear in the shrubbery. The de Beauforts held a family summit (minus Min, of course) and decided they had no option but to sell Chieverley, by then a decrepit and very smelly old house where every room contained a stash of empty bottles. Sylvie, whose alcohol habit had progressed by then to the point where she tottered around with a child's Tommy Tippee full of gin tied around her neck to prevent her losing it, was taken away to a specialist clinic. There she remained for the rest of her life, which wasn't long, under the permanent impression she was hosting a drinks party. Min, whose guardianship was transferred to the Parisian de Beauforts, never saw her again.

The Paris branch of the clan tried their best to turn her into a sophisticated, poised, well-groomed French girl. They failed totally. When Will finally met up with her again, she was dressed as though she'd thrown herself into a pile of clothes at a jumble sale, she was penniless, half-starved, and living with a man for whom the word 'unsuitable', at least to those concerned with pedigree and pure lineage, might have been coined.

Chapter Three

Having lived out the lengthy years of their adolescence separately, each pained by their inability to conform to the conventions of teenage life, Will and Min were to meet once more in very different circumstances. When Will departed for university in a blaze of glory as the first member of his family to attend such an august institution, he had chosen a degree that would cause their paths to cross again. He was to study French and Philosophy, a decision which had deeply worried his pragmatic father.

'But what use will it be?' Phil kept asking, in the hope Will would suddenly see the light and head off to study electrical engineering. 'What will you be able to do with that?'

'I'll get a job,' replied his son.

'As what?' asked Phil.

'As a philosopher,' answered the teenage wag.

Will spent an enjoyably undemanding year at a pleasant rural university where he added considerably to his life skills by learning how to give a successful party, roll a joint and tell sufficient lies to women in order to seduce them. Studying poetry soon cured him of any interest in it and his philosophical bent was straightened out by the fact that the philosophy department was due to be shut down thanks to lack of funds – not, sadly, because they had succeeded in proving the futility of their own existence. Hence they required so little of Will that his academic career was an exercise in Free Will (Do I want to write this essay?) rather than Determinism (You will be thrown out if you don't).

His French course was slightly more rigorous in that it did at least expect him to cross the Channel at some point in order to communicate with the people who lived on the other side. He went to Paris to study at the Sorbonne for a few months, something that sounded charmingly artistic but in fact was rather lonely and expensive. His student grant afforded him only a *chambre de bonne*, a room up eleven flights of stairs with a communal bathroom at the end of the hallway. In his Parisian eyrie he sat alone of an evening, drinking red wine out of a square-shaped plastic bottle – the same vintage drunk by tramps. At the weekends, he subsisted on baguette with cheese whereas on weekdays he could at least buy a 3-franc lunch in the Sorbonne canteen.

His daily budget was 10 francs (excluding cigarettes). He hopped over the turnstile at the Metro to avoid buying a ticket, only took his clothes to the launderette when they became capable of standing up by themselves, and finished up other people's leftover food and drink. He'd asked his parents for more money but they were uncharacteristically uncharitable about it. His mother didn't want him to have any spare cash as she was convinced Paris was a hotbed of drugs, and his father had decided it was time his son stopped wafting about and learnt a few hard lessons about the real world. He'd had rather enough of William's airs and graces and thought it high time his son brushed the rose petals out of his hair, found out that money doesn't grow on trees, that were wishes to be horses, then beggars would ride, and other such useful strictures.

Until this experience, Will had never quite understood how very boring it was to be poor and this he found even more depressing than the cold and constant hunger. There wasn't anything he could do that didn't involve spending money. Even, he reasoned, going for a walk eventually resulted in greater fiscal outlay because then he'd be hungrier and need more food, which would cost him more money. He wasn't managing to make any friends to share his penury with – the vast Sorbonne with its thousands of students was not the easiest place to strike up relationships so he was usually alone in his little rooftop room.

The overwhelming beauty of Paris only made his loneliness the more acute. One Saturday morning, with the whole weekend stretching in front of him like a desert, he decided to take a ride on the Metro to the flea market. A girl on one of the stalls caught his eye. She was wearing a multi-coloured knitted beret on top of her mass of dark curls and she was laughing in a way that you couldn't ignore. In one mittened hand she held a cigarette, the other she was waving around her head to illustrate whatever story she was telling in rapid, guttural French. Her sheepskin coat was falling to pieces and she wore an absurd pair of flares. She was gorgeous, captivating, and very, very familiar.

The stall contained the most awful collection of items. Its owners, the dark-haired girl and a tall, unshaven young man, seemed cheerfully aware that they would never sell anything as they were ignoring anyone who looked at their wares and concentrating on each other. Will fiddled around with a few dirty brass objects and then coughed loudly. They continued to ignore him so he coughed several times more and finally, just as he was giving a fine impersonation of an emphysema sufferer, the man looked up.

'*Oui?*' he said, quite rudely, as though Will had walked into a private room.

'I wondered, how much is this?' he said, holding up a mysterious thing he'd picked at random from the display.

The girl turned round and stared at him.

'That is verr expensive,' replied the young man.

'How expensive?' challenged Will.

'Verr, verr expensive. You cannot afford it,' the young man said arrogantly.

The girl carried on staring at Will.

'I'd just like to know,' he said, smiling back at her. 'I once saw something very like it in an old house in Berkshire, near where I grew up.'

'It is you!' cried the girl, rushing around to the other side of the stall. 'William, I don't believe it!' She flung her arms around him to give him a hug but the height imbalance between them was such that she was virtually holding on to his waist.

'It's me – Min! Don't you recognise me?' she said, her little face beaming up at him from under its mass of black hair and crazy hat.

'Of course I do,' said Will gently, wrapping his long arms round her. 'I've missed you. We all missed you. You never came to see us after you'd left.'

Once Chieverley had been sold, Min had no remaining ties in Berkshire save with the Gadgets whom the French de Beauforts didn't see as suitable companions for the girl. Mrs Gadget had written and written, asking her to come and stay in the holidays, but Tante Véronique, who had taken Min under her wing, had vetoed the plan. While the Gadgets were, she thought, worthy, kind and eminently capable of looking after a small child, she had no intention of letting a grown-up Min cultivate them as social acquaintances. After all, she had heard they lived in a terribly modern sort of house, had no connections and were not at all *comme il faut*. To save argument with her niece, who was entirely malleable most of the time but had an uncanny knack of digging her heels in when least expected, she never told Min of the correspondence between Paris and Purley. It had come to an abrupt halt some years ago when

Véronique, bored of inventing excuses, finally wrote firmly to the Gadgets to ask them not to contact Min again.

It was a chilly and insulting letter. When poor Mrs Gadget read it at breakfast one morning, she burst into tears, dripping salt water on to her grapefruit segments.

'What's up, love?' said Phil, putting down his copy of the *Telegraph*. Will had never seen his mother cry before. Her face seemed to collapse out of its regular pattern of pleasant features into a messy, twisted mask. He sat rooted to his chair with fear. Tears were splashing on to the cherry-patterned vinyl cloth his mother always spread for use in the morning. The toast had popped up, the kettle boiled and the eggs were starting to smoke but neither of his parents noticed, another alarming sign.

Burying her face in a tea towel, not something usually allowed under the strict regime of household cleanliness and hygiene, she passed Phil the letter.

'I see,' he said grimly, once he'd read the short missive. 'We're good enough when they want something. When they don't need us, they don't want anything to do with us.'

'But I wanted to see her again! I want to see her grow up,' said Mrs G, through her sobs.

'Hush, lovie, hush,' said Phil, putting his arms around his wife who cried her broken heart into his beautifully ironed shirt. 'Don't fret now. There, have a good cry,' he continued, stroking her hair.

'Oh, Phil,' said Mrs Gadget. 'She was our little girl.'

'There,' he said, wiping her eyes and nose on a serviette. 'She wasn't even ours, Joannie, we always knew they'd want her back.'

Will sat through this, bug-eyed. Until that moment his parents had appeared to be one entity that went under the composite name of Mum-and-Dad. It had never occurred to him they had a relationship with each other independent of him. All he'd seen of that so far was that, occasionally, they'd peck each other modestly on the cheek, and sometimes one would display mild irritation when the other failed to appear from the garden shed in time for dinner or took too long to get ready to go round to the neighbours'.

This display of raw emotion, coupled with the mystery of who 'they' were and why his parents thought they'd want Min, was extremely unsettling for a young adolescent. As his parents continued to hold each other in a tight embrace, he slipped out of the kitchen, got his bag and set off for school on his bike, disturbed again to discover that neither of them cared he'd gone off without a shred of breakfast inside him.

By evening, the Gadget household was back to normal, tea was on the table, and the only perceptible difference was the redness around Mrs Gadget's eyes and a crossness in Phil's manner, which he combined with excessive tenderness towards his wife. Something big had happened, concluded Will, but he clearly had no chance of finding out what so he went to his room to play his new The The single fifteen times in a row until his father banged on the door and told him to change the record.

'But I would have come, if you'd invited me,' said Min.

'We did, loads of times,' said Will, who was later shown the dismissive letter by his father as an example of why he wanted William to work hard at school and get on in the world so that nobody would be able to look down on him as they had on his parents. Phil wanted his son to hold his head high with the very best.

'Véronique wrote to my mother to tell her that you now moved in a different world where friendships with servants were not to be encouraged.'

'Bitch!' said Min in outrage. 'I loved your parents, they were so kind to me. Véronique just nagged me all this time about losing weight and not biting my nails and behaving properly.'

'You should have run away,' said Will. 'You could have come and lived with us all the time.'

'I wish I had,' said Min. 'I'd have been much happier. You can't imagine, the horror of being launched into polite society.'

A cough came from her erstwhile companion.

'Oh, sorry. William, this is Christophe,' she said. 'Christophe, this is William, my oldest friend.'

'Heh,' muttered Christophe, sounding very put out.

That evening, they – or rather Min – invited Will to come to the studio flat she and Christophe shared in Pigalle, an area where by night neon signs advertised any number of lewd entertainments available for an astonishingly small financial outlay. He arrived at their address and rang the doorbell, but there was no reply.

'*Ils sont pas là, monsieur.*' Standing by the doorway was a transvestite whose bright lipstick and high heels gave a semblance of femininity which a quick look at 'her' broad jaw and large hands soon dispelled.

'Would you know at what time may they return?' asked Will, whose French was by now fluent but still rather erratic.

'Not yet,' she said. 'There's time.' She tossed her long blonde hair and sucked her middle finger, moving it in and out of her mouth. Then raised an eyebrow enquiringly.

'That's very kind on the part of you,' said Will. 'I am inconsolable with regret not to be capable of accepting the offer that you make.'

The transvestite threw back her head and laughed.

'Most men are not so polite.'

'Surely with a woman as beautiful as you . . .' Will soldiered on, hoping Min would appear soon.

'*Chéri*, you are too good to be true. Where do you come from?'

'England,' said Will. 'Would you like some smoke?' He produced a battered packet of Marlboros from his jeans pocket.

The transvestite laughed again. 'Thank you, I have some.'

She got out a flat silver case from her handbag and took a long white cigarette from it.

'But you may light my fire,' she said, looking naughtily at him through her eyelashes. This time Will laughed, grateful his parents couldn't see him flirting with a man dressed as a woman late at night in the red light district of Paris.

Cigarettes lit, the two of them lounged companionably in the doorway, one against each side of the stone arch.

'Have they lived here long?' asked Will, curious for any information.

'A few months maybe,' said his new acquaintance. 'Are they your friends?'

'She is,' said Will. 'I'm not sure about him.'

'Ah, him,' said the transvestite, spitting on the pavement. 'He is a pig,' she said in disgust. 'One day . . .' Her voice suddenly dropped a couple of octaves and her stance changed to that of a man squaring up for a fight. 'One day I am going to punch him.' The big bejewelled hand was clenched into a fist. 'One day that cocksucking, mother-fucking, dirty little bastard is going to feel what *this* is like.'

The sound of running feet announced the arrival of Min.

'I'm so sorry I'm late. I couldn't get away from work, they were short-staffed,' she gasped.

'Don't worry yourself,' said the transvestite, who'd reverted to simpering female mode. 'I have been looking after this lovely boy.'

'Thank you, Marie,' said Min. 'You are good.'

Min and Will set off up the stairs.

'Mind you have him,' Marie called after her. 'If you don't, I will. For free!'

If Will felt hard done by with his accommodation, he quickly changed his mind when he saw how Min and Christophe elected to exist. He may have had a fantasy life in which he was a French poet starving in a garret and drinking absinthe, but to see the reality of such an existence shocked him. It was cold, frightening and demeaning. He hated to see Min cheerfully heating up leftovers from a restaurant where she worked on the ancient cooker which lived behind a floral curtain drawn across one corner of their flat, or wearing five jumpers so they wouldn't have to turn the heating on. He winced when Christophe came in proudly bearing a bunch of rotten bananas he'd somehow got hold of, as though he'd bought Min some fantastic treat. He nearly cried when they told him they were taking him out for dinner and they ended up at a soup kitchen.

Even so, he found himself heading for Pigalle most evenings. If Marie was in residence, she would always let him know which of the pair was at home. When it was Min alone, she would say, '*Vas-y! Vas-y vite!* You have time to make love!' If Christophe was there, she would scowl and say, 'The pig is in his sty.' This was very useful as it avoided potentially embarrassing situations, like the time when Will, for a joke, had stood in the corridor outside the door to the flat, singing '*La Vie En Rose*', and a very grumpy Christophe had answered.

He quickly became jealous of the relationship between Will and Min. They weren't making love, despite Marie's daily exhortations, but they did have a very palpable connection. Although Will hadn't seen Min for years, he had an empathy with her that made it very easy for him to understand her. He could have told you what colour jumper she would pick out in a shop, take a sip of a glass of wine and tell you whether she would like it, predict what her reply would be to whatever he said to her. It was like a psychic tie, he just knew. He could tell Min thought she was in love with Christophe but that, without having a clue what love actually was, she had mistaken infatuation and lust for genuine emotion. He suspected she wanted to be in love and that Christophe fitted the part of romantic hero, battling against the world she had grown up in, which only served to increase the attraction.

If Will could read Min like a book, Christophe was as comprehensible to him as underwater lessons in Cantonese. Will was pretty sure that unlike Min, whose thoughts and feelings were visibly played out across the surface of her personality, Christophe had hidden depths and that these might be quite murky. He worried that Min, who couldn't possibly operate with a hidden agenda, was being strung along by someone who could.

To say Christophe was a fervent believer in his cause was to use very mild terminology for what had become a full-blown obsession. He was consumed with the righteousness of his crusade, obsessed with his own role in restoring the rights of the people to them, lucidly, verbosely convinced of the consummate importance of himself, Christophe, deputy leader of the Trotskyite Alliance. He claimed to be the son of Breton fisherfolk but Will felt sceptical about that. The whole Trotskyite Alliance caper had 'Parental Rebellion' stamped all over it and Will longed to expose him, '*J'accuse!*' fashion, as the son of a dentist or an insurance salesman or an architect or anything suitably middle-class and unsexy.

The relationship between Min and Christophe had hardly started in auspicious circumstances. Christophe had been handing out leaflets one day – or rather attempting to press bits of paper into the unwilling hands of passers by – when he'd been run over by a man on roller-skates. In those distant days before the in-line skate was invented, young men in Paris still hared around at frightening speed on old-fashioned skates strapped to the bottom of their boots. Those who had mastered the art were fairly impressive – some could go up the stairs of the Metro at a pace mere pedestrians could only envy. But not all were so proficient. It was Christophe's bad luck – or Min's peculiar fate – that he should be standing right in the trajectory of a boy whose desire for speed was not equalled by his competence. Out of control, he crashed into Christophe so fast that he propelled him several metres down the pavement before depositing him in a flowerbed, leaflets strewn to the four corners of the square. Min's first sight of Christophe was of a man with a bloody nose, lying pathetically amongst the begonias, clutching the last few of his pamphlets to his chest. To make the scene more poignant, it had started to rain.

Christophe looked vulnerable and sweet – something that didn't happen again for the rest of the term of their engagement. Min rushed over and picked him out of the flowerbed. She mopped up the blood, gathered what leaflets she could, dusted off the shreds of municipal planting and took him to a café where he hungrily devoured two baguettes, an omelette, a small steak and a carafe of red wine. Min paid the bill.

At that time she was largely purposeless. She lived with an uncle and aunt in a spacious apartment in one of the nicest *quartiers* of Paris where she did literally nothing. She had left school, having learnt little more than where she didn't want to go in life, although a certain knowledge of the finer details of French protocol was, strangely, to turn out to be one of her greatest assets at a later stage. She was ripe to adopt a cause and Christophe provided her with one.

His talk of oppression by the upper classes – which officially did not exist in France, although like everywhere else the Republic was hardly a bastion of fairness – fired Min's soul. Suddenly she saw the shallowness, the unfairness, the strife, which the current form of government forced upon the majority of its people. She cried for the salt workers, the farmers, the fishermen, the lorry drivers and their families, and their constant toil. Never having actually paid any tax, she was blissfully unaware that the French system quite successfully penalises the rich and provides a safety net for the poor. This fact not being in Christophe's interest, he stayed quiet on these matters.

It could hardly be irrelevant that he was very good-looking. He had the perfectly chiselled jaw, the high cheekbones and dishevelled dark hair of a male model. He also had flashing eyes, passion, determination and drive. His serious demeanour concealed the fact that he was an arch seducer and it didn't take him long to persuade this tempting little morsel to fall into his outstretched hands. Until William Gadget arrived by chance in Paris, Min had been singing along to the sort of song sheet rarely heard on the Faubourg St Honoré.

Will found many things alarming about Christophe, not least his complete absence of doubt about his extremist political philosophy. He did not and would not let anyone else question the fact that the workers of France might not want to live in a perfect Trotskyite society, because if they didn't now, they would when it happened. It was impossible to conduct an argument with him because he always dived under the cover of one of his faux-rational statements. Will felt sure that despite the fervent verbiage which Christophe used to put his case, he didn't really care about the workers or anyone else. Christophe only really cared about one thing and that was himself.

'So, Christophe,' Will would say as they sat in a nearby bar where Min worked most evenings, which handily meant they could get free drinks, 'when the revolution comes, what are you going to do with the people who like the capitalist system?'

'Ah,' Christophe would reply. 'What you fail to comprehend is that when the revolution happens and we have a free and fair society in which all are treated as equals and have rights which are now only available to the few rich and privileged, no one will want the capitalist system because all will be able to see how much better life is under the Trotskyite model.'

'But surely the rich and privileged people won't like it because they'll have to lose something in order for all to be equal?'

'They will come to see that they have been oppressors, and that in a properly organised society they will no longer have to subjugate their fellow man in order to get what they want. The state will provide for every need.'

As Christophe spoke, Min whirled past, carrying a pile of dirty plates and looking exhausted.

'Min,' said Christophe, 'can you get us some more wine? This one is not good.'

'I'll see what I can do,' she whispered, before setting off to the other side of the bar to tend to some real customers.

After a few weeks of observing this champion of the rights of the people blatantly oppress his own girlfriend, Will could stand it no longer. Min appeared to be entirely funding her own and Christophe's existence with a variety of jobs such as minding market stalls, working in the bar, cleaning the restaurant, while Christophe devoted himself to the cause. Will took the matter up with her one day when they were riding around Paris on the buses, he having splashed out on two tickets.

'I'll be going back to university soon,' he said as the number 24 trundled along the riverbank.

'Don't go,' said Min. 'Stay here with us – you'll have much more fun.'

'I don't doubt it,' he said dryly. 'But I have to go, I've got work to do.'

'Why do you need a degree? Why don't you just get on with your life?'

'Because there are things I want, and to get them I need a job. I can't live on air.'

'You're so materialistic,' said Min.

'Don't you want more than this?' said Will. 'Do you really want to live in some room in Pigalle for ever? It might be fun now but it won't be when you're forty.'

'William!' said Min. 'Can't we just enjoy the view?'

'I want to know,' he persisted. 'What are you going to do? Marry Christophe and spend the rest of your life supporting the Party?'

Min was silent.

'Or is marriage too bourgeois a concept for you these days?'

'You don't really know Christophe.'

'No, and guess what? I don't want to know him. He's using you, Min. He has you running around him in circles while he talks bollocks.'

'But I love him,' she said, looking hurt.

'Oh, God,' said Will. 'That's just so like you, isn't it? Why can't you go out with someone vaguely normal? Why do you have to fall in love with a disenfranchised lunatic?'

'You don't understand,' said Min.

'No,' said Will. 'I don't understand why *you* don't understand why *I* can't possibly understand. You're not even living in poverty, you're living in squalor with an egomaniac – who is possibly psychotic – who will never, ever be able to support you, love you, or even, I have to say, like you. And you wonder why I have some reservations!'

'You don't know anything about love,' said Min haughtily.

'Maybe,' said Will. 'But I know enough to know that whatever the attraction is between you and Christophe, it isn't love, Min. At least, not love as you want to know it.'

'When did you become such an expert on relationships?'

'I've had plenty of time to think, and one of my thoughts concerns your trust fund. Tell me you live the way you do because you like slumming it and not because all the money's gone?'

Min looked embarrassed.

'There's a bit of a problem with it at the moment, at least until I'm twenty-five.'

'Yes?' said Will.

'I made a donation last year which the trustees objected to so they're refusing to let me have access to it.'

'A donation. To the Trotskyite Alliance, by any chance?'

'They were very short of funds,' said Min defensively.

'And when you're twenty-five, you will have control of all of your money?'

'That's right.'

'Does Christophe know this?' asked Will.

'I might have mentioned it.'

'Listen to me,' said Will. 'Ditch him. Get out, get away, run, don't go home tonight, just get as far away from that man as you possibly can. Min, you *have* to get out of this.'

'I don't know if I can,' she said softly.

'If you don't, he'll ruin your life.'

'And if I do, my life is ruined because I won't have him.'

'Crying isn't going to help.'

'Nothing helps.'

'Well,' said Will, 'remember this. Wherever you are, whatever you do, for the rest of your life, you can always, always call me. Don't ever think you've left it too long. It could be next year, it could be in twenty-five years' time. You might have five children and I might be married to an eighteen-year-old Vietnamese bride, but you can always call.'

'Thank you,' said Min, and kissed him gently on the mouth as the bus trundled along the left bank of the River Seine.

When Will got back to Exeter University after his sojourn in Paris, he wasn't entirely convinced his student housemates realised he'd been away. They seemed to think he must just have been out a lot over the past term. Not that they weren't delighted to see him – Dallas rolled a celebration joint, Mac slapped him on the back in friendly fashion so hard that Will thought his spinal cord might burst through his oesophagus, and Jem asked him for a cheque to cover the phone bill. Very little appeared to have changed.

'By the way, don't use the washing machine,' said Jem.

'Why?' asked Will.

'We had a party.'

Seeing no reason to seek details, he moved on to other matters.

'What have you lot been up to?'

There was a small silence.

'I dyed my hair,' said Dallas sunnily. When stoned, he tended to behave like a not particularly intelligent toddler.

'That's nice,' said Will. 'What colour did you dye it?'

Dallas thought for a bit longer.

'Pink.'

'Mac got a written warning from the Dean,' said Jem.

'Yeah, that was bloody funny,' yawned Mac, lying on the sofa wearing dark glasses.

'What for?' asked Will.

'Oh, just more crimes against humanity, the usual thing,' said Jem.

'Stupid old man,' said Mac.

'Quite,' said Jem. 'I mean, if we accept the Dean was fully aware his youngest daughter was sexually active, that he had a secret longing to see Mac with no clothes on and that he thinks his front wall looks better that way, then really, he doesn't have a leg to stand on.'

'You didn't?' said Will.

'He certainly did,' said Jem.

'Wow!' said Will. 'That's impressive.'

'Thank you, thank you,' said Mac. 'I aim to please.'

'So we keep hearing,' said Jem.

'Are you going to get thrown out?' asked Will.

'Fortunately, the case of Drunken Student Idiot versus the Might of This Wonderful University has plenty of legal precedents which imply Drunken Student Idiot must continue to be tolerated provided he shows a suitable level of contrition. Either that, or the Dean is terrified of Mac's mother,' said Jem who was reading law, something he took very seriously, unlike Dallas who received his educational stimulus via the backs of cereal packets or antipodean lunchtime soap operas, and Mac who was a perfect example of Wittgenstein's theory. Just because he knew what a book was didn't mean he'd ever read one.

'Anyone for a game of Risk?' asked the recumbent Scot. Risk was his favourite game, world domination being something of an armchair pursuit for him.

'No more Risk until you do some washing up,' said Jem. 'I'm going to take the game away and lock it up if you don't deal with those three-month-old plates in the sink.'

'Bugger off, Mary,' said Mac peaceably. 'You know the reason I don't wash up is because I don't use anything from the kitchen. I haven't been in there since Christmas.' Just then the phone rang.

'Oh, God, that'll be someone wanting my body,' said Mac. He wasn't necessarily being arrogant. At six foot five and blessed with natural sporting ability, he was hotly pursued by the captain of every university team for every sport invented as well as by large numbers of girls eager to sample his famous delights. So prolific was he, his mob of girlfriends was nicknamed 'The 101 Club' by the household as that was the number of girls Mac could remember sleeping with, when asked for a headcount. He wasn't particularly dishonest in that he never promised them anything more than sex. If they chose to interpret his actions in a different way, that was their problem.

Jem picked up the receiver.

'Hello, House of Fun.'

'Mac . . . now that is a good question. I wonder where he's got to, the naughty boy.'

Jem put his hand over the receiver and mouthed 'Charlotte'. Mac shook his head furiously. Jem gave him an evil smile.

'Hang on a minute, Charlotte,' he said. 'I can hear the front door opening and I think it might be him. Shall I have a look?'

'What the fuck?' mouthed Mac.

'Washing up,' Jem mouthed back. 'Or else.'

'No!' mouthed Mac.

'Ah, Charlotte, here he comes, let me hand you over.'

Mac leapt to his feet and ran into the kitchen where the noise of running water was heard.

'Oh, sorry, Charlotte, I did think it was him but it wasn't. Silly me, what a mistake to make . . . yes, I'll tell him you called . . . Thanks, 'bye now.'

Jem wandered over to the stereo. 'Shall I put some music on?'

'Stop!' came a terrible yell from the other side of the room. It was Dallas, temporarily revived from his drug-induced stupor. 'Don't let him!'

'What's wrong?' asked Will.

'He's been torturing us with classical music,' said Dallas. 'We can't bear it any longer.'

'Yesterday,' said Mac, putting his head round the door, 'we had to listen to some Finnish bloke murder a violin. No wonder they're depressed in Scandinavia.'

'Sibelius is a very fine composer,' said Jem huffily. 'It's been a cultural desert round here without you, Will. I've had to put up with these philistines all alone.'

'Watch it, Will,' said Dallas. 'He'll have you down the Philip Larkin Appreciation Society in a flash.' With that, he lapsed back into daytime television-watching mode.

'Any plans for tonight?' Mac shouted through from the kitchen where he was attempting to clean some crockery using Persil washing powder.

'There's drinks at the Law Society,' said Jem. 'We could start there. As long as Mac faithfully promises not to head butt anyone.'

'So sue me,' he replied. 'Flora and Jen are having a toga party.'

'Interesting,' said Jem. 'Two rival members of The 101 conspire to get Mac to remove his trousers. What can it all mean?'

'Shush,' said Dallas. 'Countdown's starting.'

It was, reflected Will, good to be back.

He didn't have to wait twenty-five years and five children for Min to get back in touch. Her relationship with Christophe broke down only months after Will left Paris. What part he'd played in its demise is impossible to quantify save to say the presence of a sceptical third party is never a help to the progress of true love. By making Min laugh, by talking to her, just by spending time with her, Will broke the spell that had enchanted Min. Her dream of love, which until he came had been as bright and shiny as newly polished silver, suddenly seemed to tarnish and fade. Christophe, who had seemed so intriguing, so unlike anyone she had ever met before, started to annoy her with his demands and his moodiness. Her lifestyle, which had appeared to her to be the epitome of a romantic ideal, was revealed to be uncomfortable and exigent. Love, she was coming to see, might not be enough.

However, even unsatisfactory relationships need some form of finale and Min got hers. For a liaison which had been full of clichés – the lovers in Paris, struggling to make ends meet, family opposition on the part of the de Beauforts, youthful passion pitted against maturity and power – it was a fitting one.

Min came home early one day to find Christophe busily instructing another member of the Party in some of the more basic aspects of political doctrine. To her credit, Min left immediately and crossed the Channel in search of the one person who had yet to let her down.

Will arrived back at his student house one afternoon to find as usual the television blaring, empty mugs arranged artfully across every surface and a variety of personages inhabiting the sitting-room. Through the dense smoggy air, he spied once more a familiar small figure. Curled up on the brown polyester-covered sofa was Min. She'd come to stay.

In the curious way of people who have never really had a home, she had a knack for establishing herself in other people's lives and making it seem like she had always been there. Again, this wasn't deliberate, it was more a product of her peculiarly adaptable personality which accommodated itself to other people rather than making deliberate statements of its own. Thus she soon blended into the house on Priory Road to the point whereby she became a *de facto* part of the furniture, although a slightly better upholstered addition than most of the original features.

That she and Dallas should get on was no surprise to anyone. In those happy days, neither of them was possessed of any ambition or purpose other than the successful wasting of time. Thus they were happy to indulge themselves in endless conversations about the plotline of *Neighbours*, which Dallas fancifully used as a tool on which to sharpen his critical faculties, preferring it to the more traditional set texts such as Shakespeare, or to dither around in the centre of Exeter, playing childish games of 'I Dare You'.

The puerile level of interaction between Dallas and Min should have acted as an irritant to Mac but, strangely, he seemed oblivious. Min, in his eyes, could do no wrong, an attitude that stood in sharp contrast to the way he treated the rest of her sex. Most women who crossed his path were judged by the criterion of whether he wanted to sleep with them or not and he modified his behaviour accordingly. As in either he slept with them and then ignored them or he just ignored them. With Min, he showed a softness that no one would have suspected he concealed inside. It is a phenomenon seen in nature that large, aggressive animals will sometimes take it on themselves to protect small, defenceless creatures. With Min, Mac was like a snarling German Shepherd with a tiny kitten cowering between its paws.

Jem was more reserved than the other two. He behaved towards her with great politeness and charm but never sought her company outright. Sometimes she joined him on an outing to the theatre or to a concert and, Jem had to admit, was more intelligent than her behaviour elsewhere would indicate. She was, he discovered, more than capable of holding an in-depth conversation on a wide range of topics and never laughed at his intellectual pretensions. But he couldn't quite forgive her for absorbing so much of Will's time and attention. Until she showed up, William had been his special friend and, in Jem's more foolishly optimistic moments, his soulmate. Unwittingly she changed that so it was no longer 'Jem and Will' but 'Will and Min'.

Will and Min fell straight back into their friendship, in the way that very old acquaintances can. As soon as they were together, all their attention was entirely focused on each other. That kiss on the bus in Paris had never been mentioned but the memory of it hung between them. It hadn't been just a peck on the cheek; it had turned into a fully fledged embrace. For a few minutes, they'd forgotten everything around them and all the reasons why they probably shouldn't kiss each other. But they'd been brought back to reality with a jolt and the embarrassment had been extreme. Min had blushed the colour of beetroot and Will hadn't known where to look. They had parted rather hurriedly and only met again when she paid her surprise visit to Exeter.

The largely happy household rubbed along together quite nicely until a succession of dank, grey spring days started to exhaust the capacity of even such a proficient group of people to do absolutely nothing. Just when they were starting to get a little bored, Mac hit on the notion they should go on tour.

'Do I have to wear a kilt?' said Will at the suggestion the friends might like to visit Mac's estate in Scotland where his mother would be holding a ball.

'It would be nice if you could try and get into the spirit of the thing,' said Mac mildly.

'It's all right for you,' grumbled Will. 'With your great muscular tree trunks for legs.'

'Er, thanks, but count me out,' said Jem. 'Just not my kind of thing.'

'What I don't understand,' mused Dallas, 'is why you chose to come to university in Devon when you live in northern Scotland?'

'I can tell you the answer to that,' said Will. 'Mac thought he'd applied to Edinburgh and only found out when it was too late that he'd ticked the wrong box and had a place at Exeter instead.'

'No!' said Min. 'You must be joking?'

Mac looked rather sheepish. 'That's completely untrue,' he claimed unconvincingly. 'I just wanted to put some distance between my mother and me.'

Mac's mother, Lady MacDougal, was a somewhat controversial figure. On the few occasions that she'd visited, she had always contrived to cause maximum impact. On her first trip she had mistaken the Dean, a very introspective geologist, for a waiter at the inaugural party and spent all evening haranguing him to get her another drink. On her next trip, she had parked in the President's space and refused to move. She was so impressively sure of her own importance that the idea of kow-towing to anybody else never entered her mind.

That year's ball was to be the first Lady Mac had held since her husband had crept quietly off into death, breathing his last in a profound sigh of relief that their long and peculiarly un-intimate union was over. They had been married for thirty-five years, a pairing which had deteriorated into formal companionship once their only son, Dougal, was born. Twenty-seven years older than his wife, Lord MacDougal had become increasingly transparent-looking over his last few years, giving the impression that someone was rubbing out his outline with an eraser. Eventually, like all old soldiers, he faded away.

Mac, who'd been largely brought up in boarding schools, externally resembled his mother, sharing her striking good looks and strident manner. Although the former had come to him naturally, the latter was an acquired response to the rigours of the British education system into which he had been dumped at an early age. At school he soon learnt not to show the soft, dreamy nature he had inherited from his father, and finding attack the better part of defence, imitated his mother's hectoring, decisive demeanour. Only at home, in the beauty of his native Scotland, did he let his guard slip and his gentler side show through.

It seemed to take days to get to Scotland in Mac's revolting old Ford. Once they'd caused serious road rage on the motorway thanks to Mac's insistence on driving in the fast lane, they drove on ever smaller roads, twisting and turning through endless forests and mountains, until at the end of a gravel drive the beautiful pale grey house, Caithness, came into view. Lady Mac was standing imposingly by the front door. Dallas and Will, quite uneasy anyway at the prospect of spending a whole weekend under the aegis of the harridan, were not reassured by her welcome. As they scrambled out of the back of the car to greet her, a hot waft of the bad banana and rank feet stink of a long journey flew out with them, causing her to take a step back in disgust.

But when Min appeared and was introduced by her full name, smiled prettily, took Lady Mac's hand and thanked her for her very generous hospitality, the old bat melted, partly from relief that Dougal had at least one friend who was socially acceptable.

The ball was, admittedly, magnificent. Caithness House was lit by a thousand torches which blazed right down to the loch below the gardens. Inside, the grand old house was decked with candles and great wreaths of fir. Tartan-clad dancers whirled faster and faster, and the piper gave a rousing encore.

Mac and Min, who'd both had the sort of education where Scottish dancing is considered more important than chemistry, were jigging around with great energy. Dallas and Will, who'd crashed into each other and the few partners they'd managed to procure, weren't quite so enthusiastic. After reeling towards disaster, they slipped away to their bedroom to smoke a quiet joint.

From the four-poster bed where they lay they could see out over the loch, a view which faded into darkness as it stretched away from the brilliance of the house. In the far far distance shone a pinprick of light.

'What do you think that is?' said Dallas.

'Must be the sea – a lighthouse perhaps,' said Will, inhaling deeply. 'God, this kilt is uncomfortable. Do you think wearing it is a test of manhood?'

'Och,' said Dallas. 'Depends what you wear underneath.'

'I'm not sure about Scotland,' said Will. 'It's not really my kind of place.'

'Don't worry, mate,' said Dallas. 'We'll swap the five-star

castle for student squalor again tomorrow. Not long to put up with feather beds and butler service.'

'Oh, thank God,' said Will dozily, drifting off into a dope-fuelled sleep.

The door opened and Mac and Min came in.

'Guessed what you were up to,' Min said companionably, settling down on the large, comfortable bed.

'Pass it over, son,' said Mac, reaching for the joint.

'Oi, MacDougal,' said Dallas. 'Why don't you share a little of your heritage with us?'

Mac thought for a second and then started to sing, a surprisingly melodic Gaelic ballad about a woman who loses her lover to the sea. As he sang, the others gently left the real world and entered a hazy, harmonious, peaceful state, a pleasing trance from which it was but a short step to the land of oblivion.

The foursome arrived back in Exeter, strangely refreshed by the bracing air of Scotland and invigorated by the bond of friendship they had formed. Poor Jem, who had instantly regretted his churlish refusal to join the trip but was too proud to go back on his word, felt even more excluded. It was his idea that the Exeter house should have a party, his hidden agenda being an attempt to try and rekindle a sense of union between the original housemates. In that respect, it was an abject failure.

By 2 a.m. the party had deteriorated into chaos. Some drunken youths were trying to dig up the garden in search of the emergency booze they'd buried on their way in, in case supplies ran short late into the night. Sadly they had entirely forgotten where they'd placed their cache and were deeply into some impromptu earthworks. A couple who for no discernible reason had come dressed as Spiderman and Wonder Woman were exercising their superhero powers across the three-piece suite. The kitchen was awash with men in rugby shirts and someone was throwing up in the bathroom.

Will and Min retired to his bedroom. They lay down on his bed.

'When I shut my eyes, the room spins,' said Min.

'Keep them open,' said Will.

'But what will I see?' asked Min.

'Rising damp.'

'Is it contagious?'

'Most certainly.'

'How will we escape it?'

'We will put brown paper bags over our heads. And then we will be safe.'

'Good idea. Do you have any?'

'No. We should improvise with my duvet.'

Will, at this point, had no intention of taking it any further. But once the two bodies were snuggled together under his coverlet, inevitably a union of sorts took place. While they were both drunk enough to make sex a more or less impossible mission, they did still manage to cross a boundary in their relationship from which there would be no going back.

When Will woke up with a head that felt as though someone was repeatedly stabbing it just above his left ear, he found he was alone. At first this didn't surprise him as he usually woke up by himself. But then it occurred to him that last night there had been someone else there. In a wave of absolute horror he realised he had, while drunk, made love to Min. And that she was no longer there.

He didn't leap out of bed as that would have been asking a bit much, even given the severity of the situation. After about ten minutes of lying still and groaning, he staggered out and blundered around his room, trying to put together the disparate images in his mind. It was, without a doubt, one of the stupidest things he'd ever done. Actually, it was worse than stupid as that implied he was a person of limited intelligence and couldn't be held to blame for what he'd done. Will might be many things but dim he was not.

It wasn't that he hadn't wanted to have sex with her. Over the past weeks he had become increasingly aware that quite the opposite was true. He was torn apart by conflicting urges – one of them shame that he could fancy someone who was practically his sister, the other a conviction that he was in love with her.

Whichever of those prevailed, getting drunk and pouncing on her was not what he had intended at all. He certainly hadn't wanted her to flee which, it was becoming clear from a cursory search around the house, was exactly what she'd done. There were plenty of people downstairs, mostly comatose and snoring, but none of them was Min.

Mac shuffled in wearing a sleeping bag which made it seem as though a very large red caterpillar had just entered the kitchen. He bunny-hopped over to the fridge and opened it, only to close it very quickly when he saw what was inside.

'Jesus! Who did that?'

Will, who was sitting at the kitchen table with his head in his hands, did not react.

'Earth to Gadget,' said Mac. 'Come on, man, you can't be feeling that bad. You didn't even drink any of my Elephant Spunk cocktail.'

He looked up. 'Mac,' he said quietly, 'have you seen Min this morning?'

'Nope,' said Mac. 'She's probably sleeping it off.'

'No,' said Will, 'I don't think so. I mean, I know so. I think she may have gone.' He met Mac's eye.

'Gadget,' said Mac slowly, 'I may not be famed for my powers of perception, but are you trying to tell me something?'

Will nodded miserably.

'You fucking moron,' said Mac. 'Even I wouldn't have done

57

that. Mind you, I have wondered . . .'

'Oh, shut up,' said Will viciously.

Dallas tooled in, looking rumpled.

'Hey, guess what?' said Mac. 'Gadget's screwed Min and now she's left.'

'Mac, shut up!' said Will again.

'No, I won't because you deserve it. You are a prat,' said Mac. 'That was a really dumb thing to do, and now because of you she's left us. Brilliant party trick, Will. Well done.'

He tried to stomp out but found this a hard manoeuvre to pull off while clad in just a sleeping bag.

'I never thought I'd hear myself say this,' said Dallas, 'but for once I agree with Mac. Wonders will never cease.'

The atmosphere in the house was strained after that, and not helped by Mac's leaving the room each time Will walked in. The first few times this happened, he fervently hoped it was a coincidence but the slamming doors and stamping feet that accompanied Mac's hasty exit from anywhere Will entered soon showed him it was deliberate. Dallas, whose perpetual good humour was exacerbated and not caused by his impressive pot habit, was unusually cold as well. When Will tried talking to him, Dallas just kept upping the volume on the television until Will got the message and left him alone.

Jem was secretly pleased by the turn of events but tried not to show it. Now he had Will to himself again, he embarked on a campaign of diverting nights out for the pair of them, which to his dismay was greeted with utter disdain by Will. Jem retreated to his room to gaze sorrowfully at the very expensive tickets he'd bought for *The Beggar's Opera* and curse Min for turning up and ruining everything.

Matters inevitably came to a head. Will walked back in one day to overhear Mac on the telephone.

'No, he's gone out. Nope, don't know when he'll be back . . . oh, shagging his sister again, I expect, that's the sort of C3 activity these Home Counties types get up to. All right then. 'Bye.'

'Who were you talking to?' said Will.

'Fuck knows,' said Mac. 'Some loser wanting you.'

'Mac, that could have been my tutor. Or my mother.'

'So?' he said rudely.

'When are you going to stop this?' said Will. 'I've said I'm sorry. What more do you want? It was a mistake, for God's sake. Can't you see I'm already being punished enough without you lot treating me as though I'm a leper?

'I don't know how much more of this I can stand,' he ranted on. 'I put up with you and your stinking socks and your endless women and Dallas watching crap on the telly and acting like his mental age is under four and Jem blithering on about the Pre-Raphaelites – and then *I* make one, just one, cock-up and you all turn on me! Who needs fucking friends, I ask you?' he finished bitterly.

He and Mac just stood there in the hallway, looking at each other. Then Mac picked up his coat, walked past him and out of the front door. Shit, thought Will, I've really blown it now.

He trailed dispiritedly into the sitting-room and slumped on the sofa with a copy of some magazine one of Mac's girlfriends had left. 'Improve your Seduction Technique' the headline cheerily promised. Will sourly reflected that was one of the few things he didn't feel he needed help with.

As he sat staring grimly at the perky blonde girl on the cover, he heard the front door open. A rather damp Mac, wet from a brisk jog down to the off licence, hoved into the sitting-room. In his hand was a blue plastic bag from which he extracted a four-pack of lager. He opened one and gave it to Will.

'There you go, mate. Thought you could use one of these.'

When Dallas and Jem got back later that evening from the theatre, where Dallas had sat so rapt with total joy at the new world unfurling before his eyes that he had quite forgotten to eat his bag of wine gums, they found Will and Mac drunkenly playing Risk. Mac had conquered all of Africa and Asia but Will was strong in North America and held the strategic advantage in the Southern Seas.

'No, no, no,' said Jem fussily, settling down beside Will. 'You don't want to do that. Look, if we move this way, we can knock the brown shirts off the map.'

'Aha,' said Dallas in a really quite impressive German accent. 'The Führer will eat carpets tonight.'

'It's called strategy, mate,' slurred Mac. 'Surprise is my weapon.'

'Yeah, yeah, yeah,' said Jem. 'And don't forget to circle the hide and always temper your flask.' These were the great military insights Mac had once gleaned from meeting action hero Fitzroy MacClean, and always came out with when pissed.

'You laugh now,' he said. 'One day, you'll be glad you know me.'

'That day seems strangely remote,' replied Jem. 'Unless, of course, you have to hire me to get out of prison, in which case I would say you're the lucky one, not me.'

'One day,' said Dallas, 'you'll look up at the silver screen and see me and say, "I knew him once. Once, he was a friend of mine".'

'No, Dallas,' said Mac. 'One day I'll look across the counter at McDonald's and say, "Burger and fries, and make it snappy".'

'Do you think we'll ever be happy we met Will?' said Jem.

'Nah,' they all said in unison.

'Not much point to him, is there?' said Dallas.

'None I can see,' said Mac.

'Oh, well,' said Jem. 'The human race will always need also-rans. He could be one of them.'

'Cheers,' said Will. 'I love you all too.'

It took much longer for the rift with Min to heal. Eventually a scrawled note arrived in the post, baldly stating she had gone back to France where she had enrolled on a photography course. The letter gave no address, but even if it had Will probably wouldn't have followed it up. By the time he read it he was in the thick of the glorious post-finals period where the sun always shone, people were carefree and friendly, the past was over and the future was yet to begin. His days were too grassy-green and indolent for him to get worked up about anything.

With his mediocre arts-based degree it would have seemed logical that Will would go on to run a foreign language book shop or teach English to young Europeans on study tours. However, at the time he graduated the City of London was avidly sweeping around the universities of Britain for any brightish young things who could be sucked into the system and made to toil for the greater good of the rapidly emerging free market. In return for their total dedication they were promised riches beyond belief, if only they would agree to a regime which involved serious sleep deprivation, toxic stress levels, physical decline, lack of a personal life and probable hair loss. Of course, none of these items actually figured in Will's contract, which much to his surprise he was awarded after five interviews, three psychometric tests, a set of group challenges and a round of golf. The golf was the only part he failed. Nevertheless William Gadget merged with and was acquired by Pollinger's, one of London's most reputable investment banking houses.

A couple of years later, as he sat at his desk, his phone rang.

'Hello, Pollinger's M and A,' said Will, who was much too junior to have his own secretary.

'William!' squeaked a breathless little voice. 'It's Min! How are you? It's been so long!'

'Min,' he muttered into the receiver, hunching himself down in his cubicle. He was also far too junior to take personal calls at work. 'How did you get this number?'

'You won't believe it, but I ran into Dallas! I just saw him in the street. I'm in London and wanted to get in touch with you so I thought I'd call your parents, but then I turned a corner and there was lovely Dallas, just standing there, as though he was waiting for me.'

Will was acutely conscious of his boss standing behind him while Min prattled aimlessly on.

'Yes, very well,' he said curtly. 'I understand the situation and think the best way forward would be to meet and take care of this person-to-person.'

'What are you talking about?' said Min in surprise.

'Let's set up a rendezvous, shall we? Say six-thirty this evening. And call me later on in the day with an update. Good to work with you. 'Bye.'

'Everything all right?' said Will's boss suavely.

'Fine, sir, fine. Just dealing with a client.'

'An important client?' asked his boss.

'Yes, very, that is, er, no, not really,' said Will.

'Good. As long as you're in control,' said his boss, gliding away to spook other trainees.

Will and Min met that evening in a City bar where the air was heavy with prosperity. The rest of the country might still be in recession but this corner of it most certainly was not. Little groups of bespoke suits stood nose to nose, jabbering away furiously while necking glasses of alcoholic fluid. The first person Will saw was his boss who raised one eyebrow in greeting and went back to his conversation. The second person he saw was Min.

Immediately Will realised his mistake. In this world of sharply defined tailoring, her long, tatty coat, woolly jumper and wild mass of black hair made her stand out like a bag lady on the catwalk. Just for added contrast, next to Min stood a cool, Nordic blonde, immaculately kitted out in a designer suit who, to make matters worse, Will had been pursuing for several months now. The thought of Nina seeing him with someone as scruffy as Min filled him with horror as he feared it could destroy the image of himself he had been carefully cultivating, as a sophisticated, contemporary icon. He was tempted to turn and run but Min spotted him and started waving furiously. Nina looked down at the pint-sized apparition, sneered and then looked to see who she was gesticulating at. When she saw it was Will, her eyes widened in amusement and she turned away with a supercilious look on her face.

'Will! Will!' Min was squeaking, practically jumping up and down with excitement. He forced himself to walk towards her and stiffly kissed her on the cheek.

'Hello, Min,' he said. 'Look, why don't we go somewhere else? It's very crowded here.'

'But I got us a bottle,' she said. 'And, God, it's so expensive, we must drink it.'

Her emphatic voice carried right across the bar and Will was painfully aware that several of his colleagues were now watching. He took her firmly by the elbow and led her to the furthest corner of the bar he could find.

'Let's sit,' he said, stuffing her into a booth by the entrance to the men's room and returning to the bar for the bottle and glasses.

'A friend of yours?' asked Nina as he passed.

'Oh, just an acquaintance,' he said, hoping to breeze onward.

'I must say,' said Nina, 'I had no idea you moved in such . . .' she paused for effect '. . . Bohemian circles.'

'Creativity,' said Will sternly, 'is the currency of the future. Ideas, Nina, they're what will make us rich in the end.' He bowed to her smartly and walked away, leaving the girl looking confused. She sneaked another look at Min and tried to work out what he meant. Was he on to something big? Was she missing out on some vital development?

★ ★ ★

Will poured Min a glass of wine and sat down next to her.

'Why is that blonde girl staring at me?' asked Min.

'Can't think, Ambrosia. Unless she's wondering where you bought your outfit.'

'Sorry, Will. Should I have dressed up? I didn't realise it would be like this.'

'Don't ever change,' he said, shaking his head in resigned amusement. 'Come on then, now we're here, tell me what you've been up to.'

'Well,' said Min, 'look at this.' She got a copy of a magazine out of her battered rucksack and opened it at a well-thumbed page. It was a spread of black-and-white photos of children. The pictures were stunningly beautiful yet every child had some terrible deformity or disease.

'What is this?' said Will.

'It's my first commission,' said Min. 'I took them in an orphanage in the former Soviet Union where children with disabilities are sent to die. They've got no money now that the Soviet Union has broken up and no one is looking after these kids. It's tragic, Will. They need so little in terms of funding and yet nobody wants to help them.'

A drunken banker tottered past to the loo, braying into his enormous mobile phone. 'Well, I'm buggered if I'm going to pay tax in both countries.'

Will quickly closed the magazine.

'You don't know anyone who might donate some money?' she said hopefully.

'It doesn't quite work like that round here,' said Will, who had seen out of the corner of his eye Nina accosting Joren, his boss. Sure enough, a moment later he approached their table.

'William. Will you do me the pleasure of introducing your friend?'

'Of course,' he said. 'This is Miss Ambrosia de Beaufort

Haskell, a journalist who has recently returned from a very interesting trip to the emerging markets of the former Soviet Union. We were just discussing conditions for business,' he continued, keeping a tight hold on the magazine so Min couldn't open it to show it to his boss.

'Ambrosia, this is Joren Thorsted, or should I say the legendary Joren Thorsted, of whom you will no doubt have heard?' He kicked her sharply under the table as he made his last statement.

'Ow! Yes, absolutely,' said Min. 'Quite. I mean, hello.'

'What conclusions do you draw from Miss Haskell's information?' said Joren.

'That the infrastructure is severely debilitated,' said Will. 'And this may have serious implications for the Russians' ability to do business.'

Joren smiled and patted him on the shoulder. 'You will go far, Mr Gadget. Have a nice weekend and I look forward to your presence on Monday morning. Miss Haskell.' He left them.

'It's been a long week,' said Will. 'Come on, Min, let's go and get plastered.'

They got very, very drunk indeed that night and found themselves in an after-hours bar behind a kebab shop in Camden Town where they washed garlic-rich humus down with vile retsina and danced to some very Greek music. When they were finally thrown out, they tottered home to William's flat where they both fell into a sleep so deep neither of them heard the doorbell ringing after William's flatmate had locked himself out and he consequently spent the night on the doorstep. The next morning, neither Will nor Min dared ask the other one if they had kissed the night before so both found it easier to assume they hadn't and carry on regardless.

After the publication of her first photographs, Min found herself enough in demand to keep her out of the country for most of the year. She drifted around the globe taking photos, concentrating on women and children, usually of subjects living in poverty and squalor against backdrops of some of the world's most amazing scenery. The key to the success of her pictures was the natural, unposed quality of her subjects which in turn came from Min's ability to hang out with Navaho Indians – or whoever – and have them accept her as one of their own. Each time she found herself in London, she headed straight for wherever Will lived and bunked down with him until the next job presented itself. Just as she tried to impress on him the conditions in which the rest of the world lived in order to give him some perspective on his increasingly lavish lifestyle, so he attempted to move her towards a more business-like attitude to her work in the hope that one day she might actually make some proper money out of it. Both sides failed repeatedly but never gave up trying.

Will worked like a demon, day in, day out; had a succession of short-term liaisons with beautiful, clever, hardworking, highly educated girls which always failed thanks to both sides' devotion to their careers. If either Min or Will had met the love of their life, the other would doubtless have been extremely put out, even though they maintained a pretence they were friends and nothing more. The lack of a physical dimension to their relationship, something both parties scrupulously avoided, allowed them to keep up the fantasy that they were not deeply involved with each other. To the rest of the world, it was quite clear that here was a couple. Only the duo themselves remained unaware of it.

Chapter Four

Once all of his guests had departed into the Notting Hill night, the random girl being the last to leave after Will had politely but firmly turned down her kind offer, he sat on his sofa, mindlessly finishing off all the stray bits and bobs of alcohol left in various cans or bottles. When the open booze was finished, he searched the kitchen for more and took a somewhat eccentric cocktail back to the sofa with him. Having smoked all his cigarettes, he attempted to light a very choice dog end from the ashtray but only succeeded in singeing his eyebrow and inhaling pure dirt.

His body desperately needed sleep but his mind was still whirling from the puzzle he was trying to put together. The Paris trip had thrown up another worrying anomaly in the deal he was working on. They had hoped to close the matter that day and consequently had taken all the documentation with them. When Percy had given it to him, at the very last minute in the conference room, Will had been taken aback to see there was only one signatory for Pollinger's and that was him, William Gadget. Ever since Percy had taken over, he had been adamant that he was in charge and would brook no argument. So why was it Will who got to sign, not Percy? As it turned out, the deal had faltered, and then Christophe's unlikely interruption had ended any chance of finalising it. But Will knew this had only bought him time and not saved him.

When the Eurostar train they'd taken out of Paris was stopped just before the Channel tunnel for a routine check to see if there were any desperate immigrants attempting to hang on to the undercarriage, Will had taken up the matter with his superior.

'Perce,' he'd said.

'Percy to you,' snapped his overweight boss.

'I was just wondering . . .' said Will, treading carefully. 'I am sure there is a very sound reason and one that you will be able to explain in clear terms to me, but I'm afraid I don't understand why I should be the only person to sign on behalf of Pollinger's?'

'Gadget,' said Percy, 'there is indeed a good reason and it's called your bonus. Either you want it and you sign, or you don't and you don't get it.'

Will gulped. With this deal in the bag, he was looking forward to a bonus payment of nigh on a million and as a result had been spending very freely of late. Without the bonus, his bottom line would take a serious knock.

'Now, no more impertinent questions, I need a nap.' Percy put on a ridiculous inflatable neck collar and a pair of eye-shades and started to snore.

To add to the strange business of the signature, William's last conversation with Joren was still playing in his head, as though on continual video loop. Just before the freak biking accident, his boss had summoned him into his office.

'Mr Gadget,' said the leather-faced Swede, standing with his back to William, looking out of his plate-glass window which gave a view over the muddy River Thames and various industrial developments.

'Joren,' said William cautiously, wondering if he was about to be sacked.

'William Gadget,' said Joren without turning round. 'As you

know, we have worked together for many years.'

'Yes?' said William.

'In that time, I have developed considerable respect for your ability and intelligence. I believe you to be a man of your word, of discretion and honour.'

Oh, shit, thought Will. I'm definitely getting the push.

'Thus you must take my current decision as no reflection of my feelings about you personally.'

Will sagged into a seat.

'You are to transfer from the deal you have been working on with me. From tomorrow I wish you to start on the proposed merger of Deck and Elbatrop.'

'But . . .' was all Will had time to say. Joren turned round and glared at him with very bright blue Scandinavian eyes.

'Good evening, Mr Gadget,' said the Swede formally, extending his hand. 'Please go home immediately. I shall see you after the weekend.'

As Will shook his hand, he felt a scrap of paper fall down his sleeve, pushed there by the other man's hand. He caught Joren's eye but knew better than to say a word.

Once home, he opened up the scrawled note. It read: *William, please forgive me but the less you know the better. For this reason I am taking you off the deal. You must cut all ties with the companies involved as must anyone who can be traced back to you. Sell any shares you hold or are held for you. All will become clear. Yours respectfully, Joren.'*

Except it never did become clear. When Monday came, Joren failed to turn up for work. He was absent for three days before the M & A team were gathered together and told the bad news – that he had had a near-fatal accident, was currently in a coma but there was a glimmer of a chance for his recovery. Only close family were allowed to see him and flowers and cards were discouraged.

The general shock at this was so intense that William

couldn't take in the news for several days. Other people in the office, like the tearful secretaries or pale-faced trainees, thought Will, Joren's protégé, was being unusually hard-hearted about the accident. But the news was so awful, he just couldn't believe it. It only sank in when he popped into Joren's office, still in the blind hope he might have reappeared, and found it empty once more. It was then that he sat down and wept.

Percy, bustling in with his new secretary, found him.

'Oh, for goodness' sake, stop blubbing,' he'd snapped. 'Yes, it's jolly sad but we've got a job to do. I need you to give me the background and history to the deal so stop being so wet and let's get on with it.'

William looked at Percy with loathing. A workman was already replacing Joren's name plate with Percy's while another measured the walls for new cabinets. 'Joren transferred me to Deck and Elbatrop,' he said softly. 'It was the last thing he did.'

'It jolly well wasn't,' blustered Percy. 'I mean, there's no record of it anywhere. As far as I'm concerned, you're still on the team. Now get your notes – and get out of my chair.'

Since that day Will had hardly slept, and when he had it had been as refreshing as snoozing inside a plastic bag, so hot and sweaty had he been when he'd woken up. He had no appetite, and when he did force food down it gave him instant heartburn as, unbeknown to him, he was now suffering from alcoholic gastroenteritis from living on a diet of caffeine and booze.

As he sat alone that evening in his Notting Hill flat, drinking his sweet Martini with grapefruit, he wondered if it was all worth it. His life was a constant battle now, against tiredness, stress, boredom and worry. Maybe he should just get the hell out, leave whatever dastardly business was going on here behind him and start again. So far he'd tried, by staying on the inside, to find out anything he could that might show a link between Joren's accident and the deal. But he'd drawn a blank everywhere and was now beginning to think that maybe it was time to save himself. He desperately wanted to talk to someone about it but the only person he trusted was two days late in arriving. Hurry up, Min, he thought to himself, I need you. As the Martini and grapefruit was too disgusting to bear a second longer, he hauled himself off the sofa and into his bedroom.

As he was getting into his pyjamas, the phone rang. He flew across the room to answer it, praying it would be her.

'Hello?' he said hopefully.

There was a rustling noise and then a man picked up.

'William Gadget?' a voice said.

'Yes?' said Will.

'Is this your address?'

'Who wants to know?'

'We just wanted to check where to send the flowers.'

'Flowers?'

'For the funeral.'

'Whose funeral?'

'Yours.'

'I don't . . .'

'What happened to your boss, Gadget?'

'Who *is* this?' said Will, his blood running cold.

'Joren Thorsted,' said the voice, 'he was a smart man. We trusted him. But he betrayed us, Gadget. And traitors pay.'

'Who . . . are you?' he said, feeling panic closing his throat.

'William,' said the voice soothingly, 'don't get upset. If you do what we say, we won't touch you. You could be fine, William, if you'd just listen. Joren wouldn't listen. He refused. Thought he knew better. Now he'll never walk again, William. Never.'

'Oh . . . oh . . . God,' said Will. 'What is this?' He had started to shake uncontrollably.

'Now, William,' said the voice, 'you think you've been very clever, don't you? And you have. So be clever again and give us the evidence.'

'Wh-Wh-What evidence?' said Will.

'I think you know,' said that merciless voice. 'I think you know what I mean. We're outside and we're waiting. Come down to the front door and leave it on the doorstep. Then we'll go away and leave you in peace. If you don't, Gadget, we'll get you.'

William flung the phone down in horror. He picked it up to dial 999 but the voice hadn't hung up and was still there. In his rush to leave the office, he'd left his mobile on the desk so had no other line to the outside world.

'We've got you, Gadget.'

He put the phone down again and gasped for breath. He was hyperventilating with panic but some ancient preservation instinct told him it was time to flee.

There was clearly no way out through the front door as that voice would be waiting for him there. He ran through to his beloved bathroom at the back of the flat and wrenched open the window. Scaffolding covered the back of the house, providing an alternative route to the communal garden fifty feet below. He squeezed out of the window and started to climb down the cold metal poles, slipping as his hands failed to find a hold on them. At one point he fell a whole floor's worth, the planks of wood that caught him reverberating with a sickening twang beneath his weight.

He was winded by his fall and felt like he'd sprained his ankle, but shinned to the bottom, jumping into a large rhododendron bush directly beneath him. He desperately wanted to stop but he knew that if the voice and his associates broke into his flat, they would instantly spot which way he'd gone. He limped through the garden to the other side where he scaled the black iron railings, dropping painfully down on to the pavement on the other side. He had two aims. First, to get as far away as possible. Second, to find a phone box and call the only person he knew who might be able to help him now.

Mac was tired. This whole business had started to lose its glamour and excitement for him. It wasn't physical exhaustion he suffered from, more a feeling of being worn out right to his very soul.

For once he was in London, on a rare trip back to HQ to catch up with some admin. It was 2 a.m. and he was in the office, an anonymous set of rooms tucked away behind Regent Street with a brass plaque at the entrance which simply read M.A. His huge frame was cramped into a swivel chair as he sat, head in hands, trying to make sense of the rows of figures in front of him.

He didn't have a problem comprehending the neat documents his accountants had provided. The reason he was going so slowly this particular day, and had been for a while, was not because he didn't understand his own business, it was because he was finding it increasingly hard to read. If he looked at anything too long, it started to blur.

A few months back he'd had the odd sensation that blue clouds were floating at the periphery of his vision. If he looked sideways to try and catch them, they vanished. As soon as he looked straight ahead, they reappeared. The headaches were getting worse, too, circling around his eyes until they felt like burning globes in his cranium. Sometimes, he would have liked to have been able to take his eyeballs out and let the bloodshot baubles roll around the desk, anything to stop the pain.

He knew he should do something about it, but he was scared. He didn't want to have his worst suspicions confirmed, that his eyesight was failing him. In his line of work, there wouldn't be much call for a man without vision. Freedom fighters don't go blind.

Pain and fear were hardly alien to Mac. Until now, he'd made a very comfortable living out of both. Occasionally he had wondered how long he could continue to trade on his immense physical strength, lightning quick reflexes and huge stamina. That he could be let down by his eyes had never occurred to him.

Mac ran his own business and very profitable it had been too. It was sparked by an idea he'd had one rainy night in Bosnia as the shells hammered down over Sarajevo. He was there with his regiment, ostensibly keeping the peace, a miserable and tricky job when there was no peace to keep. He'd left Exeter with what amounted to a BA in Rowing, Rugby and Boxing and gone straight into the Army, as he had in fact been destined to do since birth, as the eldest son of an old Scottish family.

In Bosnia, he found himself part of an international task force whose tactics in dealing with the situation had failed to progress since World War II, relying as they did on a clear front line, a defined enemy and a sense of justified moral purpose. This Balkan war which raged everywhere, with no way of determining aggressor from victim, made a mockery of the mandate the UN troops were bound by. They found themselves protecting murderers and leaving innocent people to die.

One night Mac sat in a grubby basement drinking Slivovitz with his interpreter, a softly spoken Bosnian Serb called Darko. He and Mac had become friends in the long dark hours spent under curfew or sitting in armoured cars rumbling across the mountainous countryside, wondering when the next ambush would hit.

'Hey, Mac,' said Darko. 'Will you find me a job when I come to your country?'

'Join the British Army!' said Mac. 'If you're lucky, you might get to go skiing.'

'Yeah, man,' said Darko. 'It didn't work for you.'

'I fucked up,' said Mac. 'Joined the Army and, blow me, there's a bloody war on.'

They both laughed into their plum brandy as the sandbags shook from the impact of a mortar landing streets away from them.

'What about the girls in your country?' said Darko wistfully. 'Are they nice?'

'Looking better by the day, mate,' said Mac.

'Perhaps I will become an Inglish man,' said Darko. 'Live in Inger-land with a girl to keep me warm at night and a house with running water.'

'Steady on,' said Mac. 'You clearly don't know much about British plumbing.'

'Plumbing?' said Darko. 'What is plumbing?'

'Never mind,' said Mac. 'You'll soon find out.'

'Five years at law school,' said Darko. 'Five years at Belgrade University, graduate with honours, and now my house is gone, my father is dead, I can't get a job and all I know about is war.'

'Bet you know a lot about that, though.'

'For sure,' said Darko. 'I could run a war for you. I could do it really well, you know? Much better than these idiots.'

'So could I,' said Mac. 'So could I.'

They downed another shot and their eyes met.

'Are you thinking what I'm thinking?' asked Mac.

'My friend, we think the same,' said Darko. 'Let's talk.'

That night, Mission Accomplish was born. From a drunken outline sketched by two disillusioned men in a war-torn country evolved over the following few years a formidable outfit. It ran on a skeleton staff but recruited others when needed, ex-forces usually and unashamedly delighted to be given a tougher challenge than guarding a supermarket in

Wolverhampton. If you wanted protection for a diamond mine, security in Indonesia or a small war taken care of in West Africa, Mission Accomplish were the men to call.

Darko, with his acute legal brain, kept them just inside the boundaries of international law while Mac himself ran many of the campaigns overseas, living between aeroplanes and war zones. The sense of impotence and frustration he had felt in Bosnia was replaced by pride in the work of his men. After all, he reasoned, the quicker they sorted a situation out, the less chance there was of collateral damage. This time, he really was keeping the peace, although this sort of peace came with a fairly high price tag attached. Financially, Mission Accomplish was raking it in and, while they soon spawned a host of imitators, they kept their reputation as the original and the best.

So perusing the books should have given Mac a great deal of pleasure. He loved his work, loved arriving in strange foreign airports to be menaced by men with assault rifles. His travel itinerary read like a list of the world's most dangerous places. Few people could give you the lowdown on the comparative merits of breakfast in Albania, the Ivory Coast and Tajikistan, but Mac was one of them. His client list was equally impressive and a look at it would have made any of the journalists who persistently tried to uncover the truth behind MA's activities weep with joy at the scoop they'd landed on. But no hack got close enough to find out anything resembling the truth so were left writing endless profiles of Mac instead, all illustrated with the same photo of him at a polo match with Princess Diana, and having to fill out their copy with guff about unaccountable organisations taking over the world. Which was after all deeply ironic, considering that the proprietors of the various papers that printed these articles really did hold the key to world domination, and in a most undemocratic way.

Darko, who now called himself Dennis ever since an

Afro-American client had mistaken his name for a joke in very poor taste, had come in for a 'little chat' with Mac that afternoon. He'd achieved his aim of becoming an 'Inglish man' and now commuted to work from a detached house in leafy Epsom where his sweet-faced blonde wife Annabel looked after his two heartbreakingly beautiful small children, helped by a steady stream of the Balkan relatives that Dennis continually imported. Mac often thought Annabel must have the patience of a saint to put up with the endless cousins, aunts and nephews who always seemed to be milling about, not to mention Mac himself who used the place as his base in England.

But Annabel, who Dennis had spotted standing alone, looking shy and slightly plump at a very loud drinks party and decided to marry as soon as he saw her, coped with the *va* and *viens* admirably. Dennis had wooed her with persistent adoration, taken her out of her crushingly dull job as a PA in an insurance company, given her a large house, children, and most importantly his constant love and devotion. To Annabel, a placid, comfortable and friendly woman, this was more than she had ever dreamt of. And Dennis, who had never forgotten what his former life had been like, was constantly grateful that his wife and children would never have to rummage for food in dustbins, flee an approaching army or beg for help from an unforgiving regime. He took nothing, least of all his family, for granted.

Admittedly, there were days when he wished he was Mac and could just up sticks and leave, just as occasionally, when Vera had borrowed her favourite lipstick again or Milica had fed the children too much chocolate or Goran had taken the car, it all got too much for Annabel and she had to run down to the basement to have a quick but therapeutic scream. Other than that, they were one of the few married couples Mac could truly say he envied.

'So,' Dennis had said, perching his bony tweed-covered bottom on Mac's desk that afternoon, 'we've sent them to the Democratic Republic of Congo?'

'You know we have, mate,' said Mac. 'Operation D3TY. Straight in, straight out. Leave no traces, get the goods and go.'

'Your favourite kind, in fact?'

'Not this week,' Mac had said. 'Thought I'd get some of the paperwork done.'

'But that's what I'm here for,' said his friend evenly.

'Look, I've just had enough of Africa, all right? If I want to stay in the office, I bloody well will.'

'Okay, okay,' said Dennis, holding his hands up. He tried another tack.

'Annabel and I thought maybe we could do something for your birthday next week?'

'Don't bother,' said Mac moodily. 'There's no one I want to invite.'

'Maybe you should get a girlfriend,' said Dennis abruptly. 'Someone to come home to, a place of your own, think about the future.'

'Fuck off,' said Mac. 'It's all right for you, Mr Perfect Family Man. All you do is sit on your arse being a lawyer all day. It doesn't go down well with girls, this, "Sorry darling, got to go. No, you can't call me, don't know when I'll be back or even if." Anyway, I don't want a bloody girl around, nagging me and telling me what to do. I want to be free.'

'Some people,' said Dennis, 'would say freedom is what happens when you have nothing left to lose.'

'In that case,' said Mac, 'I'm nearly there.'

'No, you're not,' said his friend. 'You could lose everything else but you will never lose us. We're here for you, Mac. And when you decide to, you can tell us what the problem is. But don't leave it too long. And we're having a bloody party for your birthday, even if you don't fucking come!'

Dennis's attempts to swear in English never sounded quite right but at least it made Mac smile, which hadn't happened for a while.

The phone ringing at 2.30 a.m. was not unusual at Mission Accomplish headquarters. It might be a dictator who'd mislaid one of his wives (the richer the client, the more they tended to use MA as a lost and found bureau or even a glorified concierge service), a frightened white farmer or a South East Asian technocrat needing software support. Anything could – and did – happen in those anonymous offices which busy shoppers routinely passed on their way to buy presents or look at the Christmas lights.

This call came from much closer to home. The 192.com software identified the location as a phone box in Maida Vale. Usually, Mac would have had someone screen the call before answering it but it was late and he was the only one there. He switched on the voice scrambler and answered personally. To his surprise, the caller used the correct code, which was changed regularly.

'Hemlines will rise this autumn,' Mac replied into the receiver. Quickly, he turned off the scrambler.

'Yeah, it's me, mate. What's up? . . . Slow down, slow down. You're not making any sense!

'Take a few deep breaths. In . . . Out . . . In . . . Out. It's okay, mate, it's okay. Don't hang up the phone . . . you can do it. Stay with me . . . stay with me, mate. Don't hang up the phone!

'Listen very carefully. I Am Coming To Get You Now. Follow my instructions . . . I don't know who they are, mate. I don't know who's after you but you're safe. I'm here. Now listen, leave the box. Don't make any sudden movements. Don't run. Turn left out of the box, and left at the corner. Stand by the hedge, out of the light. RV your location in ten.'

Before he left the office to crank up his ancient Land Rover, Mac made another call, this time to Dennis. They spoke in Serbian, the language they reserved for emergencies.

'*Situacija*,' said Mac. (Situation.)

'*Oh, bože moj!*' grumbled Dennis. (Oh, bloody hell!)

'*Dovuci to debelo dupe, odmah!*' said Mac. (Get your fat arse here now!)

'*Oh, jebem ti mater.*' (Oh, fuck your mother.)

'*I tebi isto.*' (Same to you.)

Operation Rescue Gadget had begun.

Chapter Five

The march of technology has had a well-documented effect on the evolution of the human race. New and improved communications have made it possible to stay in touch with your nearest and dearest wherever you are in the world or, conversely, to make the notion of escape impossible, depending on your point of view. Min hovered between these two opinions, still liking to vanish for long periods when it suited her yet be able to drop into rickety internet cafés the world over to pick up her mail and send the odd missive, usually to Will, to let him know she was still alive.

She had been in Marrakech for the fashion shoot then decided to stay on. She was working on a charity project, taking pictures of street children to be shown as part of an all-night celebrity telethon to raise money for kids. In Morocco, she took a harrowing set of photos of children who'd turned to prostitution, drugs and self-abuse after being abandoned by their parents, a sharp contrast to the glossy magazine work she'd done soon after arriving.

Checking her e-mail to see whether she had any new projects on the horizon, she received a most unexpected message. In a dusty café packed with pungent techno-hippies on their gap years typing out long letters full of their self-revelatory travel experiences, she opened a message from *Albert@cleanupyourlife.com*.

'My lady', the note courteously began. Only one person in the world referred to her in this way and that was Albert, William Gadget's septuagenarian cleaner and man of all work. Ever since he had discovered she was brought up at Chieverley, a house he knew well from his days as valet to the aristocracy, he had treated her with the utmost respect and politeness, figuring her to be a cut above Will's other lowlife friends. Her scruffiness didn't fool Albert for a second. He knew breeding when he saw it, and he'd had plenty of experience of tramps who were ladies. His letter continued:

Forgive me for contacting you out of the blue. As you are aware, I have been in the service of Mr Gadget for some years now and I hold my employer in the greatest esteem. I have worked for the young gentleman with pleasure, and have debated for some time what the correct procedure in this situation would be.

However, I am now of the mind that the seriousness of the current state of affairs means I may justifiably break my confidentiality agreement with him and request your assistance on his behalf. For some time now, I have been aware that Mr Gadget has not been in the best health and it is out of concern for his well-being that I approach you. I would not like to divulge any more details via this unreliable form of communication save to say I believe it would be highly advisable for you to pay him a visit at your earliest convenience.

Yours sincerely,

Albert

At the end of the e-mail was a line exhorting Min to view Albert's website, *www.cleanupyourlife.com*. So puzzled was she by the contents of his e-mail that she absentmindedly clicked on the button and found herself looking at a large picture of Albert, decked out in an apron and cheerily waving a dishcloth under the banner: 'Albert Can Clean You Up!' Outside the café, in the yellow, billowing street, a camel paused to let out a huge fart.

Min sat there for a few minutes, blankly reading the headline on Albert's advert, which promised 'discretion, reasonable rates, convenience and old-fashioned service', while wondering what on earth it all meant. Had he lost his mind? Why was he sending her e-mails about his employer? But Albert wasn't usually so indiscreet. Perhaps Will really was very ill with some mysterious disease though he himself hadn't mentioned anything of the sort in his last message. Min was perplexed.

She sent a reply to Albert, 'Coming home ASAP. Love, Min,' and went to book herself on the first flight out of Marrakech. It took a day or two for her to get a seat and by the time she reached Heathrow via an unexpected six-hour stopover in Frankfurt, the world's most boring airport, Will had already scaled the scaffolding in his pyjamas and done a midnight flit. She arrived at his flat to find it empty, the morning sun streaming in through the windows, highlighting the efficacy of Albert's rigorous programme of dusting and polishing. As it was already past eleven in the morning she assumed Will would be at work and tucked herself up on the sofa to sleep off the journey. If he had gone to the office, she thought to herself, he could hardly be at death's door, so waiting another half-day to meet up couldn't hurt.

When she woke, it was dark and she was no longer alone. A small thin man in a tweed suit was sitting in the armchair opposite. Min nearly jumped out of her skin.

'Who are you?' she said.

'Good evening,' he said politely. 'My name is Dennis. I am a colleague of Mac's. We have never met although I have often heard your name mentioned.'

'What are you doing here? And where's Will?'

'William is unavoidably absent,' said Dennis. 'He requested that I see you and that I ask you to find alternative accommodation while he is away.'

'Why? Where's he gone?'

'I am afraid I cannot tell you where he is, for reasons which relate to his and, I'm afraid, your security. For these same reasons I must ask you to leave this flat and find somewhere else to stay.'

'But why?' said Min. 'What have you done with him?'

'I haven't, as you put it, "done" anything with him. It is more a matter of what he may have done to himself.'

'I don't understand,' said Min.

'No,' said Dennis, 'I can see that this is all very difficult for you. I am sorry to say I must ask you to trust us at present. Soon all will become clear.'

'What's wrong with Will?' Min persisted.

'He is, one might say, indisposed at the moment. But rest assured, he is in safe hands and will make a rapid recovery. Now, I really cannot divulge any more details except that he suggested you might contact a Mr Jemal Haque and go to his flat this evening. I have already called Mr Haque who is expecting you around eight o' clock tonight.'

'Why does he want me to stay with Jem? Can't I stay with Mac?'

'Sadly not. He is away right now. On business.'

'And would that business have anything to do with Will?'

'I couldn't say,' replied Dennis. 'But I must ask you to leave here now. The longer we stay here, the greater the danger to both of us. From now on, this flat must be a no-go zone. I will drive you to Mr Haque's apartment now. Please collect your bags.'

Despite his unassuming figure, there was something about Dennis which made you loath to argue with him. Min meekly packed her rucksack and followed him down to his large Mercedes parked a few streets away from the flat, even though there were spaces right outside.

Jem had not been in the best of moods when Dennis had phoned him that afternoon. He'd spent all day tussling with a hysterical garden designer, some badly laid tiling and a water feature with a burst main which had flooded the back yard they were supposedly remodelling as a surprise for its owner. They'd had to stop the cameras rolling when the inhabitants of the house came home and saw what Jem's SWAT team of televisual horticulturalists had done. Tears, recriminations and the threat of court action were not quite what he wanted to broadcast at 7 p.m. on a Tuesday night.

For Jem never did become a lawyer. Born the third son of a high-caste family of Bangladeshi intellectuals, he was the most serious and studious of the boisterous crop of Haque boys and also the one who felt the least connected to their home country, which in fact was not his place of origin at all. Unlike the other two, he'd been born on the West Coast of America while his father was teaching at a Californian university. Soon after that, the family had uprooted themselves to London where they had stayed for twenty years until Professor Haque decided it was time to go back to Bangladesh and insisted it was high time that his sons became involved in the problems of their country.

The two elder boys took this in their stride. Palash, the first son, a highly successful plastic surgeon, had agreed years before to an arranged marriage, an event which had lasted for seven days, involved a bride so dripping in gold you couldn't look at her because it hurt your eyes, over a thousand guests and the union of two of the most prominent families in the region. He also had the good fortune to fall madly in love with his wife the first time he saw her – which was at their wedding – and she remained the only woman in the world he felt couldn't be improved by the use of his surgeon's knife. They flipped between Britain, where Palash overcharged rich housewives for injections into the creases between their brows or inserted sachets of salt solution into sagging breasts, and Dhaka, where he worked in a public clinic performing all manner of general surgery and fitting prosthetic limbs.

The next boy was the sort that makes mothers raise their eyes to the ceiling and sigh, while feeling secretly proud. He was a playboy, the flashy, charming type, always on the brink of making millions out of some new business venture. He zipped about London in his BMW, brokering deals, escorting beautiful women to nightclubs and living life large. When he went to Bangladesh, which he did quite often in pursuit of some maternal pampering, he always managed to persuade his parents that next year, when he'd made his money, his intention was to come back and get involved in Bangladeshi politics. Then he'd be ready to settle down and marry a nice wife. But until he was in a position to do so, it would not be responsible of him because he wanted to do things right, or so he said. Jem was always amazed that, year after year, his parents fell for the same story.

He himself lacked the talent to dissemble or the desire to spend his life in a place he didn't consider home. This in itself would not have been a problem. His parents wouldn't have minded him living in England, but they did mind his total refusal to consider marriage. In his last year at university they started to put serious pressure on him and it lifted the lid on some long-buried frustrations. He was faced with an impossible set of choices. He could tell his parents the truth, a thought which made his blood run cold just to consider it, he could bury his real feelings and go ahead with a marriage, or he could prevaricate in the hope that a simple solution presented itself. He chose the last option as the one least likely to hurt people.

However, some form of rebellion was inevitable. The law was not so much a career he'd chosen as one that had been picked for him and it was on that he vented his frustration and fury. To the amazement and incomprehension of his family, who'd never before had a minute's trouble from the docile, thoughtful, clever youngest son, Jemal took up a traineeship at a television company instead. He refused – politely, as was his way – to visit his parents at home in Bangladesh for fear he'd arrive and find himself in the middle of his own wedding, he took up drinking, dyed his thick black hair orange, threw himself with a passion into his work and found, in the space of six months, that his life had changed beyond all recognition.

The trouble with dramatic life-changing events is the unknown risk factor. As Jem was to find, if you take a sledgehammer to your existence, there is usually some form of damaging fallout and it usually occurs somewhere entirely unexpected. When he threw in the law, in which he'd been predicted a brilliant future, Jemal Haque envisaged a future of producing late-night political debate programmes or cutting-edge documentaries. However, his television career didn't quite work out as he had planned. When he came to the end of his trainee period, he was asked to oversee a completely new style of gardening programme which involved surreptitiously re-designing gardens without the knowledge of their proprietors. The show was to be fronted by a man so garishly outrageous, the concept was so flawed and the finished product so bad that Jem took the job, feeling sure another series could never be commissioned and then he'd be free to pursue other things.

He was entirely wrong. The series was such a runaway success it generated viewing figures the company could formerly only have dreamt of. Behind the scenes, Jem's name was spoken with hushed awe as the man who'd pulled off the biggest coup in popular programming since Michael Grade. His calm, professional manner, his obsession with detail, his meticulous planning and ability to deal with the star of the show, Terence Willsby-Grove, earned him the respect of his bosses but it also bound him hand and foot to *Dig It!*, a programme he came to loathe. Each time he asked to leave, his salary was upped until it was hitting stratospheric levels and he was promised that if only he would do just one more series, he would then be allowed to take on a few grittier documentaries. Needless to say, these never materialised and Jem found himself at yet another annual television awards night, wearing black tie and receiving yet another prize while other producers sniggered at him behind his back.

'Of course Min can come and stay,' said Jem to Dennis on the phone as, in the background, Terence let out a high-pitched scream of annoyance that his designs were so badly thought of and flounced off the set. 'I'd love to have her,' he said truthfully, his attitude to Min having warmed considerably over the past years. His student crush on William was something he remembered with embarrassment now and hoped he had never let slip to the others in those distant, balmy days. Little did he know they had all guessed but been too sympathetic to let on.

Jem's loft-style apartment was in a painfully fashionable area of London where young people liked to appear as scrofulous and badly dressed as possible.

'God!' said Min as the Mercedes purred through narrow streets between former warehouses now turned into very expensive flats. 'They look like people I take pictures of in famine zones.'

'Very chic, no?' said Dennis, whose thoughts had turned to home and the roast beef with Yorkshire pudding Annabel was cooking for him tonight.

The flat was tasteful in the extreme, albeit in a very modern way, meaning none of Jem's chairs were at all comfortable to sit in but they looked great as long as you were standing up. The only gesture away from minimalism was the enormous bookcase which covered one wall and was stuffed with tomes on every subject – except, of course, gardening. There were no houseplants in residence and not a shred of greenery was visible from the vast plate-glass windows. The whole place was a hymn to urban living.

As Min followed Jem in, she heard a voice declaiming from on high but could see no one else in the flat.

' "And it is a far, far better thing that I do, than I have ever done; it is a far, far better rest that I go to than I have ever known . . ." ' the voice sonorously intoned.

'What's that?' Min asked.

'Oh, it's Dallas,' said Jem. 'He likes to use the mezzanine to practise. Says it's like being on stage.'

Sure enough, Dallas's smiling face popped over the balconette.

'Hi, Min!' he said. 'Just learning my lines. I've got a part in a play!'

'You still haven't told me who you slept with to get it?' said Jem.

'Well, no one,' said Dallas. 'Last time I did an audition, I slept with everyone to try and get the part but they still turned me down. So this time, I didn't have sex with anyone and they told me today it's mine. Must mean I'm a really lousy shag.'

'Or a great actor,' said Min.

'Thank you, Min,' said Dallas. 'I think I prefer your interpretation.' He came down from Jem's sleeping area.

'So,' said Min, once the three of them were settled, more or less comfortably depending on whether they had chosen a chair or the floor to sit on, 'what's up with Will?'

Jem and Dallas looked at one another, each willing the other to begin. Just then the doorbell rang. It was Albert, bearing a bag of groceries.

'Thought I'd drop these in on my way home,' said the old man.

'Albert?' said Min. 'What are you doing here?'

'Albert works for me now as well,' said Jem, looking a little uneasy. 'He's been a great help to me now I'm so busy, and it's given me a chance to get to know him a bit . . . to have a few, er, little chats, you know, about life and stuff . . .'

'I got your e-mail,' said Min.

'Ah,' said Albert. 'Very good, my lady, very good. Well, I must be getting on. Mrs Albert will wonder where I've got to.'

'Not so fast, Albert,' said Jem. 'I think you ought to stay.'

'Would someone like to explain to me just what is going on here?' asked Min, suddenly feeling quite put out. 'I hot foot it back from Africa because Albert tells me there's a problem, I get here to find Will has disappeared, and I'm escorted out of his flat by some spooky man who says he works with Mac who's gone on a business trip, probably with Will in tow. Now, last time I checked, Will was an international banker, not a freedom fighter in waiting. I really hope there's a good story behind all this because I'm getting a bit fed up with you all.'

'Riiight,' said Dallas. 'Erm, Jem. Perhaps you'd better start off as you've spoken to Mac and I haven't.'

'No,' said Jem. 'Albert is the original source so perhaps he could say a few words.'.

'With all due respect,' said the old man, 'I am just a humble . . .'

Min cut them off. 'Someone just bloody tell me!' she snapped.

'All right, all right,' said Jem hastily. 'Here's what we know. Will has never been one to pay much attention to his own health. He smokes like a chimney, drinks as though there is no tomorrow, and his idea of taking exercise is walking faster to the off licence. On the other hand, he works incredibly hard, day in, day out, and almost never has a holiday. The strain is beginning to show.

'We thought something was wrong but didn't know how bad it had got until Albert had a word with me. He's found Will several times now, passed out on the sofa, in his work clothes, holding a bottle of spirits. The bin is always full of empty bottles and cans and there is never any food in the house.

'We're really worried, Min. That's why Albert sent you the e-mail. We thought maybe you could get through to Will. He's really changed lately and we think it must be the amount of alcohol he's taking in. We can't think of anything else it could be. He has mood swings, he's unpredictable, can turn nasty with no warning . . .'

'We tried confronting him,' said Dallas, pre-empting what Min was about to say, 'but he said I was a useless actor, Jem a sad poof, and Albert a silly old man. We were to sod off and mind our own business in future.'

'Ouch!' said Min. 'That doesn't sound at all like Will.'

'That's the point,' said Jem. 'He's changing beyond all recognition. I know he has some very big deal going through at work and he's quite stressed about that, but I can't really see how he can get any meaningful work done, not in his state.'

'Did you try doing anything else?' asked Min.

'All we could do was keep an eye on him by going round as often as possible and drinking as much of his booze as we could work through to stop him having it,' said Dallas selflessly. 'It's played havoc with my voice.'

'Albert,' said Min, her eyes brimming with tears, 'is this true?'

'Yes, my lady,' he replied gently. 'I'm afraid it is.'

Jem took up the story again.

'Mac phoned me. Last night he got a call from Will, who was delirious. Mac found him hiding behind a hedge, wearing pyjamas covered in mud, saying that they were out to get him and that he'd been threatened. He said he'd had to run away from his flat because these people had been waiting outside and now they wanted to kill him.'

'Oh, my God!' said Min in horror. 'He's gone mad.'

'It looks like it,' said Jem. 'What we were most afraid of has actually happened. He's flipped. Mac's taken him to a rehabilitation home to get well again. He said he'd be in touch when he had more news.'

'So I was too late,' said Min sadly. 'If only I'd been a day earlier.'

'Don't blame yourself,' said Dallas kindly. 'You weren't to know. None of us thought it would happen so soon.'

The little party of four broke up soon after that. They had all lost their taste for the wine they'd been drinking and poured it down the sink. Jem made Min a cup of tea while Dallas and Albert let themselves out. It wasn't much of a homecoming for her and Jem wondered how long she'd stay now that Will wasn't there.

Chapter Six

The sun was rising, turning the dark hills to mixed shades of blue and green as the first shafts of morning sun fell on them. The water in the bay, circled by mountains which dropped straight down to the shore, was still and placid although further out, beyond their protection, foaming white horses could be seen leaping joyfully across the open sea. A small castle sat marooned on an island with gentle waves lapping against the rocks. Linking the castle to the mainland was an ancient causeway, although in high tide the only way out from the island was by boat.

Inside the castle at least one of the inhabitants was oblivious to the spectacular natural beauty that surrounded him. So far, he was having trouble just coping with the room he was in; anything more dramatic than the four plain white walls that surrounded him might have caused sensory overload.

He had awoken from a sleep so deep that coming out of it was like floating to the surface from the bottom of the sea. How long he had been under he could not have said. It could have been one night, it could have been three years. When he opened his eyes to the pure light streaming through the tiny window high up in the wall, he was engulfed in brightness. For a few moments he could see nothing but blinding brilliance.

In the distance he heard the plashing noise of waves and then faintly, faintly, the sound of voices singing a choral work, a light haunting tune he didn't recognise.

He lay still, listening to the singing, the voices drifting in at the window on the breeze, and then he knew. This was it, the end of ends. He had died and this was the afterlife. How else could he explain the angelic choir, the white light, the feeling of total release and calm which stole through his whole body? Now he thought about it, he couldn't actually feel his body at all. Although it was still visible, it was as though every ache and pain had evaporated, leaving him free and weightless.

The man reviewed his last moments on earth. His memories were confused, full of dark pictures of night terror, of pain and excruciating fear. He could see a long, dangerous climb, hear a threatening voice on a phone, and remember the dazzling headlights of the car that had come for him. After that it was a blank. Whoever had got out of that car, he surmised, must have killed him because, try as he might, he could not remember a single thing between that moment and waking up in this little bed in the pure white room.

He contemplated death for a few moments and found the thought remarkably relaxing. The only reason to fear it, he thought, was the agony that accompanied a slow death or the brutality of a quick demise. He, however, seemed to have passed from one state to another without suffering, despite the fact that some act of unspeakable violence must have been visited upon him. He wondered if people on earth were mourning him. Imagining his own funeral – his relatives, his weeping parents, a girl with long black hair sitting sorrowfully on his grave, holding a single white rose – actually moved him to tears, so poignant was the scene.

The door to his chamber opened and two men clad entirely in white – angels, presumably – entered. Tenderly, one of them mopped away his tears with a soft cloth. As seraph to seraph, the man in bed smiled beatifically at his brother angel.

'You had us worried for a day or two there,' said the angel.

'But you look much better now.'

Somehow this struck a wrong note for one in an ethereal state.

'It's been a while since someone came to us in such a bad way. But you came – or were guided – to the right place.'

Angel two chipped in, 'You're quite safe. Don't worry, brother. We will help you now.'

The man's otherworldly calm was seeping away from him. It occurred to him that perhaps he had not reached heaven and was still in the land of the living after all. This was a deeply worrying prospect. If he wasn't in the afterlife, then where the hell was he?

'You mean, I'm not dead?' he queried.

'Brother, you have died in one sense. Your life in the world outside is over. But your life in Berriemore has just begun. From today, you are reborn inside our community. Welcome, brother, to life!'

At this, the two angelic impostors suddenly broke into a little song. When they had finished crooning they stood there beaming at the man, as if they really were his parents and he their newborn babe.

'Now,' continued Angel One, 'you have been asleep for many hours so we think you may be in need of nourishment.'

He indicated a bowl of gruel and a cup of water.

'When you have rested more, we will take you to the main hall where the rest of the community waits to welcome you. There you will be accepted into your new existence as a brother of Berriemore. We will celebrate the end of your former life and your passing into the new.'

The man had no idea how to process this new piece of information. While he was quite prepared to accept the concept of physical death as something irreversible and, after all, inevitable, and his new abode as the place souls went to await their final resting place, to find he was in fact still alive but had somehow wandered into this strange and unfamiliar environment where they meant to claim him as one of their own was not exactly welcome news. How had he got here? Where was here? Who were these people? And why was his last memory of a pair of headlights in a dark, rainy street?

One of the angels propped him up in bed and spoon-fed him grey gruel. To his great surprise, he found he was hungry enough to gulp down the mess eagerly. The water he followed it with was the sweetest drink he had ever tasted. When the bowl and glass were empty, they levered him out of bed, one of them supporting each shoulder, swiftly stripped him of the white robe he didn't know he was wearing and clad him in a fresh one.

Once he tried to stand, the man found he was so weak, he needed the support of the other two. Running away when he couldn't even stay upright was clearly not an option. He had heard that the only way to behave with lunatics, as he was starting to suspect these people might be, was to humour them. So he decided – not, frankly, that he could have done anything different anyway – to go along with it for now. He collapsed back into the bed.

'Rest,' said the strange men. 'We will come for you when night falls.' They left him and he fell straight back to sleep but this time it was a fractured, disturbed repose. He woke many times, tangled in the sheets, each time with a fresh layer of cold sweat broken out across his body. He saw more dark images, heard voices, had nightmarish dreams. When the men returned, this time with a bowl of steaming water smelling freshly of herbs which they used to sponge him down, he was entirely disorientated. The daylight had gone and the men carried candles which sent a warm flickering glow across his cell.

'Come,' said the elder, 'it is time.'

Putting one shaky foot in front of the other, Will followed them out of the door.

★ ★ ★

Min hadn't been sleeping well. The narrow leather sofa she had for a bed at Jem's flat might have been the last word in Philippe Starkian style but it was totally unsuitable for a good night's rest. However, even in the most comfortable of surroundings, she would still have felt like the Princess with the Pea, unable to fall asleep because of a small, hard knot of doubt in the back of her mind.

At first, she had been deeply shocked by the revelations that Jem and the others had sprung on her. She had long suspected Will's lifestyle was not sustainable long-term, but on the other hand had always assumed that one day he'd have the sense to get out before it got too much for him. She had certainly never expected him to fall to pieces in such a dramatic fashion. She felt terribly guilty that she hadn't seen him for a while and wondered whether she could have helped by coming home sooner. And yet, the more she considered it, the more she started to think that something in this peculiar and sad tale didn't make sense.

She had last seen Will in the spring when they had sat in a riverside pub, drinking away the afternoon, on one of those rare days which hold more warmth and sunshine than the rest of the summer put together. Seagulls circled above them as little boats chugged up and down the Thames, which for once had shed its sluggish brown appearance and was silvery-blue.

'So, Mademoiselle de Beaufort, what gives?' said Will, smiling at her over his pint glass.

'Bof!' said Min. 'Took a few pictures, gave away my fortune, married a revolutionary, had three children and contracted cholera. What about you?'

'Lately I've been repressing some minorities,' said Will. 'I plundered a pension fund – just for a laugh, you understand – and then I pulled the plug on a small third-world country by downgrading their credit rating.'

'Glad to hear you're keeping up the good work. If I was a country,' said Min thoughtfully, 'which one do you think I'd be?'

'Tricky,' said Will. 'I'm tempted to say Angola but there are a few central American economies which might suit you to a T.'

Min rummaged around in her bag and found a pair of light purple shades which she put on against the pale-gold sunshine streaming out of the baby-blue sky. The sunglasses should have made her look ridiculous but, framed by her mass of corkscrew black curls and perched on her straight little nose, they looked surprisingly chic.

'Another beer, *chéri*?' she asked, noting that his glass contained only a faint smear of froth.

'I'll get it,' he said.

'I can afford a drink for you,' she said. 'Though I know you think my earnings are pathetic.'

'I pay double in tax what you make in a year.'

'Rub it in, fat cat,' she replied.

'I'm not,' said Will. 'I'm just pointing out why I buy the drinks and you don't. Anyway, it's nice to have someone to spend money on.'

'What happened to . . . um . . .'

'Anastasia-Louise?'

'I still can't believe you actually went out with someone called Anastasia-Louise!'

'We split up.'

'Why?' said Min. 'Did she look under your bed?'

Will laughed. 'I might reconsider letting you have a key if you're going to snoop.'

'It was just a guess,' said Min.

A few drinks later, he started to get pensive.

'Do you ever wonder,' he suddenly asked her, 'where you'll be in ten years' time?'

'Nope,' said Min. 'Ten years ago I couldn't have told you I'd be here so I've no way of knowing what will happen over the next decade.'

'But don't you ever ask yourself,' persisted Will, trying a new tack, 'if this is all there is?'

'Is it not enough for you?'

'I don't know,' he said. 'Sometimes I wonder what would have happened if I'd done something different with my life. Maybe been more . . . involved. I don't know. Look, I don't really understand what I'm talking about. I've got everything I could want. I must be rather pissed.' He smiled at her but it didn't quite work. 'Maybe I'm just a bit lonely.'

'You've got plenty of friends,' said Min.

'Hmm,' said Will. 'It's not the same, is it? Maybe if you lived here all the time, it would be different. Maybe then we could . . .' he trailed off. 'We could,' he reprised, summoning his courage, 'finally get round to . . . We might perhaps . . .'

'What might we do?' asked Min, who could hardly speak for terror mixed with the delicious anticipation of what he would say next.

'This,' he said, leaning across the table and kissing her.

Her phone ringing at 6 a.m. the next morning was not something she felt should happen in a perfect world. Reaching a slim arm out from under Will's goose-down duvet, she located her mobile with the aim of turning it off before it disturbed his Sunday morning slumber. But when she saw the number on the display, she knew she had no choice but to answer it. Slipping from his bed, she took her mobile into the living-room, shivering a little as she sat naked on the sofa.

''Allo?' she said. 'Oui, c'est moi . . . Il est où? Quoi, maintenant? Oh, putain de merde . . . vraiment? Alors, j'arrive.'

The last time she'd slept with Will, she'd taken fright and run away in the very early morning, before she'd had to confront what they'd done. This time she had no such fear and yet, by some strange quirk of fate, was compelled to leave in the grey light of dawn once more. She considered writing him a note but there was so much to say that she didn't know where to begin. Instead, she let herself out of the flat, silently promising both herself and him that she'd be back as soon as she could, and that when she was they'd pick up where they'd left off.

Min could not have been more wrong. That damp Sunday morning when she had taken a stand-by flight to North Africa, and even in the departure lounge had not had the courage to phone Will in case the sound of his voice made her change her plans, she'd had little reason to suspect her latest assignment would take quite so long, nor that when she did make it back to London circumstances would be quite so different. It was up to her to try and pick up the pieces now.

'If you were in trouble,' she said to Jem as the two of them walked around the opening of an installation at an art gallery near his flat, 'who would you call?'

Jem paused to look at an enormous sculpture, entirely composed of dried varnished turd, called 'Out Put'.

'Incredible,' he said. 'That is the nastiest object I have ever seen. Do you think someone really will pay £32,000 for it?'

'I doubt it,' said Min. 'Not when you could have this lovely lot for a bargain £21,000.' She pointed to a heap of rumpled clothing, festooned with condoms, which went under the title 'The Long Afternoon of Adultery'.

The gallery owner, a serious young man with heavy-framed spectacles, hurried over to Jem. 'What do you think?' he said in great excitement.

'I am just blown away by it,' said Jem. 'It is so raw, it gets right to the heart of the human condition. It's so . . . so . . .' he floundered.

'Frank,' said Min, jumping in to help him. 'The quality of

truth is what strikes me most profoundly.'

'I'm so glad,' said the owner. 'It's hard to know sometimes how art this ground-breaking will be received. You sometimes wonder if people will see the genius in work such as this. Or whether they'll just think it's a pile of old rubbish.'

'You've done a wonderful job, Hegley,' said Jem. 'It's . . . astonishing.'

'Thanks,' said Hegley. 'I haven't slept for weeks, I've been so worried about it.' He turned to Min. 'The gallery's new,' he said. 'It's my baby. Oh, you wouldn't believe the dramas we've had. That one there,' he said, lowering his voice and pointing to 'Out Put', 'broke in transit and we had to glue it together once it arrived. The problem was we didn't quite know what it originally looked like so we had to guess which bit went where.'

'You'd never know,' said Min.

'Someone's bought it,' said Hegley. 'So I must have Yoo-Hooed in all the right places. Oops, there's the man from the *Standard*. Do hope he didn't hear that. Have lots of 'poo and enjoy yourselves.' He dashed off to chat up other punters.

'It's all right,' said Jem, deftly sliding two glasses off a passing waiter's tray, 'he means champagne.'

'What a sweet man,' said Min.

'Hegley? Charming chap,' said Jem. 'If he didn't have such shocking taste, I'd marry him.'

They wandered on a bit further and admired a few paintings composed of blocks of primary colours.

'Look,' said Min. 'My first painting, aged four and a half.'

'Now, now,' said Jem. 'Just because you favour the photographic art form. I happen to think that is quite attractive.'

'Hmm,' she said. 'Does it speak to you?'

'Loudly and clearly,' said Jem. 'Now, what were you asking me before the lovely Hegley interrupted?'

'Oh, yes. Imagine you had to call someone because you had a problem – who would it be?'

'Erm, well, not you because you're never around, and not Dallas because he's not much use. I would have said Will, but now I'd expect him to be too plastered to be any help. It would depend on the type of problem, I suppose. If I had a leak, I'd call a plumber. If it was a burglar, I'd call the police.'

'What sort of problem would make you call Mac?'

'My diamond mine was collapsing? I suddenly need to do a heist in the Antarctic? I don't know.'

'Or there was someone outside who wanted to kill you?' said Min.

'Ah,' said Jem. 'I see what you're getting at. You're thinking, what if Will hasn't gone mad? What if there really is someone out to get him? In which case, he'd call Mac. In such circumstances, that would be quite a sensible thing to do. Not mad at all, in fact.'

'Exactly,' said Min. 'You see, otherwise I think he'd have called you. When did you last see him?'

'The same night, just before he totally lost it.'

'How was he when you left him?'

'Twitchy. And very drunk. But no, now you mention it, I wouldn't have said stark raving mad. Though heading in that direction, maybe.'

'Then how did he go from not-so-bonkers to completely insane in what sounds like just a matter of hours? What do you think he did? Drink a bottle of neat spirits and have an impromptu nervous breakdown? And why is his flat off limits now? Why did shady Dennis make me leave and promise not to go back? There's more to this than meets the eye, Jem.'

He sighed. 'You're making too much of it. If you'd seen Will recently, you'd know that anything was possible.'

'I think we should talk to Mac, get him to tell us what really happened that night. Can you call and get him to meet us?'

'To make you happy, Ambrosia, anything.'

'To make me shut up, you mean,' said Min.

'That too,' said Jem, taking out a minuscule silver phone.

As he was talking into his mobile, Hegley shot past once more, spotted Min and ground to a halt.

'I'm so sorry, I didn't catch your name,' said the affable gallery owner.

'Ambrosia, Ambrosia Haskell,' said Min, wishing once more that she was called something sensible. 'But most people call me Min.'

'Do they?' said Hegley. 'I get called Hedge. As in "your bets", I think, although this time I can't be accused of that. I've put everything I have into this. Do you think it's going to work?' he asked anxiously.

'I'm sure it will,' said Min, smiling at his sweet, concerned expression. 'There are red stickers on almost everything.'

'What do you do?' asked Hegley.

'I'm a photographer.'

'Ever do exhibitions?' he asked. 'Perhaps I could help? Oh, no, that child is about to cause trouble.'

He raced off to where a celebrity toddler who'd come with his celebrity parents was about to dismantle one of his exhibits. Jem came off the phone.

'Chatting up Hedge, were you, Min?'

'Not at all. He asked if I wanted to do an exhibition.'

'Think you might represent rather too much gritty reality for him, darling.' There was a slightly acid edge to Jem's tone. Min wondered what exactly he meant.

'Mac will be over in an hour. It sounds like you may not be so far off the mark after all.' He looked at her speculatively. 'You're a strange one, Ambrosia. I never know quite what to make of you.'

'Is that good?' said Min.

'It's just you,' said Jem. 'Come on, let's go before I find myself saddled with a very expensive piece of crap.'

103

'How nice of you to come in through the door,' said Jem, letting Mac into his flat.

'What?' said his friend.

'We expect you derring-do types to leap through a skylight at the very least,' said Jem, who'd drunk more champagne than he'd realised at the gallery.

'Whatever,' said Mac, who clearly wasn't in the mood. He leant down a couple of miles and kissed Min on the cheek. 'Hello, sweetheart. Always a pleasure. Hi, Dal.'

'Hello, Mac. Why are your eyes so red?' asked Min.

'Contacts playing up,' he lied.

'I didn't know you wore glasses?'

'Just leave it,' said Mac. 'It's not an issue.'

As it very obviously was, no one dared refer to it again.

'Right,' he said, changing the subject, 'I take it you want to know what our friend Gadget has been getting up to, and why he is having an unscheduled holiday? Here's what I know. I was at work when the phone rang. I knew it was him by the voice but he sounded completely loopy. He was crying and gasping for air. I told him to calm down and went to get him.

'He wasn't standing where I'd asked him to. I looked around for him, and in the end put the car headlights on and saw him running away across this little park. He fell, and when I reached him, he was babbling and covered in mud. At first he didn't recognise me – tried to fight me off, saying, "You can't take me, you bastards."

'I took him to the office where I met Dennis. I'd given Will a tranquilliser in the car to try and calm his nerves down. It made him crash out almost instantly.

'He came round a few hours later. I can only tell you what he told me but, please remember, he was hardly coherent. Apparently he was in his flat when the phone rang. He picked it up, thinking it would be Min, but it was an unidentified voice saying there were men waiting outside and unless he gave them the "evidence", they would break in and kill him. He kept saying, "Joren didn't have an accident. They did it, they told me. They tried to kill him." And then he kept saying, "I won't sign! I won't sign it, it's not right." When we asked him what he wouldn't sign, he started sobbing. I asked him if he would like to go somewhere safe and he said, "No, no, I must go back and save Min or they'll get her too." Then he drifted off again. He was clearly exhausted and the sedative was still at work in his body.'

'What did you do then?' said Jem, horrified but still fascinated by the tale.

'Dennis and I talked it through. There seemed to be two explanations. Either Will had gone stark raving mad and it was all a nasty delusion, possibly brought on by too much stress and alcohol, or something really had happened. Either way, we felt it best to get him somewhere safe as fast as possible, where he could dry out and come back to life. But we couldn't take the chance that it was entirely a fantasy on his part. So we hid him.'

'Why do you think it might not have been a fantasy?' asked Min.

'In my experience,' said Mac, 'people can be close to the brink for a long time but still not fall over it. It takes a traumatic event to push someone into the state he was. I believe he was seriously frightened, and that something bad had happened to make him that way.'

'What could it have been? And why would someone phone him in the middle of the night and threaten to kill him?' said Jem, who was getting really quite excited.

'I wish I knew,' said Mac. 'You understand my first priority was to get him out of London, to somewhere nobody could find him? I didn't have time to bring him round and get the story from him, and frankly I thought it could take a while before he came back to his senses.'

'Where is he?'

'In Scotland. In an ashram.'

'A what?'

'A Yogic community. They have a philosophy of total acceptance. You have no life before you come, no name, no possessions and no past. No questions asked either. I took him there and asked that they gave him sanctuary. If you say that, they are bound by their code to look after you.'

'How did you know about the ashram?' said Min.

'It borders on Caithness – it's in a castle at the mouth of the bay where it meets the sea,' said Mac. 'About six months ago, the owner, our local fruitcake, gave it over to the Yogis and they've been there ever since. Very peaceful people. Quite admirable, really. Completely self-sufficient.'

'Who would have thought it? Mac is a hippy at heart,' said Jem.

'Sod off, I'm not.'

'When can we contact Will?' asked Min.

'We can't. There are no phones, no internet, no nothing up there. And anyway, none of us should try. If someone is, and I'm still not convinced they are, looking for him, then the last thing we should do is try and see him. Not until we know what's going on.'

'But what the hell *is* going on?' said Min.

'Search me,' said Mac. 'It's not quite my bag, all this.'

'I thought you did loads of kidnap and ransom stuff?'

'Yeah, but I don't normally do the detective work too. I work to a brief with clear-cut objectives. This one is all over the place. And, we should remember, it could all be a fuss about nothing.'

'Then what do we do now?'

'I hate to tell you this, guys,' said Mac, 'but I have to go away.'

'You can't leave us!' said Min. 'What if we meet a bunch of murderous criminals? What are we supposed to do then?

Advise them on their lobelias, recite a bit of Shakespeare and take a photo?'

'Sorry, darling,' he said. 'I haven't got a choice.'

'You always have choice,' said Min hotly.

'No, there's an operation in Africa I should have led and didn't. Now they're in trouble and I have to go and get them out.'

'But Will is in trouble . . .'

'These are my men, Min. They're in danger of their lives. I should have left already. I have to go right away.'

'Well, I still think you're a wimp,' she said petulantly.

'Christ!' said Mac, who could feel one of his headaches starting again. 'Please don't do this to me, Min. Please. I have to go, but I will be back. And as soon as I get back, I will sort everything out, I promise.'

'And what should we do until then?' said Dallas, who had been unusually silent all this time. Keen as he was on dramas on the stage, he wasn't sure how much he liked them in real life.

'FA,' said Mac. 'Nothing. And, Min, I mean *nothing*. If anything suspicious happens, you are to contact Dennis straight away. Do not get involved, do you read me? If something has gone wrong, you will not help Will by amateur sleuthing. If it's serious, we'll need to get the experts in.'

'Shame we don't know any,' said Min under her breath.

Mac shot her a look but decided not to take it any further. 'I call you the minute I land,' he promised, and then walked out without saying goodbye.

As soon as he'd gone, Min turned to the other two.

'We *so* need a plan,' she said.

'I've *so* got one,' said Jem. 'We do absolutely nothing and in a few days Will will reappear, fit and well and hopefully having had the fright he needed to pull himself together, Min and Mac are exposed as the pair of paranoid conspiracy theorists they really are, and life goes back to normal. And if he doesn't, we leave it until Mac comes back and let him deal with it.'

'He's right, Min,' said Dallas. 'I mean, what can we do anyway? We're hardly a force to be reckoned with.'

Speak for yourself, thought Min. But didn't say it.

Chapter Seven

Will's night had been an odd one. The men in white had escorted him to the Great Hall, which was, as the name implied, fairly big and pretty grand with arching oak beams supporting a vaulted ceiling and flagged stone floor worn by the footsteps of centuries. The only light came from a fire burning in a hearth large enough for a man to stand in, the skies outside the diamond-paned windows having turned to night. It was an awesome sight.

Dotted around the hall was a selection of white-clad persons among which, when Will's eyes accustomed themselves to the gloom, he spied a number of women. If this was the asylum he feared it might be, then at least it wasn't for men only. He felt slightly cheered when he spotted a very pretty girl giggling at the back. She was waifishly slender, with long, rippling blonde hair and pink cheeks. If she was insane, then he was quite happy to be mad with her too. His physical strength was still so precarious he couldn't stand up for long and had to sink on to some cushions by the fire. A knot of concerned people immediately gathered around him, one massaging his head, another taking up one of his feet and pressing their fingers into it. The sensation was blissful and Will briefly thought that had he known how nice it was to have some kind of breakdown, he would have done it years ago. It certainly beat the hell out of working for a living.

He was drifting away into his own private world, the hands on his head and his feet pulsing on his most tender points, when he felt the atmosphere in the hall change. The mood darkened as the earth does when the sun is suddenly eclipsed by the moon. The magical hands drew away and he was gently helped upright.

A man had entered the Great Hall. Not a very tall man, not a very good-looking man. But he had a presence of the sort that makes everyone else fall silent when it enters the room, that draws every eye to it, that has people hanging off its every word.

He stood with his back to the fire so Will could only see him in outline, a shaggy mop of hair on top, the inevitable white robe beneath. The brothers and sisters formed lines to either side of him. Will was led up the middle, feeling like a lamb to the slaughter. When he reached the apparition, it immediately motioned for him to kneel. Dutifully, he obeyed.

The strange man put his hand on top of Will's head and he felt a little jolt of electricity run through him.

'Welcome,' a deep voice throatily intoned. 'Welcome, brother, to Berriemore.'

Here a chorus of voices joined in.

'Home to the homeless, light in the darkness, succour to despair and path to on high.'

They all sighed happily at the end of this little homily.

'Brother,' the man continued in his mesmerising voice, 'you have been led to us. You are now our care and duty, to love and nurture and guide towards the knowledge of the life the spirit lights within.'

'Er, thanks,' Will squeezed out, but even this was wrong.

'Do not thank me,' the shaggy-haired one said. 'Thank he who led you here! This is the ashram of Berriemore. We have all been led here for a purpose, and that purpose is to give ourselves over to the Higher Power which rests within us.

110

Because our lives are pure and unsullied by the outside world, we have no communications and no distractions of the sort the other world thrives on. How can you hear the voice of the spirit if all the time you are among noise?

'Here we are quiet, thoughtful, meditative. We live simply, on the produce we raise in our farm and gardens. We work, all of us, ceaselessly, for the survival of our way of life,' he droned. 'What we cannot produce ourselves, we buy with the humble amounts we gain from selling wares on the mainland.'

Will perked up at this. 'I'm good at selling,' he said eagerly. 'Perhaps I could lend a hand on market day?'

The interruption was ignored. 'We have no individual traits here, no one is good or bad at anything, we have no possessions, no names, no past, no future. We exist solely in the present, for now, with no attachments.'

'You will work with us, brother. You will live amongst us. You will become a part of the ashram of Berriemore and we welcome you into our number!'

With that, he let out a blood-curdling shriek and everyone threw their hands up, cried out loud with joy and hugged each other. Will was at a loss to know how to respond to this expression of unbridled emotion. He had been muted for so long, so careful only to show a façade to the outside world, one of mild cynicism, boredom or superiority, that this kind of letting rip was very alien to him. He shuffled his feet, bowed his head and looked from side to side in an attempt to catch someone's eye. When it became clear to him they all believed whole-heartedly that he had been saved, he gave up and sank back into his cushions once more.

Down in London, Min was feeling rather lonely and rejected. Her brief visits to the capital city were usually a chance for her to refuel, catch up on some sleep in the bijou comfort of Will's flat, do some light shopping and spend all evening, every evening, monopolising his time. It wasn't that they did things she couldn't have done with any of her other English friends – go out to dinner, take a walk in the park, get drunk and have a fried breakfast the next day, or catch a film. The point was that without Will she felt no urge to do any of these things. She was strangely lethargic and unenthused, slobbing around Jem's flat all day, wondering why she felt quite so wrung-out and exhausted when she'd done precisely nothing.

Mentally, she was getting quite ground down by thinking only of Will and where he might be. She couldn't get out of her head the notion that something was terribly wrong and yet she had very little to go on. It all boiled down to Will leaving in the middle of the night, claiming his life was in peril, the fact that his boss Joren had had an accident, that there was something Will wouldn't sign, and that, out of all the people he could have chosen to contact, in a crisis he'd picked Mac. To Min, this was the most significant factor. She knew the two of them didn't regularly speak to each other and that their friendship had lapsed rather since university. Mac wasn't exactly the sort of man you called if you wanted a hotel recommendation. You only called him if you were deeply, deeply in the shit and needed to be rescued. Will might have been on the edge of some kind of breakdown anyway but if so, then there had to be some underlying reason for it and, as Mac himself had said, something must have happened to push him too far. What she needed to find out was what Will had been doing recently, and why.

Fortunately his life was as minimalist as his flat. He only did two things, which were to work and to drink. She doubted it was only the drink that had got to him, which left work – the bank – as the other option. After all, Oddbins was hardly going to call in the middle of the night and threaten to assassinate one of their best customers.

Jem wasn't being much help. He seemed to have decided

Will had been suffering from severe alcoholic delusion and had lost his mind. Mac's suspicions did not alarm him too much as he believed that in Mac's line of work you lost the ability to take anything at face value and were forced always to consider all options. Whenever Min raised the topic with him, he would sigh irritatingly and say, 'Just wait a few more days, Min. He'll be back. And until then, I've got plenty to be getting on with.'

Shrewder than most, Jem had also been firmly convinced for years that Min was in love with Will, even if she didn't realise it herself. The way so many of her sentences started 'Will thinks', or 'Will was saying the other day', for instance, and the way no one else got near him when she was around. Her insistence on trying to find him sprang, Jem felt sure, partly from a certain pique that anyone else should play a part in her precious Will's life and partly from the fact that she was just plain missing him.

Thus he dismissed the topic from his mind and got on with his job. As it was summer, the pressure was on for *Dig It!* to film as many episodes as possible, so that viewers could be entertained throughout the dark winter months with cheering pictures of sunny English gardens full of blowsy roses and humming bees. The reality wasn't quite so idyllic. It had rained pretty solidly that summer, turning the little patches of Planet Earth that Jem and his team tussled with to try and make them paradisiacal into slippery mud flats instead. For the umpteenth time, as he oversaw the systematic destruction of a back yard in Colchester, a bleak and depressing town made even less attractive by the presence of sprawling Army barracks, he cursed his younger self for foolishly taking on the yoke of *Dig It!* If only he'd known, he thought. You come to the crossroads of life and turn in one direction, imagining you can get off the road you are on whenever you want. And then you find yourself travelling at 200 miles an hour on a five-lane *autobahn* where the only exits marked are 'Death' or 'Poverty'.

So given Jem's obsession with the drainage problems of the south east, and Dallas's new rehearsal schedule which seemed to necessitate an awful lot of group trust exercises, largely involving hurling other actors around a small church hall in the name of art, Min was pretty much left to her own devices.

'Albert,' she said one afternoon as the old man hoovered around her feet.

'My lady,' he replied, switching off the vacuum cleaner in order to fit a new suction nozzle.

'The e-mail you sent me . . .'

He quickly turned the hoover back on and set off to deal with the dust situation in the far corner.

'Albert!' Min tried to shout over the buzzing noise. 'Your e-mail!'

'Sorry?' said Albert. 'Can't hear a thing.'

'Turn it off.'

'What?'

Min ran to the socket and pulled out the plug.

'The e-mail you sent me . . .'

'Ah,' said Albert.

'I want you to tell me exactly what you meant.'

He looked very unhappy.

'Let's start with why you sent it,' said Min.

'Well, I . . .' said Albert, looking flustered. He smoothed his silvery-grey hair. 'I am not very familiar with modern ways of communicating. I sent you a message by electronic mail, only to regret swiftly afterwards that I had been quite so forward. It's not my place to interfere.'

'But you were clearly concerned about William?'

'Mmm.'

'Come on, Albert, I'm not going to tell you you're overstepping the mark. I want you to!'

The old man was miserably twisting his hands together. He sat down heavily on the low sofa and sighed deeply. When he spoke, his carefully formal manner had gone and he reverted to a gentler, more natural mode of speech, his Norfolk origins clearly showing through.

'You do understand, my lady, what with my pension being very small and Mrs Albert not well, it's the cleaning as sees us through. If it got out that I talked indiscreetly, then I'd never be allowed into a house again. I mean, there isn't a place I go to I couldn't tell you a tale about. They're all up to all sorts, and far worse things than Mr Gadget. He was a gent, even if he wasn't really . . . not by birth, I mean.

'Ooh, I could tell you some things that would shock you! The ways they carry on . . . At least in the old days they had the grace not to do it in front of the servants. It's all different now. They're snorting cocaine off antique tabletops and expecting me to clear up after them! Some of them think because they pay me, I don't have eyes and ears.'

'I'm sorry,' said Min. 'I didn't realise it was so difficult for you. How is Mrs Albert?'

'She comes and goes. We have our good days and our bad.'

'Who looks after her when you're at work?'

'Her sister Beryl comes in, but she's getting on a bit herself these days. We get a carer from the agency sometimes but they're not reliable. We've lost all her rings already and her Rolex is gone. I gave her that for our silver wedding.'

Min thought Albert might cry.

'And then,' he carried on, his old hands shaking, 'we found someone was cashing cheques in her name. They'd taken the last couple out of a new book and tried to get money from her account.'

'Who had?' said Min, confused.

'One of the nurses who'd come in to see her,' said Albert. 'She'd taken the cheques when she was working in the house. She thought we'd never notice, on account of Mary being so tired now and me always working. It's not right, is it?' he said, raising watery blue eyes to Min. 'I mean, we had the war and everything, and we've worked all our lives. We'd just like a bit of dignity now we're old.'

'Of course you would,' said Min, who thought she might cry too.

'Your Mr Gadget's been a great help,' said Albert. 'I'm saving to take Mary on a cruise, and he gives me advice on the stock market.'

'Does he now?' said Min. 'He doesn't usually discuss work with anyone.'

'I know,' said Albert. 'But when he found out about the cruise and how I've got to pay for three, so Beryl can come and lend a hand, he tried to give me some money towards it.'

'Dear Will,' said Min. 'He'd have bought you the liner, if you'd let him.'

'I couldn't take it, of course,' said Albert. 'People take advantage of Mr Gadget's generosity, but I'm not one of them. He wouldn't let it rest, though. Said if I wouldn't take money from him, he'd give me share tips instead.'

'Albert!' said Min. 'Have you been insider dealing?'

'I have,' said Albert, his face sagging with worry. 'And, oh, my lady, I'm so sorry. Now he's gone and I think it may be all my fault.'

'How can it be your fault, Albert?'

'He said if I didn't tell anyone where I was getting the information from, we'd be fine. And I didn't, I swear I didn't! But someone must have found out he was advising me and kidnapped him.'

'Er, Albert,' said Min. 'What sort of money are we talking about here?'

He closed his eyes. 'Hundreds of pounds, my lady.'

Min stifled a giggle. She didn't want to hurt the old man's feelings. 'I don't think that's got anything to do with his disappearance,' she reassured Albert. 'But I would still like to know why you sent me that e-mail in the first place?'

'Are you sure it's not my fault?' he said, opening one eye.

'Absolutely,' said Min. 'One hundred per cent guaranteed. So go on, spill the beans.'

'Well,' he said, 'Mr Gadget's always had a bit of a taste for it, if you know what I mean? Likes a drink or two. But something else worried me more.

'He's never been wrong about a share. I've bought low and sold high every time. He's always been spot on, he has. But then he told me I must sell some shares. Said it was very important I get rid of them. He'd said to buy as many as possible, a few months back, and then some weeks ago he insisted I sold them. He said it was very, very, very important that I did. So I went and sold them and made a bit of a profit, but now they've gone up again. And again. They keep on going up. That's what made me think he was getting ill in the head, so I wrote to you.'

'I see,' said Min. 'So all the stuff about the empties in the bin and finding him asleep in his work clothes on the sofa, holding a bottle of whisky, was that true?'

'Well, yes, actually,' said Albert firmly. 'I did think he was getting out of control in that way. But I thought there might be a reason for the drinking, and that if he was going to tell anyone, it would be you. And that you could help him to sort out whatever it was so he'd feel better.'

'Ah,' said Min. 'Now let's get this quite straight. You were alarmed because William seemed to have changed. He was drinking quite heavily, he'd made a mistake about an investment he recommended and you thought he was in danger of losing the plot altogether. But you didn't want to have to explain about the shares to Jem, even though you wanted to alert him that William was not well, so you put it down to the booze?'

'I'm sorry, my lady,' said Albert. 'I didn't know what else to do. But you've always seemed such a nice person. I thought I could talk to you. I should have said something earlier, but I didn't, and now he's gone and . . .'

'Albert, stop worrying! At once! That's an order. Now, tell me, what were these shares in?'

'Tellcat,' he said. 'You know, telephones.'

'Telephones?' said Min. 'How dangerous can a phone company be?'

'In the old days,' said Albert, 'when the phone rang, they would gather all the family in the drawing-room before it was answered. It was quite an event, a telephone call. We'd still be talking about it weeks later.'

'How things have changed,' said Min reflectively.

'Indeed,' said Albert, in much the same vein. 'When I think, Chieverley is now a health spa . . .'

'Funny, isn't it?' she said. 'I saw the brochure. It said, "For generations Chieverley has been a centre for rest and relaxation, with special healing powers". It didn't mention that the previous inhabitants had been bankrupt alcoholics.'

'Put them right off their pedicures, that would,' said Albert. 'Well, must get on.' He hauled himself off the sofa and went back to hoovering.

'So must I,' said Min decisively. She had just had an idea.

She found him lying alone on a white bed, his chest rising and falling as rhythmically as the ventilator to which he was attached by a complex series of tubes. The only sound in the little private ward was the regular 'swoosh' as air was pumped into and extracted from his lungs. His face was covered with an oxygen mask, his body with a sheet. Without the notes at the end of his bed, Joren Thorsted would have been identifiable only as another body hovering on the threshold of death.

'You're not family and this isn't visiting time,' snapped a nurse in a pale blue starched uniform, bustling in to take readings from the bank of flashing machines behind Joren's bed.

'I was just going,' said Min, placing a small pink rose in his flaccid hand where it lay still on the coverlet. 'God bless you, Joren.'

The nurse, whose fervent Catholicism had given her the unshakeable belief in a just God and the existence of an afterlife which allowed her to move unconcerned through these rooms of the half-dead, softened slightly. After all, this girl was wearing a cross round her neck. She decided not to report Min after all.

'Get on with you now,' she said. 'Doctor's on his way.'

Chapter Eight

At the ashram it was breakfast-time, an event Will was looking forward to with more than customary zeal. He was absolutely starving, but that wasn't the point. He was determined to try talking to some of his fellow inmates and to find out a few pieces of local information. Where he was would be a good start. And what he was doing here. How he had arrived might be useful. In short, what exactly had happened to him? As hard as he tried, he couldn't remember anything more detailed than some blurred images of darkness and panic. It was as if someone had short-circuited his brain. One minute, as per usual, he'd been in his flat having a dull but acceptable evening; the next he'd woken up in bed in a castle. Try as he might, he couldn't find the link.

He entered the breakfast room cautiously. The leader from the night before wasn't at the table so conversation seemed more cheery. True, the topics discussed were a bit odd – the benefits of urine-drinking, whether the goat needed a homeopathic poultice for his corns, how rose quartz crystal improves the quality of sleep – but the rise and fall of chattering voices was a huge improvement on the mystic statement mode these people seemed prone to fall into with little warning.

He took a seat on one of the long benches set to either side of a massive table. A tiny little woman next to him patted him on the hand.

'Goodness, you look better,' she squeaked. 'Poor little love, I thought when I saw you, who's been doing what to you to make you look like that? Don't worry, poppet, we'll have you right in no time.'

On the other side of him, and the reason for his choosing that particular spot, was the very pretty girl he'd seen the night before. Close to, she was even more stunning than she'd seemed under candlelight, with a complexion as soft as a mound of peony petals. Her long hair waved just slightly as it tumbled down her back in a waterfall of golden strands. She was so lovely-looking that at first, Will could only gaze at her. A picture of Min flashed through his head then, sitting by the river in her violet glasses, a breeze from the water ruffling her black curls. Then he remembered the bleak days he'd spent after she'd left, waiting for some kind of word or note or sign which would explain why. Just the memory of that time caused his heart to shrink with sadness.

'Are you all right?' said the girl. Will's eyes had just gone out of focus.

'Oh, fine, fine,' he said, turning to his swiftly congealing porridge. 'Yes, quite, great. Never better.'

'Are you sure?' asked the Vision.

'Why shouldn't I be?'

'Well, you haven't been here long.'

'I haven't?' said Will.

'Not really. You only arrived about three days ago.'

'I've been here three days?' he said in horror. 'What have I been doing?'

'Sleeping, mainly,' said the girl.

'Oh, no,' said Will.

'What's wrong?'

'Look,' he said, 'there some things I need to ask you about.'

'Like what?'

'Like, where are we?'

The girl was now staring at him in open astonishment. 'You mean, you don't know where you are?'

'Haven't a clue.'

'Wow!' said the Vision. 'You really were in a bad way, weren't you? They said you were very sick when they brought you in, but I didn't realise it was that serious. Wow, that is amazing!'

She seemed very impressed. Before he had time to capitalise further on this advantage by telling her he'd only remembered his own name that morning, a white-robed man popped up at his elbow and whisked him away. He was to undergo his 'cleansing exercises', apparently. It was important to rid the body of all its toxins, the brother explained, before the spirit could be purified.

What followed was gross. The variety in terms of texture, colour and viscosity of the fluids forcibly expelled from his various orifices was quite shocking. Surely, thought Will, these substances were somehow necessary to the internal function-ing of his organs? What if the sticky malodorous glues were in fact holding him together, and without them he would fall, bit by bit, to pieces? It was a prospect only slightly less pleasant than the method of expunging the internal mucal overload which involved a bamboo pole and a bucket of cold water.

However horrific Will found the process, the end result was that he left the cleansing room with an unaccustomed spring in his step. Cleansed and invigorated, he toddled off to the meditation room. He had, he felt, quite a good chance of being a skilled meditee, having spent large chunks of his student life staring variously at walls, windows, ceilings or floors in a state of otherworldliness. Will's naturally competitive urges also made him hope he might turn out to be the best in the group, levitating effortlessly in a swathe of golden light to gasps of admiration while others struggled to pass Key Stage 1 or whatever grade system meditation works on.

For the first few minutes, as he concentrated on the 'in-out' breath, he felt weightless and serene. A minute more and he desperately wanted to scratch his nose. He used all his mental energy to refocus and rise above the itchy nose. And then the bottom of his foot suddenly demanded attention. His shoulder started to twitch. Thoughts popped into his mind. 'I wonder if that's a verruca starting on my foot?' 'How much does a first-class stamp cost?' 'Why can't you have a fruit juice tap in the kitchen?' It was somewhat demoralising finally to get in touch with his inner life and then find it quite so mundane.

As the session drew to a close, the leader of the ashram made another entrance to much swooning all around. He stood flicking back his mane of matted hair and looking smug as the white-robed acolytes grovelled at his feet. Will found himself quite revolted by the spectacle. It was a gut reaction but a powerful one. So the news that he was to start a course of 'therapy' with the man himself was not something he greeted with great joy.

The two men sat on opposite benches in a cold stone room high in a turret, eyeing one another carefully. It was like squaring up for a fight. Will expected the leader to say something but he just sat there, watching him. Will found this quite unnerving so eventually he coughed and said, 'So! Here we are!' in a cheery fashion.

'Yes, brother,' was the reply.

Silence fell once more.

'So,' Will pressed on, 'you're obviously the head man here. How's that then?'

'We are not here to talk about me,' the leader said, a touch pompously. 'Although I have been blessed to be chosen as leader of these people, I have travelled the world to find my followers. Some have come to me, some I have been led to. It is destiny.'

Destiny, my arse! thought Will. Close up, without his props – adoring followers, firelight, majestic backdrop – he was less imposing than the night before.

'Why have you come to us?' asked the leader.

Will leant forward. 'I don't know,' he said conspiratorially. 'I have absolutely no idea.'

The other man was studying him calmly.

'Where did you come from?'

'Well, I want to say I came here from my flat in London, but as I don't remember anything about it, I can't really answer that.'

'Do you own this flat?'

'No, I don't,' said Will who'd decided to lie because he was pretty sure this wasn't the sort of question therapists usually asked. He was quite happy to talk about his mother or any other family issues he might be holding on to but he certainly wasn't interested in chewing the fat on the state of the London property market with this weirdo.

'Hmm,' said the leader. 'Interesting that you have chosen not to tell me the truth.'

Will was a little surprised.

'You are here for a purpose, and I don't yet know what that purpose is.'

'Oh, dear, magic eye misted up again, has it?' asked Will innocently.

'I will unlock the secrets that you hold,' said the leader. 'I can see into your very soul and have ways of making you tell me things you might not even admit to yourself.'

'In that case,' said Will, 'there's not much point in your asking me anything, if you know it all already.'

'Your negativity does you no credit,' intoned the leader. 'It is a poison that seeps through your pores.'

'Oh, for fuck's sake! I didn't ask to bloody well come here, you know. I don't even like it here in fact, and if you'd just point me in the direction of the nearest road I'll be on my way and you won't be troubled any longer by my negativity.'

The leader greeted this outburst dispassionately. He stroked his long beard.

'I see,' he said.

'So,' said William, 'how do I get out of here?'

'My friend and brother,' said the leader, 'it has been asked of us that we take care of you until you are well again, and that day is a long way away. Believe me, in some ways I would like you to leave this place immediately and not come back. I have said as much to the council and told them I believe you represent a threat to our way of life. But they will not listen to me. As far as they are concerned, you must be allowed to stay.'

Will had never before thought of himself as someone with quite so much power. He was rather surprised and not entirely displeased by this notion of himself as a lifestyle-changing personality force.

'I have told them I see the mark of doom on you,' continued the leader, which wasn't quite such welcome news to Will. 'I have told them you carry the quality of destruction. Some people cause death, disaster, famine, war . . . and you, brother, are among their number.'

'Now, steady on,' protested Will. 'I've never done anything like that. Frankly, that's slanderous.'

'You may not know as much,' said the other man. 'You may not yet have done so. But I see a great evil coming and I see you at the centre of it.' He was gazing into the distance and Will noticed his eyes had turned an opaque milky-blue. It was a gruesome sight.

'Can you predict stock market crashes?' he said, watching the man with horrified fascination. Saliva ran out of the leader's mouth and down his chin but he seemed oblivious.

'There is money, much money. There are many people running away in fear.' The drool was gushing out now.

'I think you ought to stop,' said Will. 'I don't think this is doing you any good at all. You really don't look well. Shall I

call someone?' The leader was foaming at the mouth, scrab-
bling his hands around in the air and twisting his body in
sharp, jerky movements.

'Oh, my God!' shouted Will. 'He's having a fit.' The man was
now thrashing around violently. Will went to the door and
yelled for help but they were in a remote part of the castle that
he'd never been to before and he doubted he had time to run
back to the main living area. Anyway, he clearly couldn't leave
the man alone, not in this state.

So Will did the only thing he could. He grabbed the man,
who was now throwing himself around the room, babbling
incoherently, and pinioned his arms to his sides. The leader
tried to resist him but Will held on, even when he was bashed
right on the nose by the leader's flailing head. Gradually, as he
hung on and made what he hoped were appropriately soothing
comments to someone in the throes of a lunatic fit, the
violence of the convulsions dwindled until they were no more
than occasional slight jerks. Will lowered the man to the floor
and put him in what he thought might be the recovery
position. His breathing had calmed right down and saliva no
longer spouted from him. After a few moments, the leader's
eyes opened.

'Leave me now,' he said.

'If you think you'll be okay?' ventured Will, desperate to
escape.

'Quiet,' said the man on the floor. He directed his gaze
straight at Will who felt his blood chill as the leader stared at
him. In the other man's eyes Will saw a flicker of absolute
hatred and contempt. It was there for just a second before his
gaze went blank once more. But Will had seen it long enough
to realise that, for some reason he couldn't even imagine, this
man totally loathed him.

Chapter Nine

'Min,' sighed Polly, 'this story just doesn't make sense.' Polly was one of her many cousins although a distant enough one to have escaped some of the more unattractive features of the de Beaufort gene pool. As a result she was – for that family – quite sensitive, intelligent and aware. As much as Min adored her elder siblings, she frequently found them overwhelming with their ruthless self-confidence, loud voices and supercilious manners.

Polly was the features editor of a well-respected middle-market newspaper that was furiously trying to distance itself from the dreaded tabloids. As a result they had recently been running some in-depth investigative pieces so Min had hoped to interest her in the story of William and his strange disappearance. The cover of being a journalist, Min thought, was just what she needed to get her into a few places to ask searching questions.

'I mean,' continued Polly thoughtfully, flicking her blonde bob, 'there seems to be a perfectly rational explanation: that he's had some kind of breakdown and has had to go away for a few days . . .'

'Ten,' said Min.

'All right, ten days, to get better again. It happens quite often, you know, to people in high-stress jobs. I really don't think there's a hidden agenda.'

Min could see from her cousin's expression that she wasn't going to be persuaded otherwise. And, actually, all the evidence had sounded quite silly when she'd presented it to the very pragmatic Polly.

'I didn't know you wrote?' Polly had said when Min approached her. 'Fantastic pix, by the way. I loved the ones of Lake Titicaca.'

'I'm branching out into writing as well,' said Min, crossing her fingers under the table.

'Are you any good?'

'It's hard to say,' said Min, very truthfully, having so far written nothing that anyone could have passed judgement on.

'I mean, has anyone else commissioned you yet?' Polly checked her watch anxiously. The days when she could spend three hours having lunch at San Lorenzo followed by a facial were long gone. With falling advertising revenues cutting a swathe through her budget, she now ate a sandwich at Starbucks, didn't dare be late by more than five minutes and was currently running with at least three fewer staff writers than she needed.

'I've got a few leads,' said Min carefully. '*Tatler* are keen to see me. I do have an idea I was going to suggest to them, but I could . . .'

'What is it?' said Polly, desperate to get her hands on anything her editor would think of as posh and upmarket. 'If it's the low-fat yin and yang diet, I've already got it in about fourteen different formats.'

'No. Although, gosh, that sounds interesting.'

'I think you mean "fascinating",' said Polly dryly. 'If you're going to be a hack, you'd better learn the right phrases. Come on, Mini, you've got two minutes to impress me.'

One minute and thirty seconds later the deal was done.

Tellcat's situation, to judge from the headlines Min picked off the internet, did not in any way justify Will's insistence that Albert must dump his shares in the company. From what she could make out, they were rising meteorically, trading at £75 apiece, up from £63 the week before. She was puzzled as to why Will would want Albert to get out. Tellcat was one of the new success stories of the deregulated telecommunications market, with a track record of wholesale expansion into internet service-providing, mobile phones, domestic and business communication systems and satellite ownership. Either Will had gone bonkers and lost his judgement entirely or else he knew something nobody else did. Under the cover of writing for Polly and her newspaper, Min started her own investigation.

Her first mission was to find out who had taken over from Will at work, which was very straightforward. She simply rang his old extension at the bank to see who she'd get through to. A recorded message in a voice that certainly wasn't Will's told her he was out of the office and that Bertrand Strader would be dealing with matters in his absence. She knew from Will that Bertrand was a slippery customer and to deal with him she would need to be sharper than a drawer full of Sabatier knives.

She followed the telephonic route to Bertrand's extension, and after two rings the phone was picked up.

'Bertrand Strader,' he drawled.

'Hello, Mr Strader,' said Min. 'This is Ambrosia de Beaufort Haskell of the *Daily News*. I am calling you about—'

He cut her off.

'You want Corporate Affairs. I'll put you through.'

'No, wait!' said Min. 'This isn't a business story. It's more personal.'

'Yeah?' said Bertrand. 'Listen, I never speak to the press so you're wasting your time, Miss Haskell.'

'I don't think so,' said Min. 'In fact, I think you might be very interested in the story I'm working on.'

'I doubt it,' said Bertrand who nevertheless didn't hang up. He had a weakness for posh English female voices and Min definitely had one of the better ones he'd heard.

'I'm looking into the ways that the high-pressure environment of the City can affect key workers. How people cope with the stresses and strains of such an intense working atmosphere. How it can all go right or maybe very wrong,' Min bluffed.

'And you were inspired to call me?' questioned Bertrand.

'As a prominent member of the banking community,' said Min, hating herself a bit more with every word she squeezed out, 'I thought you would like to make a contribution to the debate over working practice versus remuneration.'

'A prominent member of the banking community?' said Bertrand, lingering over every syllable. 'Miss Haskell, or perhaps I can call you Ambrosia, I think maybe you should find someone else.'

Min went for broke. 'But my sources tell me you are one of the fastest rising stars in investment banking. So if anyone has a valid opinion on the state of the industry as a whole, it would be you.'

'Sources?' said Bertrand. 'What sources?'

'I never reveal them,' said Min, quoting Polly. 'But I can promise you, we will treat your views and opinions with the utmost respect and care. The opportunity to profile you in one of the largest selling daily newspapers would be most exciting for us and our readers.'

'Maybe we should meet,' said Bertrand, who was vain enough to fall for even quite obvious flattery as it merely brought the rest of the world's view of himself in line with his own. 'Tonight, Casa Mundo, 8.30.' With that, he hung up.

Min had in fact met Bertrand years ago at a party at Will's flat, but as he hadn't even bothered to look at her when he'd been introduced, so busy had he been eyeing up a very pneumatic blonde, she felt fairly sure he wouldn't recognise her now. Just to be on the safe side, she went and had her long black mane cut off, emerging from a salon in Knightsbridge with a sleek crop of short dark hair. She also broke the habit of a lifetime and invested in some clothes that no one else had worn before her. In a little shift dress and knee-high black boots she looked nothing like the wild child photographer she had resembled before.

Despite the fact that Bertrand's suit was as creased as his face, he was still indecently attractive. He was lounging in a chair in Casa Mundo, the latest Soho drinking spot, holding a Martini glass. Min felt a jolt go through her when she spotted him. He looked very, very tired, his eyes were bloodshot and he had stubble creeping across his chin. But none of that could detract from the incredible beauty of his magnetic face, broad shoulders and long, long legs. Damn, damn, damn, she thought. I'll just have a Diet Coke, get some facts and leave.

'Mr Strader?' she said, approaching his leather armchair. 'I'm Ambrosia.'

'A pleasure,' he said, standing up to kiss her on the cheek. 'I must say, you journalists are,' he paused, 'amazing.'

'How so?' said Min, who hadn't expected such an enthusiastic response.

'Look around,' said Bertrand. 'Whole bar's full. And yet you picked me out. That's . . . skilful.'

Min saw the gleam of amusement in his blue eyes and realised she was being strung along. Real journalists, she figured, must face up to this all the time. The key was not to get flustered.

'What would you like to drink?' asked Bertrand.

'Um, a Coke . . . I mean, a glass of wine or perhaps a cocktail . . . I don't know, what are you having?' said Min.

'Martini. Vodka. Shaken. Twist,' said Bertrand to the waitress. 'So, Miss Haskell, I gather you are very concerned about suffering in the City?' The words were said innocently enough, but Min wasn't fooled. She was starting to think this might not have been such a great idea after all. Bertrand, she could see, was even more of a piece of work than she'd bargained for. She was starting to wonder if putting up with him all day, every day for the last few years might not be enough to tip anyone over the edge.

'Absolutely,' said Min. 'The conditions in which you work, the hours, the pressure, the lack of holidays, are having a terrible impact on some of the brightest young people in this country, a situation which for the good of our nation . . .'

'Actually, I'm an American,' interjected Bertrand, taking a sip of his Martini.

'For the good of all nations,' continued Min doggedly, 'cannot be allowed to continue.' She couldn't bring herself to look at him. The combination of his startling physical beauty with the sardonic expression on his face was just too much for her.

'And what do you suggest the answer might be?' murmured her inquisitor in an astonishingly intimate tone of voice.

'I would think,' said Min, her face flooding with colour as her mind leapt on to matters quite unrelated to the daily working issues which faced those within the square mile, 'that more sex would be . . . I mean . . .'

'What?' Bertrand spat out a large mouthful of Martini in surprise. He started to laugh, tears running down his face. Min sat there, mute with horror at what she'd just said. Where had it come from? How had she framed those words? It was just too awful to contemplate.

'I think I should be going,' she said, her cheeks by now aflame with a lurid blush.

'No way!' said Bertrand, still creased with mirth. 'You tell me my working life would be improved by more blow jobs and then think you can leave? Ambrosia Haskell, you are the most entertaining journalist I have ever met. I want more top tips from you – some positions which are known specifically to reduce stress perhaps. Or how bondage could salvage my career.'

'It's not funny,' muttered Min.

'Not funny?' he guffawed. 'That's just where you're wrong. I haven't laughed like this for years. You know, Ambrosia, we could seriously reduce stress levels in the City just by sending you round to talk to people.'

Min drained her glass in one and motioned for another, feeling she might as well die an expensive death as perish like a cheap date.

'You don't really work for the *News*, do you?' said Bertrand, changing tack abruptly.

'Yes, I do,' said Min, who actually was supposed to be writing a story for Polly on exactly the subject she'd outlined to Bertrand, something she was starting to see could be much more difficult than she'd thought. Especially as Polly was expecting it by Tuesday next.

'I'm writing a feature for them on how working in the City can be bad for your mental health,' she said, thinking that being a journalist for just one evening was threatening to reduce her to a nervous breakdown. 'On how you manage to keep going despite the hardship.'

'I think you underestimate how powerful the lure of greed really is,' said Bertrand, who'd simmered down a little by now. 'It's quite easy to keep getting out of bed every morning when you're paid very large sums of money to do it. Quote me on that and I'll sue your ass off. Hey, have another Martini, Ambrosia. You know you want to.' He smiled at her, a heavenly sight even if he did look like he hadn't slept for several days.

'Thanks,' said Min, who was still mortified by her slip up. It had happened to her before, that she'd said something she hadn't even realised she was thinking. But never as badly as this.

'So, where were we? Ah, yes, you do work for the *News* and this is a real story. That's good to know. We get a lot of rival analysts posing as journalists to try and get information out of us.'

'Oh, no,' said Min. 'You can phone my editor and check, if you like.'

'I'll do just that,' said Bert. 'What's her name?'

'Polly,' said Min.

'Polly?' said Bert. 'Polly who?'

'Polly Haskell,' said Min, cursing inwardly.

'No relation of Ambrosia de Beaufort Haskell then,' said Bert, that gleam of amusement flaring again in his bright blue eyes. 'It's not the sort of name you easily forget, is it?'

Damn, thought Min. She had considered using an alias but hadn't just in case, by some quirk, he had recognised her and so found her working under an assumed name.

'We've met before,' said Bert, narrowing his eyes. 'You're very familiar, young lady.'

Min squirmed. This was turning into the worst evening of her life, compounded by the beginnings of a very lustful crush on Bertrand which she certainly didn't want to feel. He reached out one hand and stroked her hair.

'Perhaps at a press conference?' she said.

'Don't go to them.'

'Look,' said Min, 'I'm writing a story and that's why I've contacted you. Now, can I ask you some questions?'

'Not till I've asked you a few,' said Bertrand, moving closer to her, his voice down to a whisper in which the rustle of bed sheets could clearly be heard. 'But we need to be somewhere a little more . . . private,' he added, taking her face in both his hands. 'My God, you are beautiful.' His thumb was stroking her cheekbone. 'What a face! You look like an angel.'

Min was having a real problem keeping up with the twists and turns this encounter was taking. She didn't think she'd ever met anyone so disconcerting. She was too drunk and too overwhelmed by him to realise this was, of course, a tried and tested ploy. By using so many changes of approach, Bertrand confused his victim into submission. He was an extremely manipulative man who searched for weaknesses in others in order to exploit them for his own ends.

'Come home with me,' he was saying while Min felt the room spin a little around her.

'No!' she said. 'That would be most unprofessional. I mustn't.'

'You must, you must,' said Bertrand, long fingers caressing her face gently.

'Why can't we talk here?' said Min, feeling her resolve slip away.

'Depends on your definition of talk. There are things I want to say to you which shouldn't be overheard. We need to be . . . alone.'

'I need to do my interview,' said Min. 'I need to ask you how the strains of working on Tellcat have affected your department.'

It was as though she had just thrown acid into his face.

'Say again?' said Bert, who had drawn right away from her.

'I think you heard me the first time,' she replied.

'What do you know about Tellcat?' Bert was looking at her in total horror. It was like he'd just kissed a princess only to have her turn into a repellent, pustulant toad and leave yellow slime all over his suit.

'Nothing,' said Min, realising she'd hit a raw nerve. 'I just thought that was what you were working on?'

'And how would you know that?'

'Sources,' said Min, who was sobering up very fast.

'If that source,' said Bertrand, in a low, urgent voice, 'is

William Gadget, then you are in deep shit, honey. I mean, deep.'

Min felt sick. It had been one matter to imagine there was some mysterious reason behind Will's disappearance, but to have it confirmed was truly horrible.

'Why?' she said.

'Do you know where he is?'

'No,' said Min, who was getting quite scared by Bertrand's freezing cold stare. 'I've no idea.'

'If you know, you better say and fast. We are missing some very important documents from the bank and word is that Gadget heisted them for his own personal reasons. They're looking for him, Ambrosia, and they will find him, trust me.'

'Will's no thief,' she said indignantly.

'Aha,' said Bertrand. 'So you do know him? I thought we'd met before, Ambrosia. Or should that be Min?'

'How do you know my name?' she said, feeling this was all getting way out of hand.

'I've worked next to Gadget for five years, lady. Should have known he'd send his girl back to the scene of the crime. Guy's a chicken! Runs away himself then sends you in to snoop. So what's he going to do with it?'

'With what?' said Min, wide-eyed with shock.

'Oh, don't play dumb with me,' snapped Bertrand. 'The Tellcat stuff, what else? I'm having to put together one of the biggest deals in history while I'm missing certain key documents. I can hardly go back to our clients and say, "Sorry, someone stole your confidential information, we can't do this." The bank'd be toast and so would I. He must have taken them, there wasn't anyone else with access. God, I could kill him with my own bare hands.'

'I don't understand,' said Min, close to tears.

'Let me put it another way, honey. Your precious William could be arrested for what's done, but here's how I'm going to cut him a deal. It isn't in my interests, yours, his and certainly not the bank's, that this gets out. One word of it in your paper and Gadget goes to jail, it's that simple.' He paused for effect.

'So, you get me Gadget, and I sort it all out.' He checked his watch. 'It is now Monday, 9.30 p.m. I have a very important meeting Wednesday at 4. I need to know what Gadget's game is by midday that day. You help me, by the deadline, and I look after him. Miss my deadline, you both pay the consequences.'

The most frightening aspect of Bertrand at that moment was that for once he was playing it totally straight. There was nothing about his manner which led Min to believe he was anything but in deadly earnest.

He stood up. 'Goodbye, Ambrosia. You know where to find me.'

Jem was rearranging his CD collection into reverse alphabetical order when Min stumbled back in, mascara streaked down her face from crying her heart out on the long cab journey back to his flat. The cabbie had felt so sorry for her, assuming that the handsome young man who'd helped her into the taxi had just broken her heart, he'd produced a small bottle of brandy and some tissues to help stem the damage.

'Don't worry, love,' he told her as he dropped her off, 'you'll find another. 'Spect he wasn't right anyway.'

'What the hell?' said Jem to the nightmarish vision that looked like it might once have been Min.

'Oh, Jem,' she said, 'I think I've done something terrible.' In fits and starts she stumbled through the tale of her disastrous evening, ending with Bert's thirty-six-hour deadline, after which Will, when they finally tracked him down, could be facing a long, lonely time in clink. She told him about Joren lying unconscious in hospital, Albert and his share-dealing, and how he had exaggerated Will's alcoholic decline in order to warn his friends that Will was in trouble without betraying his employer.

'Go on,' she said to Jem, whose kindly face was crumpled with worry. 'Say, I told you so. Say you told me not to meddle.'

'No, lovie,' said Jem. 'This is too serious for that. Look, I think we should call Mac. He's got a satellite phone, we should be able to reach him.'

He dialled the number. 'Da mobile phone you are trying to reach may be switched off,' said an African voice. 'Pless try again. Later.'

'Damn,' said Jem. 'Bloody man! Can never get him when you need to.'

'Should we try Dennis?'

Jem shook his head. 'I'm not sure I trust him. Mac's one thing, he's a mate. But Dennis – I just have this feeling that if someone came along with a larger cheque, he'd change sides immediately.'

'Jem, what are we going to do?' said Min, whose sniffles had been replaced by a creeping cold horror. 'Do you think Will really has stolen something from the bank?'

'Let's think,' said Jem, trying to frame his thoughts logically. 'He's gone missing at the same time as some very important documents have walked. But we know from Mac that Will was scared by someone who wanted him to hand over something he didn't have. This company, Tellcat, are definitely in the mix.'

'What does it all mean?' said Min.

Jem looked thoughtful. 'We can't go and find Will until we know more,' he said. 'Remember, Mac said we would endanger him if we did. We've got very little time to get to the bottom of this. I think we should . . .'

'Panic?' suggested Min.

'No,' said Jem calmly. 'I think we should go and pay Tellcat a visit. And, given the deadline, we'd better do it tomorrow. I'll postpone filming.'

'What are we going to say to Tellcat?'

'Nothing,' said Jem. 'But bring your camera. You're coming as a photographer this time. Somehow, you're not very believable as a journalist.'

Chapter Eleven

Tellcat's corporate headquarters in Croydon was a marvel of modern architecture. The building conveyed exactly the message it had been designed to. It was sleek, wealthy, modern and on an overpowering scale, to remind you that the company was greater than any mere human who crossed its portals. The long sweep of curved reflective glass that greeted visitors created the optical illusion that it was a semi-circular wall, freestanding and with no means of support. It was only when you went through a door – once you found it – that you saw this deceptive façade concealed the immense organisation behind.

'Jem,' Min tugged at his jacket fearfully as they entered the building, 'I don't think we can do this.'

He looked at her calmly. 'Of course we can,' he said, not adding that he felt exactly the same way. 'Just follow me and do as I say.'

He tugged down his shirt cuffs, shook his head briefly to clear it and said, 'Right. Let's hit it.'

He walked over to the bank of receptionists. 'Hello.' He smiled warmly. 'We are here to see Mr Andreas Jordan. I believe he is expecting me.' He produced his *'Dig It! A Production of Artichoke Television Company (ATC)'* business card and gave it to a girl wearing an air traffic control-style headset.

'I'll call him right away,' said the receptionist. 'Perhaps you could visit security in the meanwhile?'

An enormous burly man in a tight navy blue jumper took their bags off them. He dismissed Jem's beautifully organised briefcase with a cursory glance and sighed deeply when he looked into Min's chaotic rucksack.

'I'm going to have to empty this one out,' he said. 'No knowing what might be in the bottom.'

He pulled out a large, bulging diary, a packet of Tampax, two pairs of tights, a flip-flop, some mangled Kleenex, a bottle of nail varnish and a few rolls of film. Reaching into the bottom of the bag, he withdrew his hand quite fast when it hit something slimy. 'Eeew!' said the guard, looking at his fingers which were now greasy and flecked with glitter.

'Oh, sorry,' said Min. 'Some face cream got into my eyeshadow.'

The man hurriedly handed back her bag and with it they got two passes marked TELLCAT DAY VISITOR.

Andreas was waiting for them, a tall, slender young man wreathed in affable smiles.

'Mr Haque!' he said, extending one hand. 'What a pleasure! I'm so sorry, though, it's been such short notice I haven't been able to set up any meetings for you today. I can take you around the building but everyone you need to see about your project is engaged at the moment. You'll just have to make do with me, I'm afraid.'

Andreas was clearly one of life's nice people, and under other circumstances Jem couldn't have been happier to make do with just him. The thought of perpetrating a huge deception on this open-faced, friendly man was not a pleasant one.

'This is my assistant,' he said, introducing Min. 'Will it be possible for her to take some pictures, to give us some visuals to work with?'

'Ah,' said Andreas, 'I don't have photo-clearance for you. You didn't mention it on the phone this morning.'

'Who would we need to call to get permission?'

'Head of Public Relations,' said Andreas. 'But he's gone to an off-site meeting and can't be contacted.'

'What's your role here?' said Jem.

'Corporate and press affairs,' said Andreas proudly.

'Where were you before?'

'Um, nowhere. This is my first job.' He continued conspiratorially, 'You see, I'm not sure I'm really supposed to be showing you around at all at the moment – we've got an official block on visitors – but I couldn't find anyone to say "no" specifically and I thought it would be such a coup for me if I could set up something with *Dig It!* It might really help my career, make a bit of a splash, so to speak.'

Inwardly, Jem damned both Will and Min. Standing in front of him was the very man Jem had the instinctive feeling might be the answer to his lonely prayers. And yet he was never going to be able to see him again because of what he was doing for his friends.

'Shall we go?' said Andreas eagerly. 'There's so much for you to see.'

He wasn't lying. Tellcat's offices were vast. After they'd been through their fourteenth floor making admiring architectural comments, noting house plants and water features and discussing the possibility of including Tellcat in an episode of *Dig It!* on outstanding working environments, both Jem and Min were feeling exhausted. They switched to a special lift to ascend to the fifteenth floor. So far, they had seen plenty of foliage but surprisingly few people.

'Is it always this empty?' asked Jem.

'There are so many conferences on at present,' said Andreas, 'many key staff are away. Although I believe there may have been some reorganisation lately, some transfers and perhaps a few redundancies. Normally, it would be packed.' They got out at the top floor.

'This is the conference room,' he said in a whisper. 'I don't think they're here but we should be quiet anyway.'

'Hmm,' said Jem. 'I usually find this to be the case.'

'What's that?' said Andreas, looking worried.

'In a fully air-conditioned building such as this,' said Jem, 'the driest air tends to accumulate at the top. What you have here are plants which would thrive in a more humid atmosphere.' He fingered some perfectly healthy-looking green leaves. 'I suspect you need some Kalanchöe or perhaps a Bougainvillaea. Or hibiscus might work.' He opened his briefcase. 'What I need to do is take a reading of the humidity levels and temperature in all areas on this floor.'

'I'm not really sure that's possible . . .'

'It will take just a few seconds in each room,' said Jem soothingly. 'And then we could transform the important area of the company as well as providing some very high-profile publicity for Tellcat. *Dig It!* has over ten million viewers, you know.'

Andreas' olive-skinned face lit up with excitement. 'Can I be part of the consultation process?'

'We will keep you fully informed at all times,' said Jem. 'And you will be credited as well.'

'Oh, fantastic,' he said. 'This is *so* exciting.'

Min and Jem didn't dare look at each other. Thinking the damage was already done, Jem opened the door to the conference room and walked in with Min trotting behind. He took out his various hygrometers and started taking readings from different parts of the room. On a wall at the head of the table he noticed a large chart showing the corporate structure of Tellcat and how it related to its subsidiaries.

'Min,' he said, deliberately looking away from the chart, 'can you take some pictures of the room from all angles?'

Andreas looked uneasy.

'It's standard practice,' Jem soothed him. 'I thought you'd have realised that was an integral part of our recce process?'

'Of course,' said Andreas, not wanting to appear ignorant.

'We don't normally have a problem with it,' said Jem. 'Min, from both ends, please.' With his eyes he motioned to the chart. She understood instantly what he wanted. Using a telephoto lens, she trained her camera on the back wall, making it look as if she was taking a shot of the whole conference room but in fact homing in on the chart. She took a series of pictures, capturing in detail the complicated set-up which comprised the telecommunications giant Tellcat.

Jem was getting a little nervous. 'Min, if you've finished,' he said, snapping shut his briefcase, 'I think we should move on. We have a twelve o'clock today which I am anxious not to be late for.'

'Who's that with?' asked Andreas, the picture of sweet-faced innocence.

'British Telecom,' said Jem. 'Just checking out the opposition, hope you don't mind?'

'Not at all. But you will consider us, won't you?'

'I think you'll find we will,' said Jem, somewhat grimly, as they headed for the lift.

Once down at ground level, Andreas produced his card. 'Here are my numbers, call me any time,' he said, almost pleadingly. 'I'd love to get together for a drink sometime and talk about working in television. I've always been interested, and perhaps you'd know of some vacancies?'

'Thanks, Andreas,' said Jem. 'I'll definitely give you a call.'

The pair of them left the building and Jemal groaned. 'Oh, God, I feel such a shit,' he said to Min. 'Why do I have to keep telling lies to everyone? I hate myself.'

'You were brilliant,' said Min. 'And once we sort Will out, you can always apologise to Andreas and explain.'

'Hmm,' said Jemal, who at that moment wanted nothing more than to sort out William Gadget once and for all. Min let him brood in silence for a while, knowing from his glowering expression he would be even less prone to small-talk than usual.

Once they reached Croydon station, to find their train back to London was hopelessly delayed, she thought it time to speak again.

'Did we find out anything useful?' she asked as they stood on the platform in the midst of a morass of disgruntled travellers, cursing loudly or staring mindlessly into the middle distance, depending on whether they were native and so used to the regular non-appearance of scheduled trains or came from foreign countries where timetables were thought to be credible statements of fact.

'Well,' said Jemal, just coming to terms once more with accepting the unacceptable, a recurring theme in his life, 'they have a very large and expensive building there. The upkeep alone must be ruinous. Yet they seem to have hardly any staff.'

'Andreas said they were all at conferences.'

'You don't clear your desk before you go to a conference,' said Jem. 'Most of those work stations were empty. No family photos, no papers, no pot plants. No one in the conference room, a dictat of no visitors. Strange, for a company that turns such a large profit, they should do so with little outward effort. And then there's that chart. It's hard to say without seeing the photos but the company does seem to have an unusually high number of subsidiaries. Given they've been up and running for only a few years, they seem to have acquired a huge empire. We need to see your pix, they might give us the vital clue.'

'We haven't got long,' began Min timidly.

'We've still got over twenty-four hours,' said Jem firmly. 'There's plenty we can achieve in that time.'

Their train rumbled in and the crowd surged towards the

doors, a man in a pinstripe suit and a vicar fighting so hard to get on that they knocked a woman with a pushchair flying. Jem stopped to pick her up off the platform, dusted her down and lifted the buggy on to the train. Once he'd settled her into a seat, he went over to the suit and the dog collar who, as luck would have it, were sitting next to each other.

'Gentlemen,' began Jemal in his courteous, melodic voice, 'I appreciate that God and Mammon wait for no one.' They both looked up, surprised, at the beautifully dressed young man standing in front of them. 'But to assault a mother and child in the pursuit of either is clearly unacceptable. I hope in future you will consider your priorities a little more carefully.' He smiled coldly and went to sit next to Min who was pulling faces at the child in the pushchair.

'Feeling better?' she asked.

'Much,' he agreed. 'Just what I needed.'

Will himself could have done with venting his frustration but the opportunities were quite limited, living as he did in the midst of Yogic harmony and calm. If he did get uptight about anything, it was merely interpreted as him ridding himself of deeply held anger which probably related back to some event in his childhood. Useless to protest that it had in fact been happy, calm and full of love. He was immediately told he might have blocked out or suppressed some memory of dreadful trauma which he was only now able to release.

Such talk served to make Will even more infuriated, which in turn convinced his interlocutor even more strongly that he harboured some awful secret in his core being. During a reiki session, where he lay on a bed while a woman with long, crinkled blonde tresses and hips as wide as an underground entrance got in tune with his energy, he became so incensed by her insistence on his bio-energetic levels being seriously reduced due to entrenched anger that he sat up smartly and accidentally head-butted the woman just as she was gliding towards his chest in search of stress. Their craniums met with a sharp crack and the woman slithered unconscious to the floor while Will wondered if every member of the commune was going to pass out when they came into contact with him.

The irony of it was he did indeed suffer from a form of memory suppression only it had nothing to do with his childhood. It related to the time he seemed to have lost, in which he'd left his flat and life in London, travelled to Scotland, and been awarded sanctuary at the ashram. As his mind cleared, bits and pieces of his previous life were coming back to him – he could now remember working at the bank where he'd been very busy, though doing what eluded him. He could picture his old life, his friends, his clothes, his possessions, but still had no idea what could have possessed him to up sticks and leave what looked, in hindsight, like a very happy existence. Funnily enough, none of the commune seemed keen to help him with this particular problem. They were determined that his troubles had their roots in his early life and refused to pay attention to anything that had happened to him recently.

He had at least avoided the leader for several days, since the incident in the turret, which had given Will time to collect his thoughts a little. He spent his days peeling vegetables in the kitchen, chatting to the Vision who, although very pretty, was a touch alarming in her naïve sincerity, and trying to evade the attentions of the Brigitte Bardot (in her later years) lookalike who ran the place. Yet still his reasons for and method of arriving in this place were a mystery to him, as was quite how he was going to leave. He was no closer to knowing where he was, other than in Scotland, a rather vague map reference if ever he'd heard one, he didn't have any cash and no proper clothes. A quick whizz around the castle had revealed there to be no form of communication with the outside world more sophisticated than sending out a smoke signal which, he was starting to think, might be his only way out.

He was pondering this problem while dealing with the curves of a particularly baroque carrot when the kitchen door opened and an old man crept in. Slightly to Will's horror, the ancient sat down next to him and drooled companionably. Will had seen him wandering aimlessly around the castle, gnashing his teeth or grunting in corners, and had assumed he was some sort of care-in-the-community case that the ashram had taken on out of charity. For the last few days, Will had been uncomfortably aware that the old man had taken to following him around. At least, wherever Will was, he seemed to be too, accidentally or otherwise.

Will had mentioned this to the Vision but she hadn't been too perturbed. She took a much milder attitude towards the old man, saying he was just a confused soul who should be treated with kindness. Will thought she'd soon change her tune if the man started stalking her. He accused her of encouraging the old reprobate by giving him scraps of food from the kitchen but she'd replied, rather tartly Will considered, that she thought he seemed in need of a little encouragement. At that moment, 'Brigitte' had sidled up and wanted to know what they were talking about.

'Nothing,' Will had replied sulkily.

'If it's nothing, you can stop talking about it and get on with the vegetables,' she retorted, her attitude to Will having become noticeably frosty since a particular incident.

The ageing beauty had prior to this spent quite some time trying to cast a spell over him, only for her efforts to be marked by total failure. She had for some days taken to massaging his neck and shoulders as he worked at the kitchen counter. At first, Will had found this queasily alluring, but after a day or two the smell of the oil this woman evidently doused herself in started to turn his stomach when he caught it wafting in his direction.

He didn't dislike her, just couldn't find her as attractive as she wanted him to. To a man in his fifties, thought Will, she would probably look like Bo Derek, but to him, while perfectly acceptable in most senses, she was sexually terrifying.

Being pursued by someone not necessarily old enough to be his mother but certainly sufficiently advanced in years to have been his primary school teacher, was a distinct worry. When on duty, he tried to peel extremely fast as the rule was you left the kitchen once your task was completed. Nevertheless, there were several days when Will, still a novice in culinary matters, was the last in the grand old kitchen, the setting sun sending shafts of gold, red and pink light across the venerable black ranges and scrubbed wooden worktops.

On one such evening she'd come to sit beside him. Will immediately tensed up, but this time, it seemed, she just wanted to talk.

'I've been on the journey for many years now,' she said in her deep, breathy voice.

'What journey is that?' he said, gripping a root vegetable for protection against unwanted physical advances.

'The quickening,' she said. 'It came to me as a spiritual crisis when I saw that my whole life was based on material gain. I knew then I must go on a quest to attain greater understanding.'

'And how is that quest going?' asked Will politely, edging imperceptibly away from her along the bench.

'When I lived with a shaman in Peru . . .'

'A what?' interrupted Will.

'A man who can talk to the dead . . . he awoke old spirits in me and freed me from the grasp of my ancestors. But then in the Patagonian desert I attended a meeting of the tribes where we worshipped the power of the sea and the healing a whale can bring.'

'Right,' said Will, peeling on.

'In India I studied with Swami Bagravati and I meditated for many days without food or water. I learnt to look deep into my inner self and treasure what I found. Then I went to Bhutan where I walked with yaks in the mountain ranges, stopping at monasteries to receive the blessings of the monks.'

Will reflected that she had also probably also learnt to look deep into her wallet, to finance what sounded like quite an expensive voyage. He felt quite curious.

'Don't you ever want to go home?'

'My home is where I am,' she said, taking his hand and gazing into his eyes again, a trick he felt sure she had picked up from the leader.

'Doesn't it get rather costly?' he asked. She looked down her nose in displeasure at being asked such a mundane question.

'I do not trouble myself with such thoughts.'

Will smiled to himself. His suspicion that she was a well-off woman seemed confirmed. Only the rich, he thought, could put so much time and effort into being so self-absorbed.

He would hardly claim to be psychic but that same evening took the precautionary measure of moving his bed so that it lay across the door to his cell, meaning no one could get in from outside. As was his way now, he dropped straight into a deep sleep, until he was woken by the turning of the door handle. He lay very still as someone pushed, trying to enter his little chamber. The door hit the bed with a clang and he heard muttering from the other side. The door was shoved again, this time with more force, but there was no way it could budge the weight of the bed against it. His midnight visitor gave up and walked away.

The next day, it was fairly clear who the intruder had been, given the rapid sea change in the attitude of the head of the kitchen. She ignored him entirely, but then when he made no effort to attract her attention, signalled even more furiously that she was ignoring him by walking past his bench while pointedly looking in the other direction.

'I think you've upset your girlfriend,' whispered the Vision.

'She's not my girlfriend,' whispered back Will furiously.

The Vision giggled. 'Oh, dear, have you told her that? Is that why she's so upset?'

'Shut up!' he hissed. 'It's not funny.'

The Vision's face showed she didn't agree.

'In real life,' she said, 'do you have a girlfriend?'

'No,' said Will. 'I'm single.'

'Why?' asked the Vision.

'What do you mean, why? I just am.'

'So you're not in love with anyone?' asked the Vision with the relentlessness of a small child investigating the existence of God.

'Well, there was this girl,' said Will.

'What happened?'

'I thought maybe she loved me too, but I don't think she can have done. Each time it looked like we were finally getting somewhere, she'd run away from me. It's been going on for years. This last time, when I woke up and found she'd left once more, without any explanation, I gave up hope. I've been too hurt by it all to go on.'

'Did you tell her you loved her?' said the Vision.

'No.'

'Then how did you expect her to know?' asked the Vision. 'Men are so stupid. We girls may be brilliant but you can't expect us to be mind readers as well as everything else.'

'Stop tittle-tattling, you two,' said the ageing beauty, rounding on them in a manner which implied she might not be as in touch with her inner peace as she thought. 'I'm fed up with the pair of you! We're involved in a very important task here, the feeding of the community, and you two seem to think it's all a joke. It isn't good enough and I won't stand for it. I will not have this kind of behaviour in my kitchen!' With that she flounced away.

Despite his partial amnesia, Will felt quite certain he hadn't been spoken to like that since he was in short trousers and did not like it one little bit. It strengthened his resolve to escape if he had to scale the Highland Range on foot – which was, after all, just what Mac would have done in this situation.

As the thought passed through his mind, the name triggered a response. Mac . . . The headlights. Scotland. There was a connection. He was so close to it. He could feel it coming together in his brain. And then the leader entered the kitchen and said the dread words to him.

'Your therapy. It is time.'

Chapter Twelve

It was still early in the evening when Jem's phone rang. He and Min were having a nap, following a gruelling day. Once they had visited Tellcat HQ and downloaded Min's photos on to Jem's laptop, they'd made a list of the subsidiary companies nearest to London featuring on the Tellcat chart. Jem, who usually had an army of researchers to answer his merest query, found the process charmingly redolent of his younger, happier days in television when he seemed to have everything before him, unlike his current position where he now felt before him lay only more of the same.

It didn't make Min quite so nostalgic. She was horribly aware of the ticking clock. They didn't have long before Bertrand's deadline expired and he was going to expect something better than a learned discourse on the state of Tellcat's house plants. She wasn't sure quite what Jem was driving at but thought it best not to waste time by asking too many questions and got on with sourcing the information he wanted.

Jem himself didn't really know where his enquiries might lead but had a strong sense he was headed in the right direction. During the brief but delirious period in his traineeship where he'd worked on current affairs programming, he'd been told that some people had a 'nose for news'. He'd hoped fervently that he was one of those lucky few. If he was, no one had noticed, and it had been his 'green fingers' instead which had captured the imagination of the company's bosses. Working on the Disappeared Gadget story, as he termed it in his mind, was giving Jem the first feelings of excitement and mental stimulation he'd had since he'd started work on *Dig It!*

Mixed with his investigatory zeal was a not inconsiderable dose of guilt. Before Will vanished, Jem had been getting increasingly impatient with him, finding his erratic behaviour too much to cope with. Then, when he suddenly disappeared and an alcoholic breakdown seemed the most plausible explanation, there had been a little bit of Jem which had thought, Serves him right. For years, Will seemed to have been effortlessly proceeding up the career ladder, earning larger and larger amounts of pure lucre, zipping round the world in first class, holidaying in St Moritz or Juan-les-Pins. Jem wasn't jealous of Will's salary – or only a tiny bit – but he was envious of the ease with which his friend seemed to float through life, never taking anything too seriously, never making any commitment, always the life and soul of the party. By nature, Jem was much more serious and lacked this lazy charm. He didn't have the happy gift of being liked that came to Will so naturally. Life for him was much more complex and more of a struggle than it seemed to be for Will and so Jem had made the mistake of assuming that his friend's life was as straightforward as it seemed on the surface. When it looked as though Will had made a mess of this perfect existence by his own uncontrollable drinking habits, the *Schadenfreude* which lies concealed in even the best of his friendships broke free. Jem was quick to believe that Will was the architect of his own downfall because, in part, that was what he wanted to believe.

Once Min presented him with the evidence that something much deeper and more sinister was afoot, he was mortified. He had, he felt, betrayed his best friend and this made him doubly determined to get to the bottom of the matter, whatever it cost.

This had in fact already cost Artichoke Television a mint in postponed filming. Jem had made the vague excuse that conditions were not suitable. As they'd shot previously in all weathers, hail, thunderstorm, mudslides, flooding and drought, his excuse was pretty paltry, but he didn't care. In a way, he wanted them to sack him as at least that would absolve him from the responsibility which resigning would entail. He'd told them there would be no possibility of his continuing until the start of the following week, by which time, Jem privately thought, his own landscape might look rather different.

By the time he and Min staggered back through the door of the flat they were both exhausted and delighted to see Albert in his pinny, baking a cake and priming the tea pot. They had travelled the perimeter of the M25 in order to pay surprise visits to as many of Tellcat's subsidiaries as possible. They had sat in ten-mile-long tailbacks, seen more cones than Imelda Marcos had shoes, and got the jitters from too many Diet Cokes. The interior of Jem's car, usually as pristine as though it were valet cleaned weekly, was awash with empty cans, old Silk Cut packets, newspapers, sweet wrappers and lottery scratch cards. For once, he didn't give a damn.

It wasn't what they found that was the most astonishing aspect of their odyssey, it was what they didn't. With two exceptions, out of the twenty-odd companies they visited, Tellcat's subsidiaries appeared to be a figment of corporate imagination. While the main company itself held impressive offices in the larger suburban towns surrounding London, the affiliated companies listed in their conference room were non-existent. Often, the address given for these fictitious concerns was on an obscure industrial site where Tellcat must have felt expensive investment bankers would not deign to go. Of the two companies that actually were in evidence, one had a large 'For Sale' sign over its offices and the other was closed and padlocked.

'This is so frustrating,' said Jem as he sipped the hot sweet tea Albert had provided. 'We're so close and yet none of it makes sense. It's as though there's a missing piece to the jigsaw puzzle which would put it all together.'

Min, who was tired beyond the point of speech, could only nod mutely.

'Might I suggest,' said Albert, appearing from the kitchen on a waft of delicious baking smells, 'that a short snooze would restore you both? I shall stay here and keep an eye on things. In forty-five minutes I shall awaken the pair of you, and I think you will find you are refreshed and ready to continue with your enquiries.'

'That's not a bad idea,' said Jem. 'Go on, Min, hop on to my bed. I'll have a kip here.' Once the pair had drifted off, Albert picked up the phone.

'Hello, Beryl . . . yes, it's me, Albert. How's Mary? . . . Good. Beryl, I'll be late this evening. It's the young ones, they're in a spot of trouble. I think I ought to lend a hand . . . oh, bless you.' He carefully replaced the receiver.

They didn't get their full three-quarters of an hour. Thirty minutes later, the phone rang. It was Dallas. Jem answered, woken from a blissful deep snooze in which he'd dreamt he'd won the Palme D'Or for his documentary on runaway house plants.

'Ergh,' he said. 'Dal, yeah . . . what? No, mate, I don't understand at all . . . no, what are you talking about? I don't think he's in LA . . . all right then, see you when you get here.'

'Albert,' he said, 'could you wake Min? I think we have another situation on our hands.'

Dallas arrived at the door, his face a strange shade of

greenish-white. Luella, his usually irrepressible girlfriend, said goodbye to him at the door. She and Dallas bore such a startling physical resemblance, both waifish with huge eyes set in a fine-boned oval face, topped with mops of hair which changed colour every week, that sometimes they were mistaken for brother and sister.

'Aren't you coming in?' Jem said to Luella after she'd hugged Dallas and kissed him on the cheek.

'No,' she said, her enormous blue eyes looking suspiciously close to tears. 'Dallas thinks it best he talks to you by himself.' With that she vanished into the night, her exit marked only by a loud spluttering noise which was doubtless her very ancient car having another momentary lack of faith in its ability to perform its essential function.

Dallas was clutching a Fed-Ex parcel to his chest which he thrust at Jem once Albert had let him into the living-room.

'What's this?' said Jem.

'I have no idea,' said Dallas, who was trembling slightly. Min and Jem exchanged horrified glances. They were so used to happy-go-lucky, cheery, stoned Dal that they had no clue how to handle stressed, miserable, tense Dallas.

From inside the envelope, Jem extracted a video tape, a letter and a first-class ticket to LA for the night flight the following evening.

The letter, which came from a 'Danny Kravitz', read:

Thank you so much for sending in a video of your work. I am very interested in pursuing this further. I have returned your tape as you mention in your letter that it is the only copy of the extraordinary work. I have made several more and placed them in secure locations.

Please find enclosed your contract with Kravitz Inc. and your itinerary details. It is vital we discuss this matter in person as soon as possible. My secretary is setting up project meetings for you to attend. Please be aware that your contract will immediately and irreversibly become null and void if you show this tape to anyone else in the meantime.

Yours sincerely,

(Squiggle)

Danny Kravitz

'But, Dal, that's fantastic,' exclaimed Min. 'You've got a Hollywood agent who wants to make you a star and you're going there tomorrow.'

'Congratulations, mate!' said Jem. 'That's awesome. Kravitz is a huge cheese. If you've got him on your side, you're made.'

'My deepest felicitations,' added Albert. 'I shall be proud to say I knew you once.'

'Ah,' said Dal, 'there's just one problem. That's not my tape.'

'But it's got your name on it,' said Min. 'It says "My Work – Dallas Mazerat" on the sticker.'

Dallas looked close to tears. 'That's what I don't understand,' he said. 'I was at home when the doorbell rang, this Fed-Ex package arrived, the phone went two minutes later and it was this nutter Kravitz raving on about the raw quality of my work and how in all his thirty years in Hollywood, he had never encountered such originality. He wants to make the tape into a feature film, produced by him, directed by me.'

'What did you say?' asked Min.

'Well, I said yes, of course, see you in a couple of days,' said Dallas. 'Although I was starting to get a bit suspicious. I mean, who's really going to get so excited by a shot of me playing Mother Goose at the Norwich Royal? But I couldn't get a word in edgeways. The crazy guy finished off the call saying it was the most amazing piece of work, the way I'd taken *Waiting for Godot* and updated it to a modern corporate setting, using a rest

162

room, two characters on screen and one who we never see. He wants to call the film version *Waiting for Gadget*. I don't know what the hell he's talking about. There's nothing like that on my show reel.'

The others were too shocked to speak.

'I thought about it,' continued Dallas bleakly, tears now running down his face. 'I thought about buggering off to LA with the tape, pretending it was mine and seeing if I could hit the big time. This could be my only chance after all. So, I might never see you lot again, but hey, when Jennifer and Brad and Cameron are my new best friends and I've got a beach house on Malibu, I wonder if I would really care? I could have popped a large cheque in the post one day if my conscience had bothered me, or perhaps I wouldn't even have done that.'

'Dallas,' said Jem gently, 'what's on the tape?'

'Search me. I think we'd better watch it,' he said sadly.

'But it will negate your contract with Kravitz if you do that. They've probably fitted some sort of bugging device to the tape so they'll know if you play it,' said Min.

'Probably,' said Dallas. 'I still think we'd better see what this means.'

The film was shot in grainy orange and white in only one location which appeared to be a gents' lavatory. Men came in and out, pulled faces at themselves in the mirror, washed – or didn't – their hands. One man pulled a little bottle out of his jacket pocket and drank deeply from it. Another picked his nose in front of the mirror. A tall, muscular man paused to floss his teeth.

'Freeze that shot,' said Min. She looked closely at the screen. 'I can't be sure,' she said. 'But that man looks very like Bertrand.'

'Bertrand?' said Jem. 'What's he doing on this tape?'

'Perhaps,' said Min, 'that toilet is in the bank?'

Two more men came in once Bertrand had gone. They checked the cubicles were empty. Their faces were not clearly visible but their voices were easy to make out. One man was leaning against the wall while another washed his face in the basin. He dried himself on a towel, rubbing his hair and neck.

'Progress check,' said one to the other. The second man racked up two lines of cocaine, snorted one through the right nostril and one through the left. He inhaled deeply, closed his eyes and spoke.

'Everything's ready for Paris.'

'You've got rid of the stuff?'

'Deleted and shredded. We are ready to roll.'

'Christ, I hope they finish it tomorrow. I'm busting my arse keeping that share price sky-high.'

'How's the PX account?'

'Mystery investor holds tight.'

'How long will he stay in?'

'As long as we need him.'

'Where the hell's he getting the money from?'

'*Cherche pas à savoir.*'

'What the fuck does that mean?'

'It means, don't ask.'

'What's left to do?'

'One small signature from our friend.'

'He has no idea, does he?'

'God, I wouldn't want to be in his shoes.'

The second man laughed.

'When this is all over, we'll drink a toast to him, wherever he may be.'

'I'll be in the Bahamas by the time the shit hits the fan.'

'Whereas Gadget may be spending a lot of time at Her Majesty's pleasure.'

They high-fived.

'To Gadget. Going down, going down, going down.' They sang the last refrain.

'What if he won't sign?' said the first man.

'He wants his bonus,' said the second. 'He'll sign. He's not like that nosy Swede. Doesn't have his nous.'

'That was a close one.'

'Do you feel bad about him?'

'Nah, shouldn't ask questions you don't want to know the answers to.'

'I got you something.' The second man produced a wrap of coke. 'Just in case life seems a little dull after tomorrow.'

The first man pocketed it. 'Dull? Never. All right, dude, stay cool. We're nearly there.'

They exited.

The sitting-room in Jem's flat stayed silent as they tried to digest the contents of the tape.

'Let's rewind,' said Min. 'Back to the bit where they say, "Gadget".'

'To Gadget. Going down, going down, going down,' sang the men on the tape.

'Once more,' said Min. Jem turned up the volume.

'TO GADGET. GOING DOWN, GOING DOWN, GOING DOWN,' blasted forth from the speakers either side of Jem's plasma-screen television.

He pressed Freeze on the video. 'Anyone recognise these two jokers?' The rest of the room looked blankly back at him.

'I am certainly no expert,' said Albert, 'but it would seem very likely that this tape is from a security camera, given the quality of the footage.'

'According to Danny Kravitz, it's innovative use of faux-naïf camera technique,' interjected Dallas dully.

'Is that right, sir?' said Albert politely. 'The two gentlemen . . .'

'I doubt very much they qualify for that title, Albert,' said Min, who was thinking fast.

'Shall we let the man speak?' said Jem.

'The two men seem to be discussing a colleague whose downfall they appear to have engineered for their own financial gain,' said Albert. 'They've contrived a situation whereby their scheme, which involves a mystery investor, the tragic accident which befell Mr Thorsted and an artificially high share price, hinges on whether or not Mr Gadget is willing to sign a certain document. They are hoping he will oblige while in Paris, the city from which Mr Gadget had recently returned just before his disappearance.'

'Good summary, Albert,' said Jem, who always appreciated clarity. 'What else do we know?'

'When Mac found Will,' said Min slowly, 'he was shouting: "You can't make me sign." What if he knew the deal was dodgy and suspected they were setting him up?'

'Hmm,' said Jem. 'Put that together with the fact that Tellcat looks great on paper but if you go and see it at ground level, like we did, it doesn't look quite so hot. All those affiliates that don't exist, staff missing from HQ . . .'

'Dal,' said Min, 'what exactly did you think was on this tape?'

'Will said he'd get the bank's production unit to put all my clips on to one video so I could send it off,' said Dallas, still sunk in gloom. 'He gave me this tape the last time I saw him and I was so excited, I just popped it in the post and didn't bother to watch it first.'

'So without Danny Kravitz, we'd never have known,' said Min.

'We don't quite know what we know,' said Jem. 'There's still a piece missing.'

In the thoughtful quiet that followed, Dallas rolled himself a joint as long as his forearm.

'Min,' said Jem at last, 'when Bertrand told you Will had taken something from the bank, do you think he meant this video?'

'Well, no,' she replied. 'He was talking about documents that they told him Will had pinched. He never mentioned a tape.'

'And these boys have been doing some shredding,' said Jem. 'Shit! This isn't good.'

'Think about it,' said Min. 'Joren has an accident, Will disappears. What if both of them refused to sign whatever it is that would make these guys so rich they can go and live in the Bahamas? Are they just going to give up or are they going to have one more go to try and pull it off?'

'Bert's still working on Tellcat,' said Jem grimly. 'Trying to push the deal through this week.'

'What if he knows?' said Min. 'What if he's part of it?'

'No,' said Jem. 'Someone's lied to him as well. He thinks he's working blind without all the documents because Will stole them. I doubt he knows any of this. I think he's their next fall guy. We've got to show him this tape.'

'No!' said Min. 'He's a snake. He'll take it straight to the bank and then Will will be lost for ever.'

'Min, he's a snake with a strong survival instinct. And he's our only hope – we don't know anyone else who can make sense of this lot. We *have* to call him.'

'And he gets to watch the video, I suppose,' said Dallas, morosely taking a toke.

'I'm sorry, Dal,' said Min.

'So that's that,' he said. 'Ta-ra Hollywood.'

Min and Jem exchanged glances.

'Do you really think this is the right thing to do?' asked Min.

'Min,' sighed Jem, 'I wish there was another answer but I can't see one.'

Min made the call.

'Strader,' said the aggressive voice that picked up.

'It's Ambrosia,' she said, keeping it quick. 'I have to meet you. Tonight.'

'Have you got it?' said Bert.

'Yes. But if you want it, come alone. If you bring anyone with you, I'll destroy the evidence before you can see it.'

'Oh, Sweet Jesus,' breathed Bertrand. She gave him Jem's address and hung up.

Just as she'd put the phone down, the doorbell rang, causing them all to jump out of their skin.

'Bloody hell!' said Min. 'Is he Superman?'

'Albert, get the door,' said Jem. 'Don't let anyone in, no matter who they claim to be.'

Unfortunately for Jem, it was the one visitor he couldn't turn away.

'Coo-ee,' came a chirpy female voice. 'It's me! Jemal, where are you? Come and give me a kiss.'

'Oh, God,' said Jem, burying his face in his hands. 'It's my mother.'

A small, round lady in a shockingly pink sari burst into the room, wreathed in smiles. 'Ah, Jemal, there you are! Oh, my lovie, you are so thin! Look at you! Do you know, your man didn't want to let me in but I said, "Stuff and nonsense, I'm his mother, of course he wants to see me." Jemal, my love, could you pay my taxi? He's waiting in the street.'

Albert tottered in from outside, weighed down with cool bags.

'You can put them in the kitchen,' said Sharan Haque imperiously. 'But don't try unpacking them, don't touch a thing. Special food for my son. Don't mess around with it.'

Albert looked mutinous but didn't dare disobey.

'Mother! Where did you get that taxi from?'

She gave a naughty giggle. 'Oh, dear, was it very expensive? I was in such a hurry to see you, I didn't think.'

'What are you doing here?'

'Well, my love, you're so busy all the time with your television producing and so on, and you won't come and see us, so we thought we'd come and see you.'

'Where's Father?' asked Jem weakly.

'He's helping Palash with an operation, an emergency. Silly woman went to another surgeon and she's ended up with three nipples, I ask you!' Sharan giggled again. 'They're trying to put her right before her husband gets home tomorrow!' She was, thought Min, quite enchanting even if her timing could hardly have been worse.

'Now, I see you are having a party and I don't want to intrude, so I'll just slip into the kitchen and make you a little something to eat.'

'Mother, we're not having a party,' said Jem, resisting the urge to laugh hysterically. 'We are actually in the middle of planning something and we're expecting a very important guest in just a few minutes.'

'Then you must have something to offer him! Come on, man,' she said, beckoning to Albert. 'You can come and help me, but mind you do exactly as I say.'

'Certainly, ma'am,' said Albert, rather stiffly. 'It would be a pleasure.' He bowed formally to Mrs Haque as she bustled past him, a picture of domestic efficiency.

The delicious buttery smell of spices that Bertrand noticed from the street got stronger and stronger the closer he came to flat 2a, home of Jemal Haque, producer of television's most popular gardening programme, *Dig It!* If Bertrand was surprised by the evidence of exotic cookery at the meeting place where he expected to be handed the documents on which the rest of his career rested, he was even more taken aback by the interior of the apartment to which Min had requested he come.

An old man who put him in mind of the butler from *The*

Rocky Horror Picture Show opened the door. The resemblance was strengthened by his first words.

'Ah, Mr Strader. Come in, we've been expecting you.' He was shown into a living-room where the utmost chaos reigned. On the sofa sat a petite woman with long black hair gathered into a huge bun. Eye-catching in bright pink silk, she was showing a photo album to a younger woman.

'And this girl, she is lovely, isn't she? We would be so happy . . .' the lady in pink was saying. From the kitchen came the sizzling sound of frying as the old butler hurried back to supervise his next batch of vegetable pakoras. On the floor, smoking the end of what had clearly been a carrot-sized joint, sat a young man, staring blankly into space. The low table in the middle of the room heaved with plates of curry, dal, samosas, rice and pickles. The American was too flabbergasted to speak. This was so completely different from the cool, quick handover he had anticipated.

Min saw him first. 'Bertrand!' she said, leaping to her feet. 'Come in, sit down.' She put him on the sofa next to Sharan who immediately started prattling away to him.

'Not now, Mother,' said Jem sharply.

'How can you speak to me like that?' she said, her soft brown eyes filling with tears.

'I mean, we'd all love a cup of tea,' said Jem, more gently. 'Do you think you could make us one?' Mollified, she went off to the kitchen.

Bertrand found his voice. 'I thought,' he said addressing Min, 'you said you had what I asked for? And as far as I remember, that wasn't a large consignment of home-cooked Indian food.'

'That's the thing,' said Min. 'We haven't *exactly* got what you wanted, although the samosas really are very good, you should maybe try one . . . all right, sorry. We've got something to show you. With Dallas' permission, that is?'

'Go on. At least I'll keep my integrity this way,' he sighed. 'I can't be accused of selling out.'

'And then,' continued Min, 'we've got a few things to tell you and we hope it will all make sense.'

'Babe, I promise you, if it doesn't you're gonna regret it,' said Bertrand grimly.

With anxious looks at each of his friends, Jemal pressed Play on the video recorder.

Chapter Thirteen

The night in Scotland, far from the yellow glare of streetlights, was as black as the folds of an old-fashioned opera cloak. Will lay in his cot bed, which he had again placed across the door to deter midnight intruders of whom he reckoned to get at least one or two a night, when he heard someone knock gently.

'Go away,' he hissed through the door. 'I'm asleep.'

Undeterred, the midnight wanderer tapped again.

'Look, I'm sorry, it just won't work,' he whispered through the key hole. 'It's nothing personal, it's just I've taken a vow of celibacy. So please, leave me alone. I'm very tired.'

The knocking stopped. Will, who had decided that tonight would see his escape bid, got quietly out of bed. During his therapy session under hypnosis, his 'lost memory' had been fully restored. He'd realised then he had to get out of the castle, back down south and to the bank as fast as he could. He only hoped he wasn't already too late.

His conscience, however, was not making things easy for him. He had discovered that the Vision was only nineteen and had left home after an argument with her parents. He was very reluctant to leave her in this mad house, but on the other hand the matters revealed to him by the leader were so pressing he knew he must at least get to somewhere he could use a phone, in order to alert the relevant people to the danger.

A compromise solution presented itself. He would have a

look around tonight and plan a route out of the castle but wouldn't actually go. Unless, he thought guiltily, the opportunity presented itself, in which case he'd grab it with both hands and then come back for the girl, perhaps with the back-up of some policemen or the like. Having thus persuaded himself of the rightness of his actions, he prepared to take them.

Moving the bed aside, he winced as the legs scraped against the stone floor. He opened the door gently, sidled out, and was about to start tiptoeing down the hallway when he walked slap into someone, standing there waiting for him.

Involuntarily, he let out a scream which was instantly muffled by the quick reflexes of the other man, dressed entirely in black, who shot out one hand and covered his mouth.

'Sshhh!' the man whispered in his ear. 'Follow me.'

In the split second he had to decide whether to follow the man in black or to yell for help, William had another flashback to the night he'd left London. It was powerful enough to send him reeling back against the stone wall where he gasped for breath as a panic attack threatened to overtake him.

'It's all right,' said the man in black, taking off his balaclava. 'It's only me.'

Standing upright and full of vigour in front of William, not a trace of drool in sight, was the 'old man' who'd been so assiduously stalking him.

Given that shouting for help would probably have brought out the leader from whichever room he was haunting, Will thought he'd take his chances and follow this ancient madman who seemed restored by nightfall, to health if not to sanity.

They went down through the dark cellars of the castle where Will, much to his annoyance, noticed row after row of wine bottles when he had been subsisting for days on nothing more potent than herbal tea. The man in black opened a secret door and took a series of slimy, airless, labyrinthine passages down through the very rock itself. They emerged onto the little beach at the foot of the castle outcrop which, at high tide as it was now, was nothing more than a few feet of sand. But bobbing about on the still waters of the bay was the first means of escape Will had seen. It was a little rowing boat.

'Put these on.' The old man handed him a musty black jumper and pair of trousers. 'And get in,' he ordered, in surprisingly authoritarian tones. 'Don't just stand there like a stuffed eel. Get in, damn ye.'

Will was too surprised to do anything but obey. The old man rowed vigorously to the middle of the bay where he shipped the oars, produced a hip flask of whisky, took a roaring slurp and handed it to Will.

'Thanks, brother,' said Will, taking a large dose of the amber liquid which burnt agreeably through his detoxified veins.

'Fuck the "brother" shite,' said the old man. 'Ma name's Allan.'

Sitting in the boat with the moon casting an inviting path of silvery light across the blue-black water, framed by jagged mountains with stars twinkling overhead, Will again wondered how a life so very ordinary as his could have turned out this way. Having a midnight conference with a recovered lunatic in a small wooden craft while drinking single malt was not something his previous existence had really prepared him for.

'Now, I expect ye'll be asking yersel' a few questions,' said the old man, or rather Allan, looking amused.

'Er, I think it would be fair to say so,' said Will cautiously, aware that the boat was not too stable and that it was a long swim to dry land. Humouring Allan seemed to be a good idea.

'Ye'll be wanting to know what I'm up to?' he said.

'Absolutely riveted!' said Will, getting his hands on the flask once more. 'Spill the beans then, Allan.'

'Och, laddie,' he said. 'It's a long, long story.'

'We don't seem to be going anywhere,' pointed out Will, who was already slightly pissed from the whisky.

'Do you ken what it's like to have a burden in life ye cannae put down?' asked Allan, his craggy face suddenly looking wild and impassioned.

'Funnily enough,' said Will, 'I think I do.'

This was obviously not quite the answer Allan had wanted. He glared at Will for a moment before resuming his tale.

'Och, the tragedy, the drama, the pain this house has seen,' said the old man, gesticulating at the castle, a sweeping movement which rocked the boat quite badly.

'Which house?' said Will disbelievingly.

'The castle. Berriemore. Ma house.'

'So you're Laird of Berriemore?'

'Aye, laddie, that I am, and 'tis a terrible weight for a man to carry.'

'But you can't be,' said Will. 'It's just not possible.'

'Listen to ma story, laddie, and then decide.'

And Allan spun him a tale so bizarre that Will was forced to admit it must be true, although for at least the first half he remained sceptical as he had heard that true insanity could make a very convincing case for itself. Allan, or Lord McCready as he claimed he was really called, had apparently lived alone in the castle for thirty years since the death of his young bride in a car accident. So heart-broken had he been that he had resolved never to marry again but to live in solitude, which meant he had no heir to hand the estate on to. Instead of a direct relative, it was to go to a distant branch of the McCready family who lived in London and hung out with pop stars, soap actresses and restaurateurs. Although they had no time for Allan himself, they kept in close contact with his doctor, ever-eager to hear news of his last heart attack. A year ago they had asked to use the castle for a shoot and a party.

The whole business had been hell. For weeks before, the

place had been crawling with their acolytes, insisting on redecorating all the bedrooms, stripping the castle of its austere Highland dignity and replacing it with a fashionable – and totally inappropriate – gloss. The gardens and greenhouses where the commune now grew their vegetables had been pillaged of flowers to provide enormous arrangements at every turn. Allan's cellars had been plundered of wines that his grandfather had laid down, which his guests downed like cheap plonk or spilt all over his furniture. The shoot had been a disaster as the guests had behaved like badly brought up teenagers, worn brightly coloured tweeds, refused to listen to the instructions of the ghillies and, on the worst day, caused a landslide. The men of the estate had come to the Laird afterwards and told him they refused ever to have those people back again.

Allan decided to get his revenge. Anonymously, and with the express intention of scaring his relatives, through his lawyers in Edinburgh he had offered the castle to a group of Yogis. They accepted gladly and moved into Berriemore where they set up their ashram with the leader in charge. The staff from the castle, who were mostly even more ancient and decrepit than Allan himself, were pensioned off but the estate itself was kept running under the direction of his trusted lawyer.

However, Allan still meant Berriemore to pass in the end to his family so, just to check his joke didn't get out of hand, he decided to live in the castle himself, posing as a dotty old fool. This way, his logic went, he would have free access to all parts of the place and no one would think twice about speaking freely in front of him as the mentally ill are not generally given much consideration. This was, Will thought, a piece of cunning which either bordered on genius or was a sign of genuine madness.

Allan let the oars back into the water with a gentle splash and started to row.

'Where we going now?' slurred Will.

'Shush!' Allan said. 'Look at the castle.'

They rowed round it as far as the seaward-facing side where Will had undergone his therapy sessions. From the top of the same turret where he had suffered his tête-à-têtes with the leader came a very faint blue glow.

'Do you see?' said Allan.

Will nodded, perplexed. As far as he knew there was no electricity in Berriemore and yet that light certainly didn't come from the tallow candles the rest of the castle used after the sun had gone down.

'What is it?' he whispered.

'That's for you to find out,' replied Allan.

He had a plan. For a while he'd apparently been getting suspicious of the leader and his motives, something Will could only second. With his old-fashioned sense of morality, Allan disapproved very strongly of the leader's seigneurial conduct towards the women of the commune. Added to that, he had reason to believe something else was afoot.

'I heard him talking,' said Allan, 'into a mobile phone when there wasnae anyone else there. He was saying it was time to wrap it up. He'd got enough now and wanted to move on. Said to collect him on Thursday the twenty-fourth at 5 a.m. Thae's all I heard but it's enough.'

'When the hell's that?' said Will, who'd lost all track of dates or time.

'It's the day after tomorrow,' said Allan, looking at a fancy sub-aqua watch he'd produced from his pocket.

Will was not at all pleased to hear his proposed solution which involved 'someone' climbing into the turret – as the door was kept locked – by a route Allan had used as a boy to scale the castle walls. When Will protested that surely, as he knew it so well, it would be better if Allan did the break-in, he punched the younger man playfully on the arm and said, 'Och,

178

I'm an old, old man. Ye're young and fit.'

'I don't think you're giving yourself enough credit,' said Will, whose arm hurt considerably. 'What do you think is there anyway?'

'I dinnae know,' said Allan. 'But there was a lad here, just like yersel', who disappeared.'

'Oh, great,' said Will, feeling suddenly quite sober and rather cold. 'So there might be a dead body up there?'

'Nooo,' said Allan. 'I meant, ye might be in danger too. That's why I've been following ye about the place. So if we catch him, whatever he's up to, then he cannae touch ye.'

'Hey, Allan, guess what?' said Will. 'I don't actually ever have to go back there. I've got some very important business to see to in London. I could just push you out of this boat, row to land and be gone. End of story.'

'Aye,' said Allan peaceably, 'ye could.'

There was silence while he smiled at Will and nodded his old head.

'Aye,' he repeated, 'ye could do that. But ye won't.'

'What makes ye, I mean you, say that?'

'Ye won't leave that little gurl there all alone.'

'Look, Allan . . .' said Will.

'Lord McCready to ye, laddie.'

'All right, Lord McCready.'

'Och, I was just joking, ye can call me Allan.'

'Oh, look, just stop messing around, will you?' said Will, infuriated. 'Why don't you just row me to the mainland? I get the police and we all come back, force entry to the turret and find out what's in there.'

'It's a guid plan but it'll nae work.'

'Why not?' said Will.

'Because yon man'll see the police coming across the causeway or the water and he'll have time to destroy any evidence he needs tae. No, the only way is tae steal it out of the turret, take it to the police and then we've got the bastard! And if he finds ye gone in the morning, there's no knowing what he'll do. Or to whom,' Allan said ominously. 'Ye'll no want to put the lassie in danger, will ye?' he said, glaring at Will in a way that proved centuries of selective breeding can make even the most moth-eaten scion of the Highland chieftains look pretty terrifying when he wants to.

'No,' said Will truthfully, 'I wouldn't. It's just, I've got other problems to deal with . . .'

'And ye can deal with them as soon as ye've got this sorted. Now, do ye still want to push me overboard?'

'No,' said Will, 'I don't. I'm probably saying this because I'm drunk for the first time in God knows how many days but I think you're right, there *is* something nasty going on in your castle and I'll help you find out what it is. As soon as I have done, I'm gone. Do you understand, Allan?'

'Aye,' he said, smiling with satisfaction. 'I knew you were a guid laddie. That's why I chose you.' He rowed the boat gently back to the beach where he moored it carefully and helped a rather inebriated Will back through the rocky tunnel to his bedroom where he lay down and fell instantly asleep.

Chapter Fourteen

As usual Bertrand Strader arrived at the office punctually at 7.01 a.m., ready for another brisk day in the world of finance. The great cliff-face of glass in which he toiled was already churning with worker ants busying in and out of the revolving doors at the base. Looking at it that morning, he wondered how the stream stayed so constant throughout the day. Were there people employed purely to enter and leave the building all day long in order to lend an air of bustle and prosperity to the front lobby? Perhaps they were on a loop, like the music in the lifts? Unaccustomed to such flights of whimsy, Bertrand shook himself to regain control of his wandering thoughts. Today, of all days, he needed to stay sharp.

He ascended to his office where once a certain Gadget, W. had sat alongside him, planning takeovers and mergers which were to have the effect of gradually combining all the world's companies into one giant mega-corp. It wasn't an activity Bertrand had ever considered in a moral light. His job was to make money and he was very good at it indeed. That was as close to a philosophy of investment banking as he needed to get.

Strader, B. literally couldn't afford to take a sentimental attitude to what he did. A product of the US education system, he had run up a crippling backlog of debt thanks to his long, distinguished and ruinously expensive university education.

Two Harvard degrees and an MBA do not come cheap. At one stage in his career, he had felt overwhelmed by frustration that he should have been forced to borrow over a hundred thousand pounds in order to obtain the qualifications which would allow him to get a job highly paid enough to start repaying the money. He could have done absolutely nothing and been considerably better off than he currently was. It seemed a cruel anomaly that he should have been so drastically penalised for being a bright hard-working kid with a desire to better himself in life.

While he liked to give the impression his parents were patrician, east coast, old money types, the truth was quite different. He came from a small town in the mid-West where his father ran a hardware store, selling nuts and bolts to silent men who liked tractors. He didn't have a fallback position in life, there was no financial safety net to keep his creditors at bay were he to lose his job and be unable to meet his debts. To find, as Jem, Dallas and Min had revealed to him last night, that his job and income were potentially under threat through no fault of his own other than having the misfortune to be in the wrong department for the wrong takeover in the wrong year, had been a terrible shock. Once that shock had dissipated anger took its place, a seething, insidious rage which was flowing through his veins even more potently this morning than it had the night before.

For, contrary to popular opinion, Bertrand was not devoid of feelings and these had been quite badly damaged by the revelation that he was likely to become the next victim of a set-up, perpetrated it seemed from inside the very bank where he worked. His pride had taken a huge knock. That he could be so easily dispensed with was a most unwelcome revelation. True, Joren and Will were both still alive, but one only just and the other in exile, neither a state to which Bertrand aspired. What really bugged him was that he was third in line for the scam and had utterly failed to see it coming. If he'd been the first person they'd tried it on with, he could have lived with himself. But to be seen as gullible enough to be number three, and meekly go along with the vast deception, was galling in the extreme. He found it hard to accept that Will and Joren should both have worked it out when he hadn't. A cold fury built in him throughout the morning, steeling his resolve that he, Bertrand Strader, would not be taken for anyone's fool.

It had been a tough night. He sat down with a sigh at his desk and rang through to his secretary to ask for coffee. She set it down in front of him and sniffed.

'What's that smell?' she asked.

'What smell?' said Bertrand instantly, his American horror of being unhygienic leaping to the fore.

'Like . . . curry,' said Becky, the pretty young secretary to whom he loved to dictate orders.

'Don't ask,' said Bertrand, who hadn't been home and hence had slept in a cardamom-scented fog for all of two hours the night before. 'Oh, and Becky, which meeting room have you got me this afternoon?'

'I've booked the penthouse, like you asked,' she said. The bank building was thirty-five storeys high.

'Could you do me a favour and change it?' he said. 'I'll have the one on the third floor.'

'But we never use that room,' she said disbelievingly. 'I'm not sure it's even got furniture in it.'

'Becky,' said Bertrand, using his special voice, 'humour me. Just this once, honey.'

As the last time she'd heard that tone of voice, she'd been sitting astride him in the very chair in which he now lounged, she flushed and hurried away to do his bidding.

Bertrand flipped open his lap top and started to put together his presentation for later on that day. Looking through the Tellcat files now that he had a little extra information, he took a very different view of the company. Tellcat, he was coming to see, was a prime case of the Emperor's New Clothes. When telecommunications had been lauded as the great gold mine of our days, no one had been willing to square the cold hard fact with the generally over-blown perception of where the business was going. Now that his own point of view had changed so radically, Bertrand could suddenly see that the Emperor was totally bare.

It wasn't all plain sailing. Throughout the morning he suffered moments of excruciating doubt, wondering if he should maybe just go straight to the top and tell them everything he knew. Perhaps he would at least be able to salvage something from the wreckage, come out of this as a winner somehow. Perhaps the folks he'd seen last night were just plain wrong and he was about to make a total fool of himself.

But then he reminded himself of the contents of the extraordinary tape he'd watched the night before, he thought of what Jem and Min had told him and remembered that the two people who'd worked on this takeover before him had both mysteriously disappeared. And overlying all this was the memory of a pair of dark brown eyes, looking beseechingly at him and saying, 'Bertrand, you're the only person who can help.' Like all very macho men, he had an Achilles' heel, and that was vanity when it came to rescuing damsels in distress.

Jem's morning was equally troubled. He knew what his mission for the day was but there was one off-the-record task he had to achieve before he could start on his duties. He made the call.

'Hello? It's Jemal Haque from *Dig It!* . . . Yes, hi! . . . Oh, very well thank you. Look, I haven't got long and I can't explain why I'm telling you this except that it is very, very important. Don't say anything to anyone but leave. Resign now and get out of the Tellcat building . . . I'm sorry, you're just going to have to trust me . . . Please, just do it and I promise I'll do everything I can to help you get another job. Got to go. Please, take what I say very seriously. Goodbye.'

He hung up and went out to meet his cameraman from ATC who was doing a little freelance work for Jem that morning on a subject which had nothing whatsoever to do with botany.

For all her air of eccentric incompetence, Min had the ability to handle complex photographic equipment. Which was just as well as the workings of the apparatus she'd picked up that morning would have foxed any mere amateur. She had several practice runs in the shop before she felt confident that she had mastered the protocol. She knew she'd only get one shot at this subject and if she messed it up, it could spell disaster for them all.

'The trick is,' explained Banger, proprietor of Spies Like Us, a rather well-spoken young man whose nickname derived from his love of home-made explosives which had led to his expulsion from Eton after he'd blown up his window box, 'not to look in the same direction that you're pointing, if you see what I mean. It tends to give the game away, rather.'

Dennis, who Min had called for advice on undercover surveillance equipment, watched with amusement. No, he'd told her on the phone that morning against the background noise of small children shouting with glee at the Teletubbies, he didn't have such a thing as a concealed camera. He was, he gently reminded her, a lawyer, not a spy. But he could help her get one. Dennis, who was nothing if not cautious, had decided against taking her to the warehouse in Ealing where he routinely picked up surveillance equipment for Mission Accomplish. It was, after all, a trade secret and, while she was a friend of Mac's, Dennis liked to play safe at all times. He took her to a consumer retail outlet instead, a place which always made him laugh.

Banger's shop was heaven on earth for the paranoid obsessive, stocked to the rafters as it was with every form of amateur surveillance equipment invented: baseball caps which took colour photos, pens with recording devices and t-shirts which could be tracked by satellite. Privately, Dennis thought the place fit only for wannabe James Bond types, a category he was very keen to distance MA from. But as Min refused to divulge exactly why she needed such a camera, Dennis considered he was being as helpful as he could be.

'I say,' said Banger, once she'd made her purchases and checked she knew how to use them, 'would you like my mobile number? Just in case you have any problems?'

He didn't get many attractive young women in his shop, his clientele veering more towards middle-aged harpies determined to spy on their nannies or husbands or both, and personality-disorder anorak wearers.

Dennis shot him a very Balkan look. 'She will be fine,' he said. 'If she needs anything, she will call me.' He shepherded Min out of the shop. He just couldn't help being possessive about any female in his company.

By 3 p.m. that afternoon all parties were in place, having synchronised their watches before leaving the nerve centre of operations, Jem's flat, that morning. Kick off wasn't until 3.45 but Jem had insisted that they should be ready and prepared early, just in case something untoward happened. In fact, this prudent measure was counter-productive as it meant they all arrived early at the scene and then had to spend nearly an hour loitering around trying not to look suspicious, which in one or two cases was harder than others. They kept going for little walks and running into each other. As it was very important no link should be drawn between them, ignoring each other so strenuously became quite tiresome.

At 3.45 a tiny dark-haired girl in a smart suit, which seemed perhaps a touch tight around the waist, jumped out of a cab, set off up the steps and disappeared through the revolving doors of Pollinger's, one of London's oldest investment banking houses. *Les jeux*, as they say, *sont faits*.

Min approached the receptionist and smiled politely.

'Mr Bertrand Strader,' she said. The girl dialled up.

'He'll come down for you, take a seat.'

Min leafed through a few magazines, most of which were deathly dull but which she pretended to find fascinating. The equipment around her waist was not at all comfortable when she was sitting down, but if she sat with her back as straight as a ballerina's it was bearable.

She saw the lift open and Bertrand strolled casually out through the ranks of security men, now armed with metal detectors and machines to take X-rays of the inside of bags and briefcases. He came towards her, smiling lazily, which made Min catch her breath at the sheer beauty of the man. He was, she reminded herself furiously, still a total shit and only in this to save his own skin, not out of any sense of altruism or loyalty. And yet, and yet . . .

'Miss Haskell,' he said, offering her his hand. Behind her a lady of Indian appearance in a nondescript set of overalls was busily polishing the leaves of a pot plant, bucket and mop at her side. As Min stood up, an old man tottered into the bank. He was holding a large bag of what looked like two-pence pieces.

'Just got to take these up,' the old man said to the security guard, ploughed straight through the metal detector which started beeping madly and then made a sudden run for the lift. He reached it before the guards could stop him and was heading for the upper floors when yet another alarm went off. Following Bertrand, Min slipped through the metal detector which was still on red alert from the old man's sack of pennies and they went quietly up the stairs, the cleaning lady following along behind them, humming a merry little tune as she polished each step with her mop.

Security guards were pouring into reception from every area of the building. 'We've got a situation,' said one into his walkie-talkie. 'There's an unknown alien in the lift which seems to have jammed. All systems are on code red, repeat, code red. Request permission to evacuate the building, repeat request.'

Bertrand let Min into a rather dingy conference room where a collection of men were seated at a horseshoe-shaped table with a white screen in the middle. The room was conspicuously low-tech and had clearly been hastily furnished with whatever odds and ends Becky had been able to find. It had a curiously makeshift air for a high-level telecoms meeting as none of the chairs matched, the tables were of different heights and there was no executive crockery on display. Bertrand had decided against offering refreshments, thinking that the fewer items in the room that could be used as offensive weapons, the better.

'Gentlemen,' he said smoothly, 'excuse my absence. This is Miss Haskell, a consultant in visual imagery who I have asked to join us for this very special meeting. Her role in proceedings will become clear later on.'

'Do you think we could get on with it?' said a rather testy-looking man. 'You said we'd start at three-thirty and it's getting on for four already.'

'Certainly, sir,' said Bertrand. 'Let me just introduce Miss Haskell to you all.' He indicated the testy man. Bertrand spoke more clearly than usual, as if he wished no one to be in any doubt who the assembled characters were.

'Miss Haskell, this is James Walker, deputy chairman of Pollinger's. Next to him is Percy Hamilton who oversees all takeovers.'

Min took in two ample men who might once have been good-looking before a few too many corporate freebies larded their features with a wobbling blanket of flesh. James seemed to have had the misfortune to mislay his chin, possibly leaving it at the nineteenth hole after a particularly good round of golf, whereas Percy had retained all his facial features but neglected the upkeep of his body. His head looked like a pin stuck on top of a large bean bag.

'On the right,' continued Bertrand, 'we have Bradley Doyle of Amercom, the largest American telecommunications company, and his French associate Pierre de la Croix.' If the two men from Pollinger's represented Epicurean indulgence, then the Frenchman and the American were models of asceticism. Both were fleshless and hard, not characters Min would like to get on the wrong side of. She had to admire Bertrand's nerve. He was as cool and polished as the inside of a brand-new fridge.

'On the other side of the room is the admirable Simon Denby, Managing Director of Tellcat, and his deputy, Peter Crosson.'

Neither of them bothered to acknowledge Min. Crosson, she noticed, had a faint beading of sweat over his upper lip which could be due to the lack of air-conditioning in the conference room or, given the way he was fidgeting around in his chair, be the result of jittery nerves. Denby sat perfectly still, his shorn head glinting ominously in the overhead lighting. His face, which could have been cast in wax, was a shade of whitish-grey. The only movement was in his eyes, green and reptilian, which slid from side to side.

'Just get on with it, will you, Strader?' snapped Percy, unused to this hitherto efficient team member wasting time in such a dilatory fashion. It was the sort of behaviour he might have expected from that twit Gadget, but not from Strader on whom he'd always relied to deliver fast.

'Sir,' said Bertrand, unperturbed by the older man's rudeness. In fact, he was starting to enjoy himself, not a sensation he had felt for some time. He checked Min, saw she was in position, sent her the flicker of a wink and started his presentation.

'TELLCAT – The Story of Success!' Bertrand's first power-point slide proclaimed boldly. Simon Denby couldn't help smirking. It was a tale that had been featured in every business magazine and newspaper as well as most of the lay press to boot. How Tellcat had risen from a minute operation in the East End to become the largest single provider of communications in the UK. Denby was the genius with the vision to realise the opportunities the deregulated telecoms market had to offer the entrepreneur. His first-year profits alone had been enough to secure the backing of every major investor as well as pushing Denby's name on to the A-list of business people in the country. There had been some mutter-ing about undeclared donations to political parties which, married with his frequent appearances at Downing Street drinks parties, had led to questions in the House on whether he was getting preferential treatment thanks to his 'personal friend of the PM' status. Denby didn't care. Such gossip only served to increase his profile and his power. Now, at the peak of his success, he was selling out to an American-French partnership, a deal which stood to propel him out of the top forty on the Rich List and into the top ten. Min, who'd read all the cuttings, reflected that he didn't look quite as happy as a man in his outwardly enviable position should.

Bertrand gave a brief history of Tellcat, telling the assembled company things they already knew and lulling them into a false sense of security. Just as the yawns were starting from the Pollinger's contingent, he switched tack.

'Let us now consider the enormous contribution that Tellcat has made to ensure this country has the hardware needed for efficient internet connections,' he continued.

Peter Crosson shifted in his seat once more, running his finger around the back of his collar which suddenly felt a little tight.

'Tellcat's commitment to the internet is clear from the massive investment the company has made in laying fibre-optic cable,' said Bertrand blandly, not looking at anyone in particular. 'This is a costly process and involves much faith on the part of the company, its investors and those who lend the company money. Clearly, in the past, we have felt Tellcat to be a good credit risk, given its sharply rising share price, and have felt able to extend that credit.

'Now for your projections. One of the quoted figures on which the substantial loans you have taken out is based in internet traffic to double every one hundred days. "Build it and they will come," you said. Unfortunately, they didn't come in the numbers you expected. In your most bullish moments, you even predicted a yearly increase of fifteen hundred per cent. That, gentlemen, sounded very impressive. It now sounds very wrong. Annual growth has been more like one hundred and fifty per cent. Not quite so earth shattering, I think you will agree.'

Denby smiled stiffly. Bradley was looking curiously at Bertrand, wondering quite where this was leading, while James and Percy were openly tapping their fingers on the table.

'Probably something they teach them in those damn' fool business schools,' James harrumphed to Percy.

'The same pattern emerges when we look at the mobile phone market,' said Bertrand, flipping up another graph. 'Initially, sales rose very sharply. Large capital investment was necessary, so Tellcat thought, to secure a third-generation mobile phone licence. People would want to send e-mail via their mobile phone, watch television on it, run their lives from the handset. But Tellcat, and the bank who lent them money based on the projections the first few years of business indicated, failed to take into account that the day would come when everyone owned a mobile phone already and the market would be saturated. Again, Tellcat overspent drastically and found demand was not strong enough to support their investment. And yet the share price continues to rise and Tellcat continues to post a profit. How, gentlemen, can this be?'

James and Percy sat up, cautious not to betray too much alarm. Bradley and Pierre exchanged glances while Simon fixed his snake-like gaze on Bertrand as though he wished to poison him with a look.

Bertrand's next slide was the photo taken by Min in Tellcat's boardroom, showing the corporate structure.

'Tellcat is a more complex organisation than we were at first led to believe,' said Bertrand.

'Where did you get that picture?' snapped Simon.

'Please,' said Bertrand, 'humour me. Admittedly, this whole takeover has been somewhat dogged by incomplete documentation.' Bradley's eyes narrowed. 'But even so, nowhere in your official company literature was the bank made fully aware of the extent of Tellcat's holdings inside the UK and, it seems, in other places such as the Cayman Islands.' The Cayman Islands, a tax haven, were practically banking shorthand for fraudulent activity. 'As an exercise in corporate accountability, we visited some of your affiliates in this country, time being too short for us to embark on a world tour although that would doubtless prove highly interesting as well.' He flashed up more of Min's pictures, this time of the company with the 'For Sale' sign, a photo of a waterlogged industrial unit in Essex with a padlocked door, and an entirely empty office block in East Sheen. 'We can see from these pictures that Tellcat is perhaps not in the financially sound position we have been led to believe. Added to that, we have reason to suspect the share price has been held up by artificial means and is not a true reflection of the worth of this company which, on further investigation and access to the correct documentation, will be shown to be deeply in debt.'

'Strader, stop this nonsense, will you?' barked James.

'I'm sorry, sir,' said Bertrand pleasantly, 'that won't be possible.'

'You're sacked!' shouted James. Percy, meanwhile, was frantically trying to get help. He buzzed down to reception but the phone was answered by a most peculiar-sounding individual.

'I've got a gun to her head!' roared a hysterical voice through the receiver. 'And if you piss me off just a little bit more, then I'll shoot! I will, I've done it before!'

On the ground floor, the head of security was rescinding his order to evacuate the building. 'Repeat, cancel instructions. No one to enter or leave the building. We have a dangerous lunatic in reception. Repeat, dangerous lunatic.'

The head of security mopped his brow. He had just ascertained that the lifts were jammed because the old fool with the bag of small change, who presumably didn't know the difference between an investment bank and a retail one, had suffered some form of attack in the lift and fallen against the emergency button when a man in a blond bubble wig had run in and started waving a gun around. Before the guards, who were all gathered around the lift, could reach him, he'd jumped over the reception desk and put a pistol to the head of the poor girl behind the counter.

'No one moves,' he'd yelled, 'or the girl buys it!' When the phone rang, the bubble-permed man snatched it up and started shouting into the receiver.

'I think you'll find it worthwhile to keep on listening to me,' said Bertrand in the conference room.

'Carry on, Mr Strader,' said Bradley. 'I'm all ears.'

Bertrand flashed up a picture of a middle-aged man in a suit, laughing with his office companions.

'This is Joren Thorsted who originally masterminded the

takeover of Tellcat by Amercom. Sadly he has since had a very serious accident.'

The next slide was Will's official company picture which unfortunately made him look like a simpleton with terrible hair. 'Here we have William Gadget who preceded me on this deal until he disappeared in mysterious circumstances a few weeks ago. The fact that two of my esteemed colleagues have vanished or been incapacitated while working on this takeover reveals how desperate things have become at Tellcat. I put it to you, gentlemen,' said Bertrand, now truly in his stride and sounding a bit like an American version of Sherlock Holmes, 'that Tellcat is a company which, far from turning the profit it claims, is in fact deeply in debt and needs this takeover to rescue both it and this bank Pollinger's – to whom it owes, I estimate, over £500 million – from certain bankruptcy. The takeover is entirely based on fraudulent financial information. This is my firm and certain belief.'

Min almost expected him to bow and vanish in a puff of blue smoke, so theatrical was his delivery by the time he reached the end. She had to restrain herself from clapping and calling out, 'Bravo!'

Denby sat incredibly still, the same smirk still fixed on his face. Whatever Bertrand had to say, he clearly thought he could buy his way out of.

'This is a set up!' shouted James. 'You'll pay for this, Strader.'

'Calm down, James,' said Denby. 'I congratulate you, Mr Strader. You're clearly much more astute than I gave you credit for. But not *that* astute. If you were just a little cleverer, you would have realised with whom you are dealing. You will never be able to prove any of your assertions. Added to that, my political connections are very keen not to allow any form of scandal to rock the City at this delicate time. If the takeover fails, then we will receive the help of the government to rebuild our company until the point whereby the figures to which you refer, which are, after all, only projections of profit and were never meant to be read as actual statements of revenue . . .' Bertrand inhaled sharply at this patent lie, delivered with the utmost sincerity '. . . will be reality. At that moment, Mr Strader, my company will be snapped up as a valuable asset and a world leader in innovative telecommunications strategies, and you, I sincerely hope, will be begging on the street. I can assure you I will take every step possible personally to ensure you never work in finance again, or in anything else, both on this side of the Atlantic and the other. Pursue this course, Strader, and you are a marked man.

'However,' he continued smoothly, 'there is a way out of this which will benefit us all. I am prepared to overlook this regrettable incident, and even to demonstrate certain admiration for your abilities. I propose that the takeover goes ahead as it stands with the proviso that Pollinger's offers extensive credit to Amercom and the promise that their share price will remain fully supported for an indefinite period. Bradley, Pierre, I believe you both have extensive stock options and the acquisition of a major UK telecoms provider enhances Amercom's global position. In the short term Pollinger's is protected, at the very least from an embarrassing enquiry, and long term it stands to gain substantially. As for you, Mr Strader, your position at this bank is clearly untenable but I would be happy personally to guarantee you a pay off of, say, one million pounds and you may find Pollinger's happy to match that. Provided you never cross my path again, I fail to see why you should not lead a long and happy life.'

The cheek of the man was breathtaking. The attention of the whole room was focused on Denby's supercilious face as he leant back in his chair, sure that victory was his. Bertrand stood frozen to the spot. A million pounds, possibly double that, was a lot of money to reject on principle, especially given the fact he hadn't had any principles until the night before. He'd fallen in with this caper in a spirit of self-preservation, understanding that he was to be set up as the fall guy for a fraudulent deal. When the only route to salvation had seemed to be exposing the machinations at work, his path had been clear. Now he was being offered an easy and lucrative way out. If he just agreed, he could walk, a free and rich man. But then what? A life with no goals, no achievement, no focus. He'd spent so long trying to amass a fortune that he'd never seriously considered what to do with one. Start his own business? Run for President? Retire? Would that be fun?

All eyes were on him now. He gazed out of the window at the muddy river and marshland surrounding London's great financial centre and reflected what a dump England was. Stupid, small and shitty. Still clinging hopelessly to the notion it was in some way superior. And the English: with their cups of horrible tea, jokes that weren't funny, disgusting breakfast spreads, terrible plumbing and endemic snobbery. Clearly no one had bothered to tell them the race was over and they hadn't even qualified for entry. Dammit all, thought Bertrand in a rare flash of patriotic fervour, they could take everything he had, he'd still be an American. They couldn't strip him of that.

'Come on, old boy,' said James nervously.

That did it.

Bertrand faced the room. 'I accept, on one condition. That James nominates me for membership of his golf club.'

James spluttered in horror. It was the most exclusive in the country. Putting up Bertrand Strader would be social suicide.

'Just kidding,' said Bertrand. 'Having what you Britishers would call "a laugh".' He shot James a withering look. 'My old man told me never to start something I couldn't finish.' He gave them the full benefit of his devastating smile. 'So I'm going to finish you.'

'You can't prove anything,' said Denby, whose calm was rapidly slipping away from him.

Min, who had crept unnoticed out of the conference room for a few seconds, stepped forward, a tiny, brave figure, like Joan of Arc defiantly confronting her accusers.

'I think you're wrong,' she said firmly.

'I don't care what you think,' said Denby, rolling his eyes.

'I think you do,' she said. 'After all, we've got witnesses.' She gestured to Bradley and Pierre.

'Of course,' said Denby. 'Bradley. How is the beach house in the Bahamas? I hear the Family Isles are beautiful at this time of year.' Bradley looked away, furious with himself. 'As for Pierre, I doubt his English is good enough. I don't think you understood much of that, did you, Pierre?' The threat was implicit, in whichever language it had been said.

Min played her trump card.

'We've got Gadget. He's told us everything, and he's given us the tape.' She was gratified to see James's puce face gradually turn a satisfactory shade of mottled blue.

'Where is it?' Percy blurted out before he could help himself.

'Oh, so you do know about it?' said Min sweetly. 'You must have been so worried. And I expect you've been desperate to find out what happened to Will?'

'Gadget,' spat James, who'd never wanted to hire that cocky little know-it-all. 'I might have known he'd be behind this.'

'The tape,' said Min, 'contains plenty of evidence which shows that you were trying to push through a takeover before Tellcat went under, owing millions to this bank. Pollinger's couldn't afford you to fail so they were holding up the share price of Tellcat to lure Amercom. If the deal closed, the bank could have its money back, you would be very rich and would have offloaded your problem with Amercom left to pick up the pieces. You relied on the fact that once it had bought Tellcat, it would not be in Amercom's best business interests to reveal

197

what a mess it was in. They would probably come back to the bank with a complaint, but then the blame was to be put on to the individual who'd steered the merger, be it Joren, Will or Bertrand. That person would be the bank's only signatory to the deal so that in case of any enquiry the blame could be entirely attributed to them. That person would catch it in the neck and then, in a spirit of conciliation, the bank would have offered very reasonable terms to Amercom to help them out of their hole. However,' said Min, 'that tape, along with a recording of this meeting, has already gone to ITN and the Serious Fraud Office. I suggest you might want to start preparing your statements now.'

'Security!' yelled James into the phone. 'Get here now! I don't care if there's murder in the lobby!'

Min and Bertrand looked at each other and she nodded very slightly. They smiled at each other as a pair of burly men burst through the door.

'They've made a tape,' screamed James at the men. 'Find it! Search the building until it turns up! Don't let anyone out. Especially not these two.'

The flight back from Kinshasa had been a long one, especially as the first six hours had been spent in a Hercules, sitting on his backpack, with no form of refreshment or in-flight entertainment. Mac didn't really care. He was bringing his men home, not in body bags as he had feared, but live and well and ready to fight another day.

He still had the smell of the Congo in his nostrils – over-ripe fruit, urine, red mud and weeping trees mixed with the bitter smell of sweat. When he closed his eyes, he saw the thick jungle where layer upon layer of grasping greenery formed a cathedral-like canopy over the rotten cover of the forest floor. The rasping, metallic noise of a thousand insects was louder than a building site's worth of machinery, all drilling and sawing and digging and pumping at the same time. Something evil had lurked in that jungle, the birthplace of Ebola, the heart of darkness and, some said, the origin of AIDS.

The men had been fine but only just. He had found them hiding in a mud hut, wild-eyed with exhaustion, dehydration and fear. Under their feet crunched the bones of nameless dead bodies, the years-old skeletons nibbled clean of flesh as soon as the dead or half-dead had hit the ground. They were the gruesome reminder of decades of civil unrest, now being harshly clamped down on by an ageing president and his increasingly repressive regime. Mac, who'd once saved the local warlord from certain death at the hands of rebel troops, had managed to call off the blood lust long enough to get his men out.

This time he'd had enough. The devastation, the stench, the horror of war, had all suddenly caught up with him and, for the first time in his life, the idea of a quiet, peaceful existence, far from the sound of bullets, appealed. Whereas once, in his dreams, he'd seen smoke rising as tanks rolled through burning villages, now he imagined mist hanging low over a loch in the early-morning, a pale yellow sun peering through clouds which broke over purple mountain peaks. A stone house where a fire burnt in the grate and his faithful black Labrador greeted him as he came through the front door. He'd go home, he thought as the Hercules bumped over the clouds and dipped in and out of clear air turbulence, have a bit of a holiday for once, get his eyes sorted out and just take some time off. God knows, he thought, I deserve it.

Mac kept a serviced flat in St John's Wood for the times when he needed more privacy than the spare room at Annabel and Dennis's afforded him. Wanting desperately to be alone, he headed there once he'd landed with the simple aim of sinking into a long hot bath followed by a period entirely devoted to sleep. He put the television on loudly enough to hear it from his bath and wallowed happily, the bubbles soothing away the stresses and strains from his body.

A minute later he'd jumped out of the water as though someone had thrown an electric element into his bath. Grabbing a towel, he ran into the sitting-room where he caught the tail end of the lead news item. On the screen, a serious young man in a dark suit was speaking into a microphone.

'And the question everyone is asking this evening after the sudden collapse of Tellcat, the telecommunications giant, is where is William Gadget, the missing banker whose disappearance first sparked the investigation which led to the discovery of massive fraud both at Tellcat and at Pollinger's investment bank? This is Jemal Haque, reporting for ITN.'

Chapter Fifteen

Lady MacDougal thoughtfully crunched a piece of toast spread with sharp, dark brown marmalade as she listened to the 6 a.m. shipping forecast on Radio 4. 'Cromarty, south-east five or six, occasionally seven, blowing fair, showers later or fine,' droned the familiar, comforting voice emanating from the antiquated receiver sitting on the sideboard of Lady MacDougal's breakfast room, from whose windows the pink fingers of dawn could already be seen clutching at the bluish remnants of the previous night. The breakfast-room looked out over a long sweep of lawn which led smoothly down to the waters of a wide bay. From the far side a river ran out into the open sea. The bay was surrounded by a deep forest of pine trees, broken intermittently by the violent yellow of deciduous trees, already on the turn with the approach of autumn. The mountains behind still held their purplish haze of heather but the glorious yet brief Scottish summer was clearly on the wane.

About her feet lay a collection of geriatric dogs who, in theory were looking forward to their walk but in practice were finding the sedentary life infinitely preferable now they were so very old. Occasionally, one of them would thump a tail on the floor, but other than that they showed little sign of vigour.

She breakfasted alone. In preparation for her morning walk around the estate, she wore a tweed hat crammed down on her sensible haircut, an old navy blue jumper of her husband's, jodhpurs and a pair of slippers which she intended to change for the green Wellingtons that waited by the magnificent front door of Caithness House, seat of the MacDougal family these past seven hundred years. Despite being elaborately disguised by the usual unflattering paraphernalia of the upper classes, Lady MacDougal still cut a striking and strangely elegant figure.

As she ate her way through the toast, she made notes in a leather-bound dairy. 'Buy feed', read one entry enigmatically. 'Generator?' said another. 'Iris baby – remind vicar'. They spoke volumes to the writer who liked to keep her eagle eye on events on her estate. Very little escaped her notice and so she found its management, which had passed to her on the death of her husband, quite straightforward. More so, in fact, without him interfering and doing things which were just plain wrong, as even an idiot would have known.

However, that particular morning, the favourable shipping forecast for the region aside, events on the MacDougal Estate were unfolding which were, for once, outside the control of its formidable owner. Faintly, faintly in the far distance a plume of smoke was rising across the bay. Less faintly came a sudden hammering on the front door.

Lady MacDougal rang the bell for James, her trusty butler.

'Is there someone at the door?'

'It would appear so,' he agreed gravely.

'Who can it be at this hour?' said her ladyship, feeling put out at this disruption to her routine.

'Perhaps,' said James, 'I should go and see?'

'Yes, I think that would be best,' said Lady M. 'Whoever it is, don't bring them in here. The dogs won't like it.'

'Very good, my lady,' said James, evaporating away.

A few minutes later, the door to the breakfast-room was flung open and a filthy, dishevelled, bearded man wearing the torn remnants of some sort of cloth garment flew in and prostrated himself at her ladyship's feet.

'Lady MacDougal,' he panted.

'Who, might I ask, are you?' said Lady Mac, flashing a look so terrible it would have turned lesser mortals to stone.

James hurried in.

'I am so sorry, my lady,' he said, wringing his hands. 'He just ran through as soon as I opened the door.'

'There's a man dying in your woods,' said the horrible apparition through rasping breaths. 'It's Lord McCready, I think he's had a heart attack. You must rescue him.'

'Allan McCready?' Lady MacDougal was for a second seemingly overcome with relief until white-hot anger took its place. 'Do you mean to say Allan McCready of Berriemore is dying on my land?'

The apparition nodded, having run out of breath entirely.

'Well, that's just bloody typical,' said Lady M furiously. 'James, get a search party out for McCready. If he looks like he's about to kick the bucket, you can pop him back on his side of the border. I will not be inconvenienced in this manner.'

'There's a girl with him,' said the bearded man, pleadingly.

'Huh! When isn't there?' said Lady M, her fury showing no sign of abating. 'Oh, I expect you believed him, didn't you?' she said, rounding on the dirty young man who was still kneeling on the floor. 'I expect he told you he'd spent thirty years mourning his wife. Poor soul was still warm in her grave when he filled the castle with floozies! It's just one thing after another with that wretched man. This latest scheme, giving Berriemore to all those crazy people and disappearing himself, is just the final straw. I've had it with bloody McCready and his stupid jokes!'

'Please, Lady MacDougal, this isn't a joke. It's for real.'

'What did you call me?' she said.

'Lady MacDougal,' faltered the mud-splattered man.

'How do you know my name?' she shot out like a ricochet of bullets.

'I'm a friend of your son Mac's,' he began.

'My son is *not* called Mac,' she shouted. 'He has a perfectly good Christian name which is Dougal and I wish more people would use it.'

'My name is William Gadget,' he said. 'I was at university with Dougal.'

'Oh,' said Lady MacDougal, 'you're that boy from the Home Counties. I said you'd never amount to much.'

Will had forgotten quite how obnoxious Mac's mother could be. But at that moment they were both distracted by a deafening noise from the sky. Towards the ever-thickening column of black smoke rising at the northern end of the bay, a stream of helicopters flew over the roof of Caithness House, heading out over the sea.

'Berriemore is on fire,' said Will quietly.

'Oh, good Lord,' said Lady MacDougal, sitting down suddenly. 'So this isn't one of Allan's pranks?'

'No,' said Will. 'This is serious.'

'Is he really ill?'

'I'm afraid so,' said Will. 'He had a sort of attack last night and I left him in the woods with the girl and ran here for help.'

'But we're miles from Berriemore,' objected Lady Mac.

'I know,' said Will.

'Can you take us to him?' said Lady M.

Will nodded.

'Then let's go,' she said simply.

Until Allan tripped over a tangle of ivy in the forest, twisting his ankle and suffering an aneurysm, the midnight heist at the castle had been going quite well. Despite the hangover, brought on by his whisky-drinking session with Allan in the boat the night before, and an understandable reluctance to find himself yet again in danger through no fault of his own, Will had steeled himself for the onerous task of cat burglary Allan had asked of him. It wasn't something he actively wanted to do, but on the other hand Allan's suspicions of the leader chimed so well with Will's own that he felt he couldn't leave the good people – for good they were, if a bit weird – to their fate with this manipulative and bizarre individual. Maybe, reasoned Will, most of the inhabitants of Berriemore had been out of the wider world for so long their critical faculties had become blunted and their natural cynicism had deserted them. Either that or their brains were tuned to different frequencies from his as he was receiving the message loud and clear that the leader was trouble in a white robe. Will couldn't just run away.

It was a well-chosen night for crime. The moon was full, the sea was calm. In the late evening the leader conducted his monthly moonlight yoga session after which he habitually picked off one, or sometimes more, woman for late-night private tuition. Knowing this, Allan and Will thought they had a good few hours to attack the turret, find out its contents and escape in the pre-prepared rowing boat beached on the castle sands.

In undertaking this quest, Will had made one condition – that they should take the Vision with them. He couldn't abandon her to the mercy of the leader. He wasn't even sure he trusted Allan not to forget to bring her, but short of taking her on a death-defying climb to the top of the tower, he had little choice but to trust the old man. Allan was to wake her up and take her down to the boat at the same time as Will set off for the turret, with Allan returning up the rocky passage to meet him in the main hallway afterwards and guide him back down to the beach.

The climb to the turret made Will think that Allan must have been one psychotic little boy if this was what he'd done for kicks. Possibly the castle had been in better nick in those distant days, but even so it was a perilous ascent. He gripped on to bits of stone which crumbled in his hands, his feet lost their purchase and whole blocks fell suddenly and crashed into the sea, many feet below. He hadn't really registered how vast Berriemore was and how little of it was actually inhabited. Scaling the ramparts, he wondered what mental impact it would have for one man to live in such a vast place, alone, for over thirty years.

Although at moments he thought his fate would be to perish in a froth of cold Scottish sea, dashed on sharp rocks and pecked to pieces by hungry seagulls, he managed to scale the turret and slithered in through the window, which fortuitously was open. Will himself didn't quite know how it could be possible he was alive after such an astonishing physical feat. Little did he realise the twice-daily yoga classes, meditation and the relentless healthy diet he had been forced to adopt, had given his body a strength and flexibility that the man who'd staggered out of his bathroom window in a panic some weeks back could only have envied.

Once in the turret, he was deeply heartened not to find a dead body or a set of torture implements. Instead he saw something much more familiar. A lap top, a mobile phone and a neat set of files lay on a desk. Will packed them carefully into the rucksack Allan had given him and shimmied out of the window once more, gravity helping him all the way down.

As they rowed across the bay, Allan, Will, the rucksack, and the Vision who assumed they were returning her to her parents – which, quite honestly, was not now the worst option she could think of – looked back at Berriemore, its magnificent, bellicose exterior erected centuries ago to repel intruders from both land and sea.

'Goodbye, ma ain hame,' said Allan sadly.

'You'll see it again,' said Will.

'Nae,' said the old man. 'The soothsayer said my house would perish in flames and I'd go soon after.'

'Rubbish!' said Will. 'That's just a load of tripe.'

'I'm not so sure,' said the Vision. 'Look at that.'

Against the night sky, a pale orange light was blooming.

They abandoned their little coracle on the far side of the bay. With Allan in the lead, they set off through the woods which were so very dark they looked like several shades of black laid out on a palette. A cry from in front signalled that the old Laird had fallen. He lay on the spongy ground, wheezing like a steam train running out of coal.

'Can't move,' he said, forcing the words out.

'Allan,' protested Will, 'I can't carry you. You're too heavy. You've got to walk.'

'Too far,' he said. 'You go. Come back. Bring help.' His breathing sounded painful, its vagaries amplified by the rustling silence of the forest around.

'What shall I do?' Will asked the third member of the party.

'Go,' she said. 'Go and get someone. I'll wait with him.'

'Allan,' said Will urgently, 'which way do I go?'

'East,' came the reply. 'And take the bag.'

He set off at a run but kept crashing into trees he couldn't see in the dark so quickly slowed down to a jogging walk. As a little light stole into the woods, he realised that instead of going east, he had been heading north. He had been hurrying towards a yellow light over the horizon which as he drew closer he saw was not the rising sun but the flow of flames, sending clouds of billowing smoke into the pre-dawn sky. To his horror, he realised the smoggy, hot glare was coming from the direction of Berriemore. On the left-hand side of the bay, blush-coloured shafts of light announced the sun was making its daily appearance. He turned away and forced himself to move faster towards the rosy glow. When he could hasten no more, he settled into a plodding walk through the seemingly endless trees.

He found himself by the still waters of a loch with the sun rising in the east. Up the undulating curve of a grassy lawn sat a very familiar grey stone house where Will had spent many a university holiday, happily smoking pot in the attic or filching drinks from the cabinet for midnight picnics on the shore. He was looking at Caithness House, home of Mac, aka Lord Dougal MacDougal. He heaved himself up the slope and pounded on the door.

Much later that day, Allan awoke in an imposing four-poster in a room at Caithness House overlooking the bay. Lady MacDougal was sitting beside him, her half-moon spectacles perched on her nose as she read *Riders* for the umpteenth time.

'Ah, Maud,' he said, woozily. ' "Come into the garden, for the black bat night has flown".'

'Allan,' said Maud MacDougal, 'are you still delirious?'

'It's Tennyson,' he said dreamily. 'Written to his one true love.'

'Oh, stop babbling, you silly old man, and tell me what you were doing creeping around my forest having heart attacks?'

He started to laugh wheezily.

'Still the same as ever,' he said. 'Even in death, you show me no mercy.'

'Oh, for heaven's sake,' she said crossly. 'You're in my bed and I have no intention of letting you or anyone else die in it.'

'What other man would go to such lengths to get into your bed?' he murmured, his eyes closed.

'Is that Tennyson again?' she said suspiciously.

'No, Allan McCready. Original works of,' said the Laird of Berriemore.

'Honestly! You disappear for months on end, you fill your house with mad people who worship the sun, and then a friend of my son's turns up to tell me you're in the undergrowth with a girl a quarter of your age. You'd better have a damn' good explanation for this one, Allan McCready.'

'I love it when you're angry,' said Allan. 'Which is just as well, as you've never not. Why didn't you marry me, Maudie? Why?'

'Because I was already married to Alasdair when I met you, as well you know,' she said primly.

'Och, that's a feeble excuse,' said Allan, wheezing with laughter again.

'You are the most impossible man I have ever met,' said Maud, starting to laugh as well. Five minutes later, when Will popped in to see how Allan was getting on, he found the two of them sitting there, tears of laughter running down their cheeks. They didn't notice him so he closed the door again gently and went back downstairs.

Night had settled comfortably over Caithness when the estate Land Rover screeched to a halt on the gravel drive. James, the usually unflappable butler, staggered out, looking somewhat green from the unprecedented speed at which he'd been driven back from Inverness airport. Mac, who he'd gone to collect, had insisted on driving, claiming the stately pace the elderly retainer liked to move around at would waste more valuable time.

'Well, finally,' said Lady MacDougal crossly as her only son walked through the door. 'I knew this had something to do with you. And what in heaven's name is wrong with your eyes?'

'Hello, Ma. How are you?' said Mac, kissing her on the cheek. In the way that cheese goes with onion, Mac and disaster made natural partners. Wherever one was, you could safely assume the other would follow. 'You haven't by any chance got a chap called William in the house have you?'

Lady Mac erupted. 'Oh, for heaven's sake, Dougal,' she snapped. 'Berriemore's burnt to a cinder, I've got half the Aberdeenshire constabulary eating scones in the kitchen, there's some teenage girl in the drawing-room who's on the missing persons list, and Allan McCready is upstairs with his lawyer.'

'What's McCready doing here?' said Mac sharply.

'Your friend brought him. Apparently you left the Gadget boy at Berriemore a few weeks ago. I note you didn't bother to pop in and see me while you were here. It's all very well rushing around saving fuzzie-wuzzies,' ranted Lady Mac, who was gloriously politically incorrect, 'but you should be where your duty lies, here at home, looking after the estate. What your poor father would have said . . .'

'My poor father would have said, "Get McCready out of my house right now",' observed Mac dryly.

'Well, it's not your house, not yet anyway,' said Lady M. 'So if Allan wants to stay, he shall.'

'Oh, God, Mother,' said Mac. 'Not McCready. Do we have to?'

Lady Mac drew herself up to her full height, an impressive sight, and was preparing to face up to her son when a clean-shaven and freshly bathed Will popped his head out of the drawing-room to find out what all the shouting was about.

'Mac!' he said. 'At last! Someone who can tell me what's going on.'

'Gadget,' said Mac, hurrying over to give him a manly hug, 'I'm so pleased to see you, you have no idea.'

'So what's been happening?'

'It's a bit of a long story,' said his friend. 'I think you might want to sit down.' They entered the drawing-room together but Will was already comfortably installed in an armchair when he noticed Mac hadn't got any further than the door. He was standing there, just staring at the Vision – whose real name was Louise – who was sitting by the fire, wearing an old Aran jumper, her blonde hair falling around her face which through Mac's blurred vision made it look as if a halo of golden light surrounded her. She was, he instantly decided, an angel.

'Watch it, mate,' said Will, noting Mac's expression. 'She's only nineteen.'

'So?' said Mac. 'I'm only thirty-three.'

Louise, for her part, recognised him as the giant who had brought Will to Berriemore.

'It's you,' she said, blue eyes shining. 'You're real.'

'Very,' agreed Mac, coming forward and kneeling at her feet.

'But you're a hero,' said Louise.

'Sort of,' he said modestly, having wanted someone to say that for years.

'Don't mind me,' muttered Will, feeling very put out that his own, quite heroic contribution didn't earn him a sweet-faced girl with admiration streaming out of her eyes.

'I need to talk to Will alone,' Mac said gently to Louise. 'There are some policemen downstairs who want to take your statement. After that, I'll take you back to your parents.'

'Hang on a minute,' said Will irritably, 'I rescued her. Surely I should get to take her home?'

'Point one,' said Mac, who could talk in a very boring fashion when he chose, 'you are still in shock and I don't believe you've been properly checked over yet. Point two, as soon as you leave the gates of this house, you will be pounced on by a few of the thousands of people who want to talk to you. Point three, I've got a car, you don't.'

'Hmmph.' Will had to admit defeat. 'But you will tell her parents that I got her safely out of Berriemore, at great personal cost?'

'Of course,' said Mac soothingly, fully intending to play up his own role a little, to earn extra brownie points from her family. 'Don't vanish,' he said to Louise as she left the room. 'There's something I want to ask you.'

Chapter Sixteen

'The real star of the show,' said Mac reflectively a few hours later, as he and Will sat either side of the blazing fireplace, a bottle of whisky sitting on the hearth and a few dogs curled companionably about their feet, 'was Sharan Haque. I don't know if they could have pulled it off without her.'

'How did she get involved?' said Will, mystified.

'No idea,' said Mac. 'But she saved the day. She had this theory, which turned out to be true, that if you're a middle-aged woman, you might as well be invisible in the UK. Especially if you're dressed as a cleaner, which she was in some overalls Albert got her. She waited outside the conference room door with a mop and bucket, pretending to polish the parquet. Min ran out, dropped the film into her bucket – which of course was empty – and ran back in. So when Min was searched, they found the camera but they didn't get the film.

'Sharan set off down to the basement and found the cleaners' kitchen where she sat down and had a cup of tea and a chat with the other ladies. In fact, she was having such a nice time that Jem, waiting outside, thought she must have been caught by security it was so long before she emerged.'

'But she was just biding her time until the coast was a bit clearer. Knowing that however effective her disguise was, she'd still be searched if she tried to leave through the front door, she got one of the other ladies to let her out of a back entrance. She pottered around to the front where Jem was sitting in his car, having a massive panic attack over what he'd done to his own mother. She handed over the film and Jem drove like the clappers to ITN. When he rushed in, holding a tape and claiming he had footage of the scam of the century, you can imagine what pandemonium broke out. It was a very brave news editor who decided to run the story as the lead item last night. Apparently, the top brass were screaming about libel and authentication, threatening to pull the plug if the story went out. The news team were so determined to run with it they locked themselves into the studio to do it. The rest, as they say, is history.'

'What a story!'

'Remind yourself to thank Min when you see her. It was all her idea.'

'Where is she?'

'Um, helping the police with their enquiries at present,' said Mac, laughing into his glass. He had caught up with Min and Bertrand at Scotland Yard where he'd arrived to inform them of the whereabouts of one William Gadget. The rest of the details he'd picked up from a phone conversation with a ridiculously over-elated Jem. What Mac didn't tell Will was that the police had given him a fairly serious dressing down for taking the law into his own hands and had made some very trenchant observations about the role of the mercenary in a democracy. Mac, who was quite used to people shouting at him anyway, didn't take it too personally. He certainly didn't let it puncture the good mood brought on by the incredible fact that his raggle-taggle gang of friends should have pulled off such an impressive feat.

'Has she been arrested?' said Will, half leaping out of his chair.

'Relax, mate, she's fine and looking forward to seeing you. She just had a few, what can I say, things to explain to Scotland Yard. She won't be charged.'

'Jesus! Will they let her go?'

'She's not guilty of anything,' said Mac. 'Other than obsessive devotion to a certain Gadget Esq.'

'So the man who phoned in the middle of the night, who was he?' said Will, not wanting to discuss Min just at this moment.

'I doubt we'll ever know,' said Mac. 'Some thug, I expect, told to frighten you.'

'What did they think I had?' said Will.

'Ah,' said Mac. 'This is where it gets complicated. According to Bertrand . . .'

'I still can't believe that he of all people would knowingly have done something to help me.'

'Guess what? He was one of the good guys,' said Mac. 'According to him, your office was wired up by a television crew who were filming you at all hours of the day for some Corporate Reality exercise. You then took a tape from the production booth . . . .'

'I'd asked them to put Dallas's show reel together on one tape so he could send it to an agent.'

'Exactly,' said Mac. 'But there was a mix up with the tapes and the one you got was from a TV camera with overnight footage from the men's loo, where two Young Turks had conducted a very revealing conversation about how they were setting up one William Gadget to take the rap for their shady deal, and how, once it was signed and sealed they expected to be very rich and very far away.'

'Oh, good Lord, so there *was* something wrong with Tellcat?'

'As they weren't from your department, they had no idea about the Corporate Reality exercise. They only found out the next day when one of them came back to your floor, looking for the diary he thought he might have dropped in the loo. To his horror, he saw the camera and found out that, yes, the bogs had been wired for sound and pictures the night before. He went straight to the top – these two monkeys were just pawns, really, acting under orders – and they got their hands on the tape. When they watched it, they were probably far from amused to see our Dal, dressed as a large feathered bird, laying golden eggs in a provincial theatre. The tape they really wanted had already gone home with you and been given to Dallas who'd posted it to LA. That's what they were after when they came to your flat that night.'

'Wow,' said Will. 'That's unreal.'

'I nearly had a heart attack when I saw Jem on telly,' said Mac. 'I'll just got in from Kinshasa and was having my first bath in a week when I heard the reports that Tellcat had collapsed, Pollinger's looked set to follow, and a search had been started for you. I leapt straight out of the bath, didn't even stop to wash my hair . . .'

'You haven't got any,' protested Will.

'Well, cheers,' said Mac. 'I went straight to Scotland Yard where Min and Bertrand were already, explaining to many people, many times quite what they'd been doing that day, and told them where I'd put you.

'By the time they got an emergency force out to Berriemore, you weren't there and the castle had pretty much burnt to the ground. But I had a fair idea I might find you here.'

'What about the people of the ashram?' asked Will.

'Not yet all accounted for,' said Mac seriously. 'We may need your help with that.'

'I see,' said Will, who had heard about enough for one evening. 'Do you think there's anything else I could have done?'

'No, mate,' said Mac. 'You've done quite enough already. And you got the lap top out, which we've given to the police.'

'What's on it?'

'They'll tell you that,' said his friend. 'Have another whisky. I think you deserve it.'

The door to the sitting-room opened and for the first time in her life Lady MacDougal entered a room quietly. She sat down next to Mac, tears trickling down her lovely, aged face.

'It's Allan,' she said. 'He's dead.'

Upstairs in the master bedroom, where long ago he had made a cuckold of Mac's father, Allan had died, probably as peaceful as he ever had been. He passed away in a room overlooking his beloved coastline, with the woman he adored by his side, secure in the knowledge that he had stopped an evil man from perpetrating more harm.

The leader, so the police had told Allan the afternoon before he passed away, was in fact a well-known fraudster called Dezzie Blake who had been on their wanted list for some time now. Thanks to his chameleon's ability to disappear and reinvent himself, they had been unable to arrest him. Blake was a former stage hypnotist who used his impressive powers to abuse the trust he was able to inspire in simple people searching for direction and faith. The ashram was not the first time he'd pulled this stunt – there had been an incident in Cornwall in which the police believed he was involved, but they had lacked the evidence to convict him or the knowledge of his whereabouts to arrest him.

Blake's usual policy was to infiltrate a monastery, retreat or commune, where he claimed to be on a journey of self-discovery and revelation. Once there, he would gradually prey on vulnerable members of the commune, convincing them that he alone held the key to their salvation. Initially, he used his hypnotic techniques to gratify his own sexual needs but it was a quick step from there to financial gain. Once his victim was in a trance, he persuaded them to divest themselves of their worldly goods and sign them over to Blake. After three months at the monastery in Cornwall he had vanished, taking with him the contents of the safe, several people's bank account details which further investigation showed he had emptied, and an ornamental gold-plated Buddha. Blake had avoided the policy by fleeing abroad, taking a world tour which had set him up with some interesting new contacts for his next venture.

Blake had big ideas. As he saw it, the flow of money around the world was impeded by people asking annoying questions about where it had come from. He hit upon a simple way to remedy this while making himself extremely rich in the process. By setting up his own charity, ostensibly to provide shelter and nurture for those who wished to pursue an alternative lifestyle, he created the perfect vehicle for money laundering. Once he put the word out across the criminal network about his 'financial cleansing scheme' his client list quickly grew. It was an attractively straightforward notion – they made a donation to Blake's 'charity' which was then invested in the stock market, cleaned up, a cut taken, and returned to its original owner in the form of a tax-free grant. Mafiosi, drug dealers, thieves and tax evaders queued to use his services as he provided a way to bring money into the United Kingdom which could then be used to buy houses in Belgravia, reinvest in the stock market, snap up small businesses or buy strings of racehorses. Keeping your money off shore was all very well, but there came a point when owners wanted to spend it legitimately.

Setting up the ashram had been easy. Although he'd initially done it only as a cover for his other activities, Blake had found it most enjoyable to be able to dominate the simple, lost people he accumulated. The reason he had disliked Will so fervently from the start was because, thanks to his intuitive talent, he could see he would never be able to manipulate William Gadget in the way he wished.

The offer of the castle of Berriemore, which had come when the wattle and daub huts he'd persuaded his followers to build were falling to bits, had been a gift from the Gods. As a welcome extra, Blake took special pleasure in relieving certain inmates of Berriemore of their worldly goods, getting them to sign over any investments or property they owned to his 'charity'. It was a drop in the ocean compared to the sums of money that flowed in from other sources but it was fun, and Blake liked his fun.

Lately, he'd taken a gamble. He'd been helping a trader from a certain bank to reduce his tax liability when this young man had come to him with a very interesting offer. If Blake would agree to keep buying, on behalf of his clients, shares in a certain telecoms company, then with the backing of his bank, the trader would ensure that Blake was told the optimum moment to get out of the market with guaranteed huge profits. Blake ploughed everything into Tellcat, expecting to sell as soon as the deal with Amercom was announced. The person Allan had overheard him talking to on the mobile was none other than one of the traders who featured on the video, discussing the downfall of William Gadget.

However, the call from Pollinger's never came. Blake got nervous and decided to leave Berriemore anyway. He'd had enough of roughing it and a luxurious spell in the sunshine was starting to appeal.

But he had been out-manoeuvred. Once he had finished his last midnight yoga session, something which incidentally he was in no way qualified to teach, he found the turret had been broken into, his lap top, files and mobile phone gone. In order to fake his own death, he had already lit a fire on the ramparts which was eventually to burn down the whole castle. He fled to the beach where he thought a rowing boat awaited him. That too had been taken, meaning he faced a couple of miles of open sea before reaching the freedom of the mainland. Given the fact he couldn't swim, he hid and waited for the tide to turn, by which time helicopters had descended from the sky and armed policemen stormed the castle in search of survivors. It was a great irony that Blake, for whom the police had searched long and hard, should be picked up in the hunt for someone quite different. They were looking for William Gadget.

The police didn't tell Allan all of this. The scale of their discovery was beyond their wildest dreams, even if it did inspire in DCI MacKinsey, head of Aberdeenshire's Special Investigations Unit, keen hopes of a medal, promotion and drinks on the house for ever at the annual policeman's ball. Not that he fully understood what he was seeing but he knew enough to realise its import. It was only when the dust had settled that the true impact of Blake's shenanigans became clear. When Tellcat and Pollinger's collapsed, the 'charity' was left millions of pounds in debt. Blake had some very angry and very dangerous people on his trail, and suddenly a stint in prison seemed quite attractive. After all, he was sure he would find another opportunity to work his special magic inside the safety of the high walls Her Majesty had so thoughtfully provided for his personal security.

Allan McCready's funeral took place the next evening, in a small stone church overlooking the sea. Inside the white-washed house of God, the sparse, wooden pews were filled with solemn villagers at the front and London relatives, who'd hot-footed it up on the promise of hearing Allan's will after the ceremony, at the back.

Once everyone else was seated Maud stalked in, looking magnificently dignified with a lace mantilla draped over her hair. On either side of her came Mac and Will, one in a well-fitting dark suit, the other seemingly wearing a garment meant for someone several inches taller and quite a bit broader. Behind them followed a ravishingly pretty blonde girl, her perfect complexion set off by a fifties Balenciaga black dress that Lady M had found in the back of her wardrobe.

The London relatives stirred at the sight of such sophisticated people so far from any other sign of civilisation.

'Who are they?' whispered the new Lady McCready to her husband, Rory, busy text-messaging his mistress, a PR girl who promoted alcoholic drinks for teenagers, under his prayer book.

'I don't know,' he said, one eye on Maud, one on his mobile, wondering if the old girl was going to announce she was Allan's secret wife. Rory, who was not at all the gentleman he might seem at first glance, tended to credit everyone with motives as low as his.

The Presbyterian priest gave a stinging address in which he reminded those present that sin was only ever a thought away and that God saw into the hearts of all men and judged them accordingly.

'What do you think God makes of that lot at the back then?' Mac murmured to Louise, sitting next to him. They'd phoned her parents the previous night to let them know she was safe and would be home soon. Her mother had been too over-whelmed to speak but her father, usually a bluff, wise-cracking businessman, had cried down the phone to Mac and thanked him brokenly for finding his only daughter and letting them know she was safe.

As devoted *Telegraph* readers, they had heard of the daring Captain Dougal MacDougal and assumed their precious Louise had been personally rescued by Mission Accomplish and a crack team of balaclava-clad mercenaries. Mac didn't disabuse them of this thought. Will, after all, had Min to go home to, whereas Mac had fallen hook, line and sinker for Louise. In her sweetness and youth he saw the antithesis of the filth and stink of war and betrayal. He saw a new vision of his future where he wasn't constantly pandering to the whims of some of the world's richest and most unpleasant men. The soft, gentle life which he'd always rejected out of hand as dull and pointless suddenly seemed his heart's desire.

Once the coffin had been lowered into the spot pre-ordained for Allan in death since the moment of his birth, the mourners adjourned to Caithness House for the wake.

By the time they reached the home of the MacDougal family, Rory McCready was seething with rage, much to the covert amusement of the rest of his party. He had accosted Maud at the end of the ceremony to ask what she thought she was doing, arranging a funeral without consulting Allan's family, and holding the wake at Caithness instead of Berriemore.

She had looked him up and down with distaste. The family resemblance was strong enough. Rory didn't look unlike his uncle at that age: the same slate-blue eyes, straight nose and double crown which made it so hard to get their dark hair to lie flat against the head. But it was like seeing a version of Allan which had gone through a stone polisher, so smooth was the man in front of her. If Allan had been raw hide, this man was butter-soft suede. He had none of the *joie de vivre*, the impetuosity, the fiery charm or appealing insanity of his departed uncle.

Hovering nervously behind Rory was his wife, a formerly attractive, curvy good-time girl who had suffered the ravages of too many babies in too few years. Her black dress was holding itself together but only just, having turned shiny from the strain in various places. While Rory was immaculately kitted out and entirely free from sticky handprints, his wife was the opposite. Maud suspected that one of the couple spent much more generously on their wardrobe than the other. From the twitching of Rory's wife, Maud gathered he was a bully who liked to get his own way. Would Allan have turned out to be the same sort of husband had Maud married him, as he had repeatedly asked her to? Would he have broken her down, as Rory clearly had his wife? Alasdair MacDougal might not have been the most inspiring of husbands but he had been a good man in his way.

'I have been somewhat surprised by your attitude,' said Rory, a hint of steel lurking behind the outwardly polite words. 'Barging in at our time of grief. I don't know who you think you are.'

'I don't think,' said Maud coldly, 'I know.'

'The reception should be in our family home, Berriemore.'

Maud, who was a good six inches taller than him, fixed him with her steely gaze.

'You might find that a little uncomfortable.'

'I will be moving the ashram out immediately. They have no right to remain in the castle now that my uncle has – sadly – passed away.' Rory's grief was clearly not a matter he felt should be displayed in public. Either that or else the death of his close relative had made no emotional impact on him whatsoever.

'Those poor people,' sighed Maud who had seen the bedraggled, singed Yogis leaving Berriemore, wrapped in blankets, their innocent faces full of tearful, confused shock. Traumatic though their exit from the castle had been, at least, she reflected, they had been spared Rory.

'Oh, poppycock,' he spat. 'An estate which could be turning a large profit under the right management has instead been losing money for years. My uncle has presided over the virtual demise of Berriemore.'

Mac came up behind his mother and stood there, staring at the new Lord McCready in a frankly quite menacing manner. Despite his bravado, Rory was starting to feel a little out-faced by these very tall, extremely unfriendly people.

'All right?' said Mac coolly.

'Fine, thank you, Dougal. This incredibly unpleasant young man here says he is Rory McCready, Allan's nephew. He seems to think we should have held the wake at Berriemore. Clearly, no one has bothered to tell him the castle has burnt to the ground.'

It is rare to see somebody embody a cliché of popular speech but Rory managed it. His jaw actually dropped.

'Errgh?' He recovered the use of his lower mandible. 'Burnt – Berriemore? Burnt?'

'That is correct,' observed Lady Mac crispy. 'Arson, the police think. They are treating it as a criminal case.'

'By God, someone'll pay for this,' said Rory furiously.

'If you were hoping that someone would be an insurance company, you can think again. Allan didn't believe in them.'

'That wretched old bugger!' said Rory, while his wife ineffectually tried to put a soothing hand on his arm.

'Well, there we are,' said Lady Maud. 'Do come and have a drink at Caithness to remember the uncle of whom you were clearly so fond. And if you must bring all those children, please try to keep them under control.' She walked away, Mac following, keeping a hand on her shoulder.

'Well done, Ma,' he whispered in her ear. 'Great performance.' Through barely suppressed tears, she flashed him a smile.

Wakes are not occasions which can be judged by the usual social criteria of success or failure. While Allan's had all the elements of a good party – plenty of booze, a wide mix of people, a beautiful setting, a common theme – strictly speaking it was nevertheless a total disaster. No guest left wishing they could stay longer, with a new friend, or having enjoyed the company of those they came with.

It was a strange affair – one half of the room stood stiffly in their Sunday best, politely attempting to honour the dead by remembering what was good about their departed, eccentric laird: his talent as a crack shot, his fulsome generosity to those in need and ability to sort out the complex personal problems of those he cared for. His leaving Berriemore in the care of a bunch of people the locals could only view as maniacs was not mentioned. It would be, but there was enough respect for the departed for criticism to wait for another day.

The southern contingent, who stood apart as though they feared that provincialism might be catching, had no such scruples. They felt no need to hold back the acid commentary with which they graced the dining-rooms, bars and parties of London.

'But, darling, clearly the old man was completely barking!' a distant cousin in a black dress and matching feather boa exclaimed. 'Didn't you hear what happened? He got brain-washed by some strange cult who then moved in and held satanic orgies in the castle. It burnt down in one of their rituals!'

'He'd been absolutely doo-lally for years,' said her second cousin once removed. 'Rory tried to have him sectioned, for his own good of course, but the case got thrown out of court. Rory thinks he bribed the judge.'

'Lovely people,' said Mac to Louise and Will who were standing quietly in one corner of the drawing-room.

'He seems to have an awful lot of relatives who'll miss him,' said Louise.

'No, darling,' said Mac. 'Old man was as rich as Croesus. They're all hoping for their pay off.'

'You didn't like him, did you?'

'I think,' said Mac carefully, 'my parents would have been happier without him.'

The reading of the will took place in a side room. Allan's lawyer informed Rory that his uncle had in fact changed his mind and left Berriemore and all that went with it, quite a substantial bequest once the fishing rights, the forests, the farms and the castle were taken into account, to the National Trust of Scotland. White with anger, Rory left promptly, driving his two-seater sports car away in a speckled cloud of rage and abandoning his wife to the aubergine-coloured people transporter that she heaved their children and nannies around in.

Once they'd finally got rid of the last of the McCreadys, quite a few of whom were so delighted to have been on hand to witness Rory's ire that they felt the day had been thoroughly worthwhile even though they weren't the happy recipients of a windfall, Will decided to make a move as well. He wanted to go home and he wanted to see Min. He was missing her quite dreadfully and even tomorrow didn't seem soon enough.

Mac's Land Rover hadn't changed a bit in all the years Will had known him. He used it as a sort of mobile repository of stuff, filling it with old bananas, Sunday papers, riding boots, road maps of Sweden, dusty tins of travel sweets, and other such useful bits of flotsam and jetsam.

'What's this?' said Will, holding up a metal/leather combo.

'A martingale,' said Mac. 'Use it on difficult horses.'

'Thank God,' said Will. 'I thought for a minute it was something to do with your deviant sexual practices. But I expect Mac's told you about them already, hasn't he, Louise?' She was competing for space on the back seat with a large black dog.

'Does he ask all his girlfriends to wrap him in clingfilm?' said Louise innocently as the dog slurped her ear.

'Only the very special ones,' said Will. 'The rest get Bacofoil.'

'For the record,' said Mac, 'I want it to be known that no kitchen implement has ever been involved in a relationship with me.'

'You were very fond of the egg whisk once,' said Will. 'I distinctly remember it. The butter dish cried for days.'

'Mac, you must get Will to peel some vegetables for you. He's very good at it,' came Louise's voice from the back, slightly muffled by Labrador.

'Do you know,' said Mac, 'I don't remember ever eating any food which Gadget had a hand in preparing.'

'Wise man. No wonder you've done so well.'

'What are you going to do now?' asked Louise.

'There's someone I want to see,' said Will. Mac smirked but didn't say anything. 'And I'll take the rest from there.'

They pulled into a garage so Mac could fill up. Will set off to load up on Murray Mints, Marlboro Lights and Diet Coke for the journey, but stopped in his tracks. Outside the garage shop was the usual bank of newspapers, competing loudly with each other for attention. They all had the same photo, even if it was run in different sizes. HAVE THE DARING DUO FOUND LOVE? blared one red-top tabloid under a picture which seemingly showed Min and Bertrand in an embrace.

'All right, mate?' said Mac, coming past to pay for the petrol. Then he too saw the picture.

'Oh,' was all he could manage.

'Is it true?' Will asked him bleakly.

'Don't know,' said his friend. 'But you know what papers are like, they'll print anything.'

Will read out the caption. ' "Major fraud-busting is not all that's on the agenda for Min Haskell and Bertrand Strader, the intrepid pair who brought down a multinational company. It seems that love is in the air for the corporate dynamos who together make a fighting force to be reckoned with. If this picture is anything to go by, their relationship is off to a sizzling start!" '

He went back to the car where Louise was waiting.

'Have you got some sweeties for me?' she chirped.

'No,' he said.

'But I thought you were going to . . .'

'I changed my mind,' said Will.

'Shall I get some then?'

'No!' said Will. 'Just leave it.'

Mac found a rather confused girl and a very cross man in the Land Rover when he returned.

The original plan had been to take Will to his flat in London but he asked Mac if he would mind making a diversion.

'Would you take me home?' he said.

'Your parents?' said Mac, raising an eyebrow.

'Yup,' said Will, looking away from him.

'You're the man,' said Mac.

'That's just it, isn't it?' said Will. 'I'm quite clearly not.'

Chapter Seventeen

Min and Bertrand hadn't noticed the long lens of a camera trained on them and they certainly didn't hear the click as it caught them in each other's arms. Neither was sufficiently aware of their new status as celebrities *du jour* to know that for this brief period, while their faces were splashed everywhere, they had forsaken any right to privacy.

The picture was taken outside a television studio where they were to appear on yet another chat show to regale the nation with the story of how they had caused the downfall of one of Britain's seemingly most successful companies, and with it the investment bank Pollinger's.

'Min.' Bert paused outside the door. 'I just want you to know that I think what you did was amazing.'

'You were pretty fine yourself,' she replied, smiling at the neat-haired American.

'But you were so cool,' continued Bert. 'I mean, I kinda had to do it. I did it to save my own skin, but you did it for someone else.'

'You could have taken the money,' she said.

'Yeah,' he conceded, 'I coulda. But hey, how was I to know you didn't have a gun?'

'That's not really why, is it, though?' said Min. 'You did it because it was the right thing to do.'

'Shush!' he said. 'You're ruining my reputation. People might think I care.'

'I think you do,' said Min, suddenly feeling quite moved.

'Come here,' said Bertrand, opening his arms to give her a hug.

'A big welcome to our next guests who need very little introduction from me,' said Fawn, the plump blonde presenter of *Your Morning*. 'In the studio today we have none other than Min Haskell and Bertrand Strader, the Anglo-American team who have rocked the world with their revelations of high-level intrigue and fraud.'

The audience cheered uproariously as Bertrand, covered in foundation and hair gel, and a far more fresh-faced Min took their seats on the large squashy white sofa.

'So,' said Fawn leaning forward and smiling toothily, 'everyone's talking about you. How does that feel?'

'Great!' said Bertrand.

'Embarrassing,' said Min at exactly the same time. They caught each other's eye and laughed.

Fawn smiled indulgently at them before dropping her voice to a conspiratorial whisper and turning to the camera. 'Here, for anyone whose missed it, is the astonishing footage of what happened in that crucial meeting . . .'

Even though the entire audience had already seen the famous clip, showing Bertrand roundly denouncing his bosses, they sat in hushed silence as it was run one more time. When it reached the bit where Bert said, 'That is my firm and certain belief,' they rose to their feet, cheering and stamping.

Fawn clapped her hands together sycophantically and turned back to him.

'Bertrand,' she said soupily, 'when did you realise your mission in life was to expose the malpractice in investment banking?'

As his life plan so far had been to make as much money as possible in the shortest time, he was put on the back foot by Fawn's far from searching question.

'Like me,' interrupted Min who was a fast learner, 'Bertrand was horrified by the depth of the deception being perpetrated against the public at large. We simply had to act to stop these people in their tracks.'

'I understand,' said Fawn, continuing to target Bert, 'that Calvin Klein have asked you to endorse their new range of underpants?'

'That's not something I can comment on,' said Bert, who only the day before had signed a very lucrative deal to appear on billboards and in magazines, clad only in a pair of white Y-fronts under the slogan 'It's All True'.

'People out there are watching – young people,' said Fawn sincerely. 'What is your message to them?'

'Look beyond the obvious,' said Bertrand. 'Trust your instincts and have some very good friends.'

'Thank you for that,' simpered Fawn. 'And now to the woman who had twins when she didn't know she was pregnant!'

Min and Bertrand were shuffled off the sofa by a posse of headphone-wearing minions.

'Was I okay?' said Bertrand as they left.

'You were great,' said Min.

'But really?'

'Really,' said Min.

'How did I sound?'

'A bit like you, frankly.'

'Was I good enough?' he said, anxiously checking his reflection in a window pane. 'Should I keep my hair like this?'

'Bert, you're a star! Stop fussing,' said Min. Having spent so much time with him in the countless interviews they'd both done, for the authorities and the media, she'd grown quite fond of Bertrand. She'd come to see that under the bulging muscles, the gym-toned body and sleek clothes, lay a welter of anxiety which made him far more likeable but at the same time much less desirable. Bert could be quite petulant at times, when demanding skimmed milk for his *latte*, for instance, or interrogating a waiter as to the precise fat content of a certain dish which to Min, who was terribly French when it came to food and drink, was just plain cringe-worthy. He kept asking her not to smoke and telling her she should take up roller-blading to improve her cardio-vascular fitness. Their friendship blossomed as the attraction, at least on Min's part, waned.

'Ambrosia,' said Bertrand as the car took them smoothly away from the television studio and back towards central London.

'Don't call me that,' she said.

'It's a bit more dignified than Min.'

'Bert, I'm not a very dignified sort of girl. And I hate the name Ambrosia, it's dreadful. Can you imagine going through life named after a tin of custard?'

'What's custard?'

'It's a high-fat food substance,' sighed Min. 'I don't think you'd like it.'

'Aaannyywayy,' he said, hoping to move the conversation on, 'I have to go back to the States.'

'Oh, no!' said Min. 'Don't go – we've only just realised you're not the devil incarnate.'

'Gee, thanks, lady, you sure know how to flatter me.'

'You know what I mean.'

'Yes, I do,' said Bertrand. 'I can see where you're coming from. But my priorities have changed since then.' He was gazing at her again, in a manner which once would have caused Min's stomach to flip over with lust but now just made her feel rather queasy.

'What are you going to do in the States?' she asked, not catching his eye.

'NBC want to talk to me about fronting a show.'

'Wow!' said Min. 'That would be brilliant.'

'I gotta face the fact, no bank on this earth is going to hire me now.'

'You don't think there are more Tellcats out there, do you?'

'This may be just the beginning, Min. Congress wants me to speak to them.'

'Bertrand Strader, you rock the world!'

'Come with me,' he said, suddenly and passionately. 'I'm not the sleazy guy you think I am. Okay, I'm a babe magnet, what can I say? But I don't want that life anymore – it's destroying my soul. I want to love and be loved, and I want you by my side.'

Min was not at all happy that this conversation was taking place in the back of a moving motor car with a driver who was clearly listening in and no prospect of escape.

'Min, we're a great team,' said Bertrand. 'You and me, look at what we've achieved. Together we could be incredible. There's so much out there for us and I want us to do it together.'

'*Chéri*,' she said gently, 'you can't use me to accessorise your lifestyle.'

'That's not what I'd do,' said a pained Bertrand.

'I really like you, but I'm not very good at commitment.' Bert was astonished to find himself on the receiving end of the same line he'd used so many times.

'You've been quite committed to Gadget,' he grumbled.

'I've known him all my life.'

'And you could know me for the rest of your life,' said Bertrand. 'We could be huge, Min.'

'I don't want to be huge.'

'What do you want?'

She found she couldn't speak.

'Oh, my God, it's him, isn't it?' said Bertrand, striking his forehead with his hand. 'Of course it is. How could I have been so dumb? How come I didn't spot that? Look at me, Min, and give me a straight answer. Are you in love with William Gadget?'

'I find,' said Sharan, fixing Albert with her liquid eyes, 'that a little citric acid will shift the stains better.'

'Partial as I am to Cif,' he cordially agreed, 'I feel you may have a point.' They both gazed into the stainless steel double sink of William Gadget's kitchen.

'These young ones,' sighed Sharan.

Albert nodded in agreement. 'If only they knew.'

'Quite,' said Sharan. 'They think we're making it up when we try to tell them, but we only want the best for them.'

'Indeed,' said Albert. 'They have to find out the hard way.'

Warriors of the past, they smiled at each other.

Bertrand was mixing a killer Martini in the next room. In the past, he'd never been known for his grace in defeat as each setback was interpreted as an incentive to try even harder. But he had accepted Min's rejection manfully. He was so enjoying the new sensation of having friends, people with whom he was not in competition and who had no interest in the contents of his bank account or trousers, that suddenly winning everything at any cost was no longer quite so important. He'd been so determined for so long to succeed that he had bulldozed his way through life. Now, just for a few moments, he was standing still and finding he quite liked it.

'Hey, Bert,' said Dallas who'd just arrived with the irrepressible Luella in tow, a girl who well merited the term 'bombshell', so likely was she to explode with high spirits or cause structural damage to any premises she entered.

'Hi, Bertrand!' she squeaked, knocking bits of furniture

flying as she dashed across Jem's living-room to greet him.

'Hey, Luella,' said Bertrand, once he'd escaped from a highly scented hug. 'You look great.'

'I'm going to LA with Dallas,' said Luella in great excitement. 'It's going to be so cool, I just can't wait!' Danny Kravitz, who'd watched CNN in amazement a few days before, scarcely able to believe what he was seeing, was no slouch. The tape had suddenly become one of Danny's most precious assets. He'd decided to push ahead with plans for a major feature-length film. Dallas, who Danny was now representing, was to fly to LA to become consultant to the team of scriptwriters Danny had immediately hired.

'Were you pleased with the shoot?' asked the buoyant Luella.

She had styled Bertrand for a fashion spread with a glossy men's magazine who had decided that his sang-froid, coupled with his evident sartorial flair, made him an icon of urban chic.

'It was different,' he said. The eco warrior meets City banker look they'd gone for had certainly created some unusual results, a sort of Swampy dressed as Gordon Gekko.

'They're going to put you on the cover,' said Luella happily. 'Can I tell people in LA that I'm your personal stylist?'

'You can say what you like, babe,' said Bertrand, laughing. 'I'll make sure I tell anyone who asks that only Luella is allowed to dress me.'

'Amazing, man,' said Dallas. 'Do you realise you've become the poster boy for the anti-capitalist movement?'

'It's fucking unbelievable,' said Bertrand. 'It doesn't matter how many times I tell them I worship the free market, no one wants to hear it. They're determined I'm the deadly secret weapon of those opposed to globalisation.'

'Stay with it, man,' said Dallas. 'Could take you to some interesting places.'

'Look me up if you're ever in NYC,' said Bertrand, who a few days ago would never have dreamt he might volunteer to be seen in the capital of chic with two such eccentrically dressed persons as Luella and Dallas. 'I'd love to take you out.'

'Hi, everyone!' said a tall, slender man coming in through the open front door. Shyly, he offered a magnum of champagne.

'I'm Andreas. I don't think we've met yet although obviously I know who you all are. I've just spoken to Jem, he'll be here any minute.'

Jem, who had broken one of the biggest news stories for decades, was in hot demand. Artichoke had been forced by their parent company to release him and he'd been taken on by ITN as a top-flight correspondent. Now, instead of trudging around the suburbs of England, glumly viewing hydrangea plants, he was to be seen outside the House of Commons, at the Stock Exchange, the Palace or Millbank Tower, each time holding a microphone and talking to camera. For now, he was covering domestic stories but with insistent rumours of war coming from the Near East, it was commonly believed that Jemal Haque's name would soon be among those put forward for the prestigious, if dangerous, job of frontline war reporter.

A minute later, Jem bustled through the door.

'Oh, you're here,' he said, giving Andreas a hug and a kiss on both cheeks. 'Have you met everyone?'

'Not everyone is here yet,' said Dallas. 'We're missing a few key players.'

'Has anyone spoken to Min?' said Luella anxiously. Bertrand poured himself another very strong drink.

'Er, no,' said Jem. 'We have no idea if the mission has been successful.'

Bert emptied his drink down his throat and poured another. Just because he was behaving in a dignified fashion, didn't mean he couldn't indulge his hurt feelings by getting plastered.

'Anyway, this is Andreas who used to work at Tellcat.'

'*What?*' said Bertrand.

'We met him,' continued Jem, basking in the sunny glow of Andreas's beaming smile which was directed entirely at him, 'on our day trip there.'

'I take it you are no longer an employee of the evil empire?' said Dallas.

'Bertrand and Min rather saw to the end of that career,' said Andreas pleasantly.

'Hey, man, nothing personal,' said Bertrand. 'Unless of course you were the person authorised to destroy the accounts of all Tellcat's affiliates and blame their absence on a man living in disguise in a castle in Scotland, while meanwhile hiding millions of pounds of debt in a very complicated manner and fraudulently arranging for the share price to be inflated in order to push through a bogus takeover?'

'I was a bit junior for all that,' confessed Andreas.

'Sorry to have robbed you of your job,' said Bertrand.

'You didn't,' said Andreas. 'I'd resigned that morning.'

'God, how psychic!' said Luella.

'Not really,' said Andreas. 'Jem phoned me and told me to leave.'

'Did he?' said Bertrand. 'Would that be the same Jem who insisted on a total information embargo for maximum security reasons?'

Jem looked a little abashed. 'Sorry, guys. But I had my reasons.'

'You did all right,' said Bertrand.

'Speaking of that,' said Jem, 'Andreas, will you come and meet my mother?'

Andreas put both hands on Jem's shoulders and said quietly, 'It'll be okay.'

They departed for the kitchen which Albert and Sharan, who had become firm, if somewhat competitive friends, had taken over with their catering arrangements. On one side of the room Sharan was composing trayloads of dainty canapés while on the other, Albert was rolling up little morsels of vegetables and meat in floury blankets and deep frying them. They seemed comfortably companionable together, sometimes bickering mildly over methods of domestic management, a topic on which both excelled, at others swapping nuggets of hard-won wisdom with each other. The feckless nature of youth was a bit of a favourite theme to which they constantly returned. A lot of head shaking, shoulder shrugging and tutting accompanied their observations about the superficial, selfish and spoilt nature of today's young people. Funnily enough, neither of them thought to discuss the observation that old people enjoy nothing better than a good whinge, especially if it's about the next generations.

Sharan sat down rather hard on one of the kitchen chairs when Jemal introduced Andreas as his boyfriend. She was shocked to hear him say it, but not at heart surprised. She had watched Jem change from an open, happy little boy into a man who was perpetually ill-at-ease, at least with his parents. There had seemed to her to be a sadness about him which she hadn't understood, although in her franker moments she had come close to a good guess.

For all her adult life she had straddled different cultures, living in the US and England where she found she didn't fit in, only to go home and find she'd become too Westernised really to feel comfortable there either. She knew only too well what it was like to feel at odds with the world around her and it was not something she wanted her son to experience in the long-term. Sharan might have cried a few tears but the kindness and consideration these two young men were showing to her was far removed from the absence of thought which her other male relatives accorded her.

'Oh, well,' she said philosophically. 'Daughter-in-laws are nothing but trouble really, so one less will be a blessing. Only

I'm not sure, Jemal love, how we are going to tell your father . . .'

By now, Bertrand was on auto-pour. Mac and Louise had arrived only seconds after Jem, Louise looking frail and lovely in a silvery cashmere jumper Mac had bought her a couple of days earlier, after she had accompanied him on a trip to a consultant neurologist in Harley Street. She had protested that he should be the one getting presents, not her, but her pleas fell on deaf ears and they spent a happy few hours considerably enriching the good burghers of Bond Street. Mac, who liked to think he was decisive rather than impulsive, had set his heart on Louise the minute he saw her and had lost no time in telling her so.

The reason his eyes were so red, the consultant had told him, was because he had a tumour growing in his brain which, left to its own devices, could debilitate him severely. An operation was very necessary and very safe, the only caveat being that post-surgery he might find his physical reflexes considerably slower and would probably develop a persistent shakiness in his hands.

'Can't aim a rifle, can't dodge a bullet,' he said carelessly. 'So I've given it all up.'

'What are you looking so happy for then?' said Dallas, perplexed.

'There are other things in life,' said Mac, kissing the top of Louise's head while Luella and Dallas exchanged significant looks at a rate the broadband connection would envy. 'I've sold my share of the business.'

Bertrand whistled. 'Can we ask how much for?'

'Nope,' said Mac. 'But put it this way, now we can go home to Caithness and live there forever.'

'We?' said Dallas, whose perceptions were already considerably blunted by Bertrand's bar-tending skills. 'We?'

'Louise and I,' said Mac with wry amusement, noting his friend's pathetic attempts to conceal his surprise. 'Did you think I wanted to spend the rest of my life on my own?'

'We really rather assumed,' said Dallas, 'that you'd drive your Land Rover over a mine one day.'

'Do you have life insurance?' asked Bertrand, genuinely interested in the reply which never came. The last two guests had arrived.

Chapter Eighteen

Will's parents could have been forgiven for thinking their son had been struck deaf and dumb by the time he came home from Scotland, so uncommunicative was he. Thinking it best not to pester him when he'd obviously had such a testing time, his mother tried not to worry that her thirty-two-year-old son was lying upstairs in his bed, his face turned to the wall, stone cold cup of tea next to him. She contented herself with making rejected plates of scrambled eggs while Phil got on with a little gardening.

Will could hear the drowsy sound of his father mowing the lawn percolate through the autumn afternoon. He lay there, looking at the fifteen-year-old poster of Belinda Carlisle on his wall, unable to escape the private hell his thoughts had taken him to. Min and Bertrand, he just couldn't believe it. Had she been in love with him all along? Will had to admit that next to Bertrand's sculpted physique he himself would look a bit of a speccy twerp. Did Min like men with muscles? It was so bizarre. They were two people he would never have put together.

He didn't know what to do. He felt absolutely certain that Bertrand would be very bad for Min, that she didn't have the strength of personality to put up with the endless flirtations he felt sure life with Bertrand would involve. Bertrand's ego, his insecurity, his desperate desire to impress, were sides of him that someone fragile and chaotic like Min would never be able to handle. Bert needed a very firm woman, imbued with total self-belief and complete devotion to him, for a relationship to work out.

There were two options available. He could wait until Bertrand and Min came to the disaster he could see looming in front of them, at which point yet again Will would be there to pick up the pieces of another failed romance, or he could intervene.

In different circumstances he would not have hesitated. He would just have told Min that she was making yet another enormous mistake. He might have got quite angry about it, in fact. Given her a piece of his mind and told her he wouldn't be around for ever. He loved her, God knows, that wasn't an issue. But her treatment of him was intolerable. She couldn't keep landing in his life and then taking off unexpectedly. This time he rehearsed in his head what he would say. He was going to demand that she show him more consideration. No more running away in the early morning, no more bombing about the globe. Settling down and leading a normal life was what he would insist on in return for his heart and soul.

The problem was, he couldn't say it. Bertrand had saved him, Will had to admit. How could he now stab the man in the back by breaking up him and Min? And if it was what she wanted, did Will have any right to interfere anyway? After all, what could he offer her? He had lost his job and his chances of getting another were slim. The City was already showing signs of nose-diving into a long-overdue recession, a move precipitated by the wholesale collapse of a large bank and with it a major telecommunications company. With his recent track record, the jumpy and superstitious City was unlikely to welcome Will back with open arms. He doubted he could meet his mortgage repayments, meaning he might have to sell his flat and live with his mum and dad for a while. He hadn't even managed to come out of this as a popular hero – that role had been taken by Bertrand whom William was starting to hate though he knew he shouldn't. Surely Min deserved better than an unemployed loser who lived with his parents?

'Love,' said his mother, popping her head round the door, 'would you nip to the shops for me?'

'Oh, Mum, do I have to?' said Will, sounding about eleven years old.

'Well, love, yes, you do,' said Joan Gadget with unusual firmness. 'Your father's busy and I'm all out of, er, gravy granules for supper.'

'Let's not have gravy then.'

'Don't be so daft,' said his mother, whisking the duvet off him. 'You can't eat roast chicken without gravy. How ridiculous!'

Will sighed. His mother appeared to have changed somewhat in the time he'd been away. He couldn't remember ever being ordered to undertake a domestic task before.

'You can look in the window at the Help Wanted notices while you're at the shop,' she said, rather cheekily he thought. There was clearly no way of getting out of it. He sighed and hauled himself off the mattress.

It took him ages to get there and back, so grudgingly slowly did he walk. He had wanted to take the car but found it was in the process of being waxed by his father, something he found unreasonably annoying.

'Can't you do that later?' Will snapped at Phil.

'No, William, I can't,' replied the mild-mannered man. 'I need to do it now.'

Will had set off in a funk of bad temper which was only exacerbated by the signs in the shop window looking for people to sew mail bags or stuff envelopes, occupations he thought reserved for those residing at Her Majesty's pleasure.

When he got home, the drive was empty.

'Where's Dad gone?' said Will to his mother.

'He needed to pop to the station,' said Mrs G, accepting the gravy granules without commenting on the fact that he had deliberately bought the wrong brand.

'Then why didn't *he* buy the sodding gravy then?' shouted Will.

'I'll thank you not to swear in my house,' said his mother sharply. 'And he is your father and I will not have you speak of him like that. Actually, we thought you needed a little walk.'

'For God's sake, I am not a child.'

'Then don't behave like one,' retorted his mother.

Will was utterly flummoxed.

The sound of the Rover Saloon coming to a very precise halt on the driveway announced the return of Phil.

'Go into the sitting-room, William, and I'll bring your tea in,' ordered Mrs Gadget or rather the Goebbels-like alien which had somehow assumed the external form of his mother. Too defeated to care, he sat himself down on the sofa element of the three-piece suite. The door opened, but standing there was not Joan Gadget with a cup of hot tea but a small girl with crazy black curls. It was Min.

Will stared at her and shook his head.

'If you've come to invite me to the wedding, I'm busy that day,' he said, his voice thick with tears.

'What wedding?' said Min.

'Yours,' he said.

'I'm not getting married,' said Min. 'At least, I hadn't thought about it. But maybe you're right. Maybe that would be the answer.'

'Glad I've been able to help,' said Will miserably. Now he'd inadvertently managed to persuade the love of his life to marry his arch enemy. Brilliant work, Will, brilliant, he thought. What a total prat you are.

'It makes perfect sense,' she continued. 'That's such a good idea.'

244

'Min, please, if you came here to gloat, then you've done it and you can go.'

'I came,' she said, 'to take you to a party. But now I think there's another reason for my visit.'

He had his head in his hands. 'Please make it a brief one.'

'It's certainly that,' said Min. 'William, will you marry me?'

The party had been swinging along for only an hour by the time the newly engaged couple showed up but already the guests were no longer in a fit state to operate heavy machinery, supervise small children or give accurate evidence to the Constabulary. None of these tasks, thankfully, was expected of them, but they had all, somehow, got much drunker, much faster than they'd intended. Bertrand was the only person who knew quite how potent his Martinis were and he had been knocking them back as though Prohibition might be reintroduced before midnight. When Will and Min had come in together, their faces radiant with the unmistakable shine of true love, Bertrand had known with piercing certainty that he had no hope with her today, tomorrow, next year or ever. Sensibly, he had decided to drown his sorrows and was soon liberally dousing everyone else's too by filling up their glasses at five-minute intervals. The announcement of the impending nuptials fuelled the raging fires of insobriety as now they had even more to celebrate than before.

'About bloody time,' said Mac when the couple broke their big news. 'God, I've have knocked your heads together if it had gone on any longer.'

'Congratulations, Mr de Beaufort Haskell,' said Dallas, clapping Will on the back. 'Where are you two lovebirds going to live? Here, with the faithful Albert waiting on you hand and foot?'

'Oh, no,' said Will. 'Ambrosia has worn out her quota of

normality by agreeing to get married and so we've got to go and have a bizarre chain of adventures until she feels better.' He may have said it jokingly but he meant it. There was to be no settling down for the new Mr and Mrs Gadget. Min, who had turned out to be the last living descendant of one of France's most noble counts, wanted to go back to France to join the resistance against the new President, Le Maître, who had been voted into power just days after William's fateful trip to Paris.

The reason, she had explained to Will, but only after there had been many tears and hugs and kisses, as well as a few other activities which the sitting-room would not have been familiar with, that she had left so abruptly in the spring was thanks to a revelation which Christophe of all people had unearthed. Le Maître, the new President of France, had long been looking for all the possible claimants to the throne he could find, or so Christophe's intelligence network had learnt. Le Maître, they believed, wished to handpick from among them his favourite candidate for the reintroduction of the French monarchy, a move which his enemies were searching to understand. Even before the election, Le Maître's opponents were desperately seeking more information about his activities. Now he had become president, their quest was even more urgent. They needed spies on the inside and Christophe thought he might have found the perfect one.

That grey and inopportune morning, Min's ex-boyfriend had disrupted the start of her romance with Will by a phone call to tell her that living in Morocco was an old man who might hold the clue to her past. However, she had to hurry because he was critically ill and might not last longer than a day or two.

Christophe had been spot on. The old man was Min's great-uncle Anton who'd lived for many years in self-imposed exile in North Africa. She'd been born illegitimately, he told her, to Mathilde, only child of the Comte de Bresson

Moncourt, one of France's grandest men. He'd been furious, Anton had told Min. The disgrace, the scandal, the stain on the family name couldn't be tolerated. Mathilde couldn't marry Min's father, partly because he was her riding instructor but mostly because he was already married. Mathilde was concealed throughout her pregnancy and once the baby arrived, she was shipped off to live with de Beauforts in England and be brought up as one of their own.

The Comte had expected Mathilde, who apparently looked exactly like Min, to marry and have children legitimately but she had confounded his expectations by dying young. The old man had been heartbroken, but too proud to admit he had been horribly wrong so he never asked to see his only granddaughter, although he left her his fortune when he died.

As Min was a very strong claimant to the French throne, Christophe, who in the intervening years since she'd left him had taken some hard knocks, lost much of his crack-pot vocabulary and learnt to fight real battles instead of imaginary ones, hoped to use her to infiltrate Le Maître's inner circle. He had asked her to return to France to become a secret agent in the war against fascism, a highly dangerous role which she had instantly accepted.

'So having practised by bringing down a telecommunications company and a bank, you're going to have a shot at a government now?' said Will, stroking her hair.

'Will you come with me?' she asked her newly betrothed.

'Everywhere you go,' he said. 'With just one condition.'

'What's that?' said Min, who was so delirious with happiness that she would have agreed to anything.

'Don't make me spent too much time with Christophe.'

At 42 Cornwall Crescent the party was still raging. Someone had unearthed an ancient set of Twister, a juvenile game where participants seek to entangle themselves hopelessly with each other in the hope of not crashing to the ground, a premise which seemed all too appropriate given the circumstances. Even Sharan was persuaded to join in, on condition that Albert played too. Currently Bertrand was manning the controls, which consisted of a plastic arrow on a dial which he had to flick around to give the contestants their next move, something he was finding quite taxing in his advanced state of inebriation.

With a groaning roar, the Twister edifice imploded, leaving the participants lying on the floor in a spaghetti tangle of limbs. Sharan was lying under Albert, helpless with snorting giggles, Andreas was snogging Jem, Luella was smoking a large joint, Bertrand had passed out on the floor while Mac exhorted him to temper his flask and always to circle the hide, Dallas explaining again to a rather cross-eyed Louise the dos and don'ts of Hollywood, while the future Queen of France and her consort sat floating on a little cloud of pure joy. Just at that moment, an older man crashed through the front door which no one had thought to close properly and into the sitting-room.

'What,' thundered the man, 'is the meaning of this?'

'Father!' said Jem. 'We can explain. Everything . . .'